Praise for *Would You Rather* by Allison Ashley

"A pitch-perfect mix of all the best romance tropes, *Would You Rather* is what happens when friends to lovers, fake-dating, and mutual pining are elevated to perfection. Allison Ashley gives me all the feels, and I love every one of them!"

—Ali Hazelwood, *New York Times* bestselling author of *The Love Hypothesis*

"Sweet, sexy and smart, *Would You Rather* is an absolutely un-putdownable book, a slow-burn so rich with pining and genuine emotion that I dare readers to do anything other than devour it in one sitting."

—Lynn Painter, author of *Mr. Wrong Number*

"I adored this lovely and heartfelt friends-to-lovers story. Noah and Mia have very real reasons to stay apart, but you'll be rooting all along for them to wake up, abandon their significant personal baggage, and realize they're perfect for each other already!"

—Julie Hammerle, *USA TODAY* bestselling author of *Knocked-Up Cinderella*

"An emotional and heartfelt journey that will have you laughing, crying, and falling in love. Trust me, You Would Rather get this book than miss out."

—Mariah Ankenman, bestselling author of the Mile High Happiness series

"A dynamic page-turner from the very first chapter. Allison Ashley has a masterful way of lighting the kindling in a slow, deliberate burn between two stubborn best friends who refuse to admit what everyone else sees clearly. I laughed out loud as Noah coveted the way Mia looked at chicken wings—any partner would be so lucky to receive such a longing gaze."

—Taj McCoy, author of *Savvy Sheldon Feels Good as Hell*

"Has all my favorite things: a marriage of convenience, only one bed, and chicken wings. I couldn't put it down!"

—Suzanne Baltsar, author of *Trouble Brewing*

"A heartwarming page-turner filled with scorching tension and all the best tropes. An ode to those who struggle with vulnerability, this romance captures the beauty in accepting another's unconditional love."

—Amy Lea, author of *Set on You*

"Delivers all the delicious anticipation of friends-to-lovers, plus the swoony yearning of a marriage-of-convenience. Noah and Mia's chemistry sizzles—this book is the perfect mix of laughter and feels."

—Chandra Blumberg, author of *Digging Up Love*

"Allison Ashley absolutely delivers with this swoony friends to lovers romance. The pining and the yearning and the kisses swept me off my feet and I couldn't help falling in love with Noah and Mia. I loved every second of this book!"

—Falon Ballard, author of *Lease on Love*

"A sparkling, warm romance that reminds us why the friends-to-lovers trope is superior! Allison Ashley skillfully delivered a chemistry-filled, happy-hug-of-a-book set against the backdrop of real-life struggle. It's the kind of story I've been waiting for!"

—Sarah Adams, author of *The Cheat Sheet*

"*Would You Rather* made my heart burst in the best way. It hits every emotional high note with moments of laugh-out-loud humor, scenes that will bring you to tears, and cuteness that will make you squeal out loud. Allison Ashley will charm you with this affecting and engrossing love story."

—Sarah Echavarre Smith,
author of *Faker*, *Simmer Down* and *On Location*

"From stolen glances to the sweeping euphoria of the first kiss, Allison Ashley writes love stories you feel in your soul. *Would You Rather* is a masterful mix of adorable, heart-wrenching, hilarious, and unforgettable. Make sure you have caffeine for the morning, because you'll be up late unable to put down this incredible book."

—Denise Williams, author of *How to Fail at Flirting*

"Sexy and sweet, with a fresh twist on friends-to-lovers, *Would You Rather* is the type of romance I wish I could read again for the first time. Allison Ashley draws the reader in and holds tight with a carefully woven story, sparkling chemistry, and unforgettable characters. It's pure, swoony, flirty, romantic bliss."

—Lauren Accardo, author of *Wild Love*

ALLISON ASHLEY

Recycling programs for this product may not exist in your area.

ISBN-13: 978-0-7783-8649-0

Would You Rather

This is a work of fiction. Names, characters, places and incidents are either the product of the author's imagination or are used fictitiously. Any resemblance to actual persons, living or dead, businesses, companies, events or locales is entirely coincidental.

For questions and comments about the quality of this book, please contact us at CustomerService@Harlequin.com.

Mira
22 Adelaide St. West, 41st Floor
Toronto, Ontario M5H 4E3, Canada
BookClubbish.com

Printed in U.S.A.

For Amber and Fransen,
for being the first to encourage me to keep writing.

Would You Rather

1

Mia Adrian stared at her phone screen, wondering what in the hell she'd just read.

Noah: Would you rather—text message edition. Daily messages with strange animal facts OR positive affirmations?

What kind of question was that? She frowned and leaned one elbow on the arm of her chair before tapping out a one-handed response.

Mia: ???

Noah: It's a question. Would you rather receive daily animal facts or positive affirmations?

Mia: Um.

Mia: Neither?

Noah: Both it is.

Mia: Don't you dare.

A banner appeared at the top of her screen, alerting her to a message from an unknown number.

When I breathe, I inhale confidence and exhale timidity.

She groaned and waited, hoping for some additional message that would give her instructions to opt out of whatever service he'd just signed her up for. Her gaze darted to her computer screen for a second, then back to the phone.

Nothing.

Would she seriously get something like this every day? How the hell was she supposed to stop them?

The text alert dinged again. Another unfamiliar number.

Elephants are the only animal that can't jump.

She pressed a fist to her forehead.

Mia: I'm going to kill you.

Noah: Should have done it before you taped a banana under my desk. I've been wondering what the smell was for days.

She couldn't help the laugh bubbling up, and glanced around to make sure no clients were around. Noah might be her best friend, but they teased each other at the office like elementary school rivals. She liked her job, but it was still work—and their games usually helped her get through until five o'clock.

This, though? This was her personal cell phone.

He'd taken it one step too far.

Mark my words, Noah Agnew. I'll get you back for this.

Yet another chirp sounded, but this wasn't a text message. It was the alert reminding her she needed to leave in fifteen minutes for her weekly infusion appointment.

She smiled at the thought that followed. Thursday meant a trip to the infusion center, but more importantly, it also meant chicken wings for dinner.

She closed her eyes and leaned back in her chair. What would it be today? Louisiana Rub? Lemon Pepper? Maybe she'd go wild and try the Mango Habanero.

They all sounded *good*—but which sounded best?

When it came to food—chicken wings in particular—Mia didn't mess around.

"You're thinking about chicken wings, aren't you?"

Mia's eyes popped open and she lurched to a sitting position. Noah stood on the other side of her desk, arms folded across his broad chest.

He had on the baby blue dress shirt. Blue always had been her favorite color on him—she'd told him so no less than fifty times. And yet he only wore the hue once a month, maybe not even that often.

She didn't mention the ridiculous text messages. Best to let him think they didn't bother her that much and get him back when he least expected it.

She flicked invisible lint from her black skirt. "It's Thursday, is it not?"

"It is. But even if it wasn't, I'd still know. Nothing else puts that look on your face."

"What look is that, exactly?"

He slid his hands into his pockets. "Pure, unadulterated longing. I've never seen anything like it."

"Only every Thursday for the last nine years." She leaned forward and dropped her elbows to the desk. "It's your fault, you know. You're the one who introduced me to them."

Noah reached out and moved her nameplate several inches to the left. It drove her crazy.

No matter, she'd rearrange the items on his desk tomorrow morning before he came in.

"I didn't know I was creating a monster."

Mia laughed. "Too late for hindsight. Want me to bring some over tonight?"

"Sure."

She didn't have to ask what flavor he wanted. Noah was as consistent as her doctor's appointments. When he found something he liked, he stuck with it. Long ago she'd noticed he usually ordered something he'd had before when they went out to eat, and once asked him why he never branched out.

"What if I try something new, and it's not as good?" he'd said.

"What if it's better?" she'd returned.

But he wouldn't be swayed. Wasn't worth the risk, he maintained, and she'd let it go.

She made a mental note to add a ten piece of plain wings to her order tonight, and swiveled aimlessly in her chair. "How's your day been?"

"Boring. Full of client meetings, but you know that."

"If not, I'd be the world's worst administrative assistant. Speaking of meetings, you've got one more in—" she checked her watch "—ten minutes."

"I do?"

"Darcy Lane, here to discuss her new fitness center."

"Right." He put his palm flat on the desk and leaned in a little. His eyes brightened with excitement. "So I had lunch with my dad today."

She smiled, ignoring the pang of jealousy at his casual mention of spending time with his dad. There was a time she and her parents got together for regular meals, too. Now, she couldn't even remember the last time. "Yeah?"

"He's going to announce his plans to retire. This week, probably."

"Really?"

They'd been expecting it. Mr. Agnew had been dropping hints about retiring for the last three years. Mia didn't blame him—he was in his sixties and had built an impressive architecture firm of fifty employees that had become known around Denver for modern, sustainable designs. He'd earned a break.

"Yep. Said the principals would look to promote one of the associates after he left."

When Mia had started this job many years ago, it had taken her a while to learn the titles and hierarchy structure of architects at the firm. CEO, principal, associate, architect, intern... but eventually she'd gotten it straight.

Mia rubbed her hands together. "Which means a junior principal position will open up, and it will have your name on it."

He shrugged. "Maybe. I don't want them to pick me just because I'm the founder's son."

She snorted. "Son or not, you're the best candidate. No contest."

"Thanks," he said, chewing on his lower lip. "I'd love the opportunity. And I know it would make my dad proud."

He ran a hand through his hair, leaving an errant lock sticking straight up in the back.

"Noah," Mia scolded. She stood and beckoned him to lean over. He obeyed and she smoothed his hair down, a ritual they performed at least twice a week. "Better."

"Thanks." He turned toward his office. "You'd better get out of here."

"I will as soon as your three o'clock arrives."

He started down the hall to his office just as Julia and David, both architects like Noah, came from the opposite direction.

Julia paused and flashed him a smile. "Hey, Noah."

He offered a polite greeting but kept moving, and Mia scowled at his back. No matter how many times she brought it up, he always brushed off the suggestion Julia was interested in him.

Julia, looking poised and elegant in a gray dress and heels, veered off into the break room while David turned to where Mia sat. "I can't find the Trodeau file."

She blinked, disarmed by his clipped tone. She shouldn't have been, though, because he always spoke to her like that. "Um, I thought I filed it last week. Did you check the black file cabinet?"

He looked at her like she'd just asked if he knew right from left. "Of course."

"Oh. I'm sorry, I might have misplaced it," Mia said, unease filling her stomach. Every time she messed up—which wasn't often—it always seemed to involve David. The man thought she was a complete idiot. "I'll find it."

David just stood there and arched a sardonic brow.

Mia glanced to the side, then forced herself to regain eye contact. "I can't do it right this minute, I'm about to leave—"

"Right," David said disapprovingly. "It's Thursday. Make sure it's on my desk first thing tomorrow. It's important."

"Yes, I can do that. I'll get it to you tomorrow."

He didn't reply and went back the way he'd come.

A subtle chime sounded, alerting Mia to a newcomer in the office. A young woman with long brown hair stepped into the foyer, and Mia stood.

"Good afternoon." She smiled, trying her best to shake off the interaction with David.

The woman came forward. "Oh, hello. I'm Darcy Lane—I have an appointment?" It came out like a question.

"Yes, at three o'clock with Noah." She should probably refer to Noah as Mr. Agnew to clients, but that had always been what she called Noah's father. "I'll just let him know you're here. Can I get you anything? Water, coffee?" Serving and chatting with clients while they waited was one of Mia's favorite parts of her job.

"I'm okay, thank you." The woman sat in the chair farthest from Mia and pulled out her cell phone.

Guess she wouldn't be one of the chatty ones, but that was probably best since Mia had to leave, anyway. She picked up her desk phone and hit number one on her speed dial.

"Client's here?" Noah asked by way of greeting.

"Yep. Should I set her up in the conference room?"

"Not yet. I need a couple of minutes to get her stuff together. I'll come get her when I'm ready, you need to head out."

"Relax. I won't be late."

"You will be if you don't leave now."

"Okay, okay. See you tonight." She hung up and locked her computer screen. Just as she was about to turn to the woman, she heard Noah's voice and looked up to see his head poke around the corner.

"Darcy? I'm Noah. I'm just finishing something up, and I'll be with you in a few minutes."

The woman seemed stunned for a second as she looked at Noah, blinking several times. "Um, sure. Yes, that's fine. I know I'm a little early."

Mia smiled to herself. The woman had no idea how much Noah appreciated that. Tardiness drove him crazy.

"I look forward to our meeting." Noah's expression was polite and businesslike, and he ducked back into his office.

Mia forwarded her phone to the office manager and gathered her purse. She went around the desk and stopped in front of Darcy. "I have to head out for an appointment, are you sure there's nothing you need before I go?"

Darcy's cheeks were flushed. "No, thank you."

This wasn't the first time a woman had become flustered around Noah. The firm did mostly commercial design, and the majority of their clients were men. But occasionally women came through, and they'd had several female interns. It was quite clear the effect Noah had on women, even if the man himself was oblivious.

Despite their long-standing friendship, Mia could still admit her best friend was hot.

Really hot.

At thirty-one, he looked his age, which she would argue was when men hit their prime. He was old enough to appear masculine and worldly, his jaw defined and always covered in a light layer of facial hair, but youthfulness still rounded his features in the best way. Like he hadn't become hardened by what life had thrown at him.

He was healthy and fit, as much as one could tell in his dress shirt and slacks. Based on his frequent trips to the mountains for rock climbing expeditions, Mia knew it was even better underneath.

But the thing that caught people off guard was his hair. Noah was a redhead, his thick hair like a muted sunrise. Not the vivid orange associated with a brilliant sky that prompted #unfiltered hashtags on social media posts, but rather the soft glow brushing the horizon just before the sun appeared. In certain light some might call it strawberry blonde, but Mia never liked that term. Noah pulled off the redhead look beautifully.

She supposed it could have also been his eyes—an ice blue that drew people in like water in a parched desert. Those eyes were the reason Mia told him to wear blue more often.

He was hit on every time he wore blue, without fail.

As she started her car and drove to the infusion center, she wondered idly if Darcy Lane would uphold that convention. Even if she did, Mia knew what Noah would say.

Dating was a topic they rarely discussed. Having been close friends for more than two decades, there weren't many subjects that were off-limits. She knew almost everything about him, and he, her. But whenever she asked about his love life, he shut down, or turned things back on her, which she couldn't argue against.

She didn't date much, either.

They were different, though. Noah had nothing to hold him back.

Mia? She had a damn good reason to stay single, and she intended to keep it that way.

★★★

"If it isn't my favorite patient." Natasha approached Mia's recliner with a smile.

Mia rolled her eyes good-naturedly. "You only say that because I bring you food."

The middle-aged nurse shrugged, unapologetic. "Wasn't that your plan? To butter me up so I'd make sure you were always with me?"

"I heard you were the best at starting IVs."

"I've never stuck you more than once, have I?"

"I keep bringing you food, don't I?"

"I guess we've got the perfect arrangement, then," Natasha said, her eyes searching around Mia's chair. "So, what is it today? Pumpkin bread? Muffins?"

Mia reached into her purse and located the small paper-wrapped package. "Scottish shortbread."

Natasha put the back of her hand against her forehead dramatically. "Mercy, I love shortbread."

"You love anything with sugar."

"Truth." Natasha tucked the proffered package into her scrubs pocket. She took Mia's hand and tugged gently to straighten her arm, palm up. She tapped two fingers along the crease of Mia's inner elbow. "Veins still look great, even after all this time."

"Someone told me to chug water the day of each infusion. Works like a charm."

"Not everyone listens to me, but I'm glad you do."

Mia smiled and watched as Natasha wrapped a tourniquet around her bicep and swabbed the blue vessels with an alcohol pad. She had to look away when Natasha pierced her skin, though. No matter how many times she did this, she still couldn't stomach the moment the needle went in.

Once the IV was in and the clear fluid was running, Natasha peeled the gloves off and disposed of them. "I'll go get your drug."

While she waited, Mia unlocked her phone and pulled up her personal email. One caught her eye, and her stomach flipped. She opened the message and her eyes flew over the words:

Ms. Adrian,

Congratulations! From an incredibly talented pool of applicants, I'm delighted to inform you that you've been chosen for the Ignacio Return to Learning Scholarship. We look forward to welcoming you back to campus...

Her heart leapt with excitement, but it was as short-lived as the rush of the downhill slope on a roller coaster. Her brain quickly admonished the surge of joy with a harsh reprimand.

What were you thinking?

She'd applied for the scholarship late one night when she was feeling sorry for herself. She'd had a couple glasses of wine and started researching what it might take to go back to school to finish the dietetics degree she'd started more than a decade ago, despite knowing it would be a challenge while working full-time. She already had medical bills to deal with and was averse to taking out significant school loans, something that had held her back on multiple occasions.

Hence, the scholarship. She'd found one specifically for adults going back to school and on a whim, decided to go for it.

When she'd filled out the application in her mildly buzzed state, she poured out her heart, explaining what happened during her third year at CU and why she'd had to put school on hold. She talked about her lifetime goal of becoming a pediatric dietician after being such a picky eater as a child that she was in the fifth percentile for weight, and only improved after beginning therapy with a dietician who worked exclusively with kids. Her desire to do the same for others hadn't faded since leaving halfway through the program. She disclosed her financial hardships, and that she'd do almost anything for the opportunity to finish her degree and pursue a career she was passionate about.

It had been therapeutic. An exercise in putting herself back out there and considering the possibilities for her future.

She didn't think she'd actually get *picked*.

The scholarship required she enroll in at least twelve credit hours per semester, and there was no way she could do that plus work full-time at Agnew Design Group.

And there was no way she could quit, because she needed their generous medical insurance policy.

She laid her phone in her lap and bit the inside of her cheek, pondering any possible way she could accept the scholarship. She came up empty-handed, and an hour later, when her infusion was finished and she walked out of the treatment center, her disappointment ran deep. She headed to Wings To Go, glad she was meeting Noah tonight.

If she could pick one person to sit with while wallowing over how much this sucked, it was him.

2

He shouldn't have worn this shirt.

It was Thursday, and Noah knew he'd have client meetings. Hell, he even knew one was with a woman. Not that he shared Mia's assessment—he wasn't so arrogant to think the color made him irresistible.

But he *did* seem to get more attention when he wore blue, as evidenced by the look Julia had given him in the hallway that afternoon, and the awkward rejection he'd just delivered to Darcy.

His phone vibrated as he left the office a little after five, and he fished it out of his pocket.

"Hey," he greeted.

Graham, his friend since college, got straight to the point. "You up for a kick-ass climbing trip next month?"

Noah reined in the flurry of adrenaline and told himself not to get too excited. "Where?"

"Why is that always your first question?" Graham asked. "You know I only plan trips to the best places. I do my research."

"I know." But it was the thing that mattered most. Noah unlocked his car and sat down. "So, where?"

"Washingt—"

"No." He started his car, and the audio automatically switched to his speakers.

"Come on, man!" Graham's voice was three times louder, and Noah quickly dialed down the volume. "It's Index. A hidden gem of climbing glory, and May's the perfect time to go. I've got two other guys who are in."

The desire to say yes—to climb the magic land of granite that was Index, Washington—pulled hard on his willpower. He was careful to keep his voice steady and firm. "That sounds incredible. You can tell me all about it when you get back."

A heavy sigh echoed through the car.

Noah said nothing.

Finally, Graham said, "Can I say one thing?"

"Whatever it is, it won't change my mind."

"Nathan always wanted to climb Index."

Noah paused before pulling out of the parking lot and rubbed a hand across his forehead. "I know," he said quietly. "It's still a no."

"So you're just gonna climb in Colorado for the rest of your life? That's it?"

Noah shook his head, even though Graham couldn't see him. "Not for the rest of my life." He paused. "At least I don't think so. But for now? Yes, that's how it is."

Graham grunted. "Fine. We still on for tomorrow night?"

That was one thing Noah appreciated about his friend. He was easygoing, didn't hold grudges, and could move on to another subject in a heartbeat. Noah and Graham in particular knew how to dance around difficult conversations, and smoothly maneuver topics that could cause pain and regret.

Graham was the only other person who'd been there the night Nathan died, yet they never spoke of it. The fact that he said Noah's brother's name at all during this call was a step further than usual.

"Yep."

"Great. Let me know if you change your mind, okay?"

"I will," Noah said.

But he knew he wouldn't.

"So, was I right about the blue shirt?"

Noah scowled at the coffee table centered in his living room—currently covered in chicken wings and carrot sticks—and didn't respond.

Mia grinned and nudged his shoulder with hers. They sat beside each other on his couch, eating wings and watching *The Bachelorette*. He thought the show was beyond ridiculous, but Mia loved it. "I knew it."

"I don't know what you're talking about," he muttered, reaching for another wing. If he didn't covet the look in Mia's eyes when he wore blue, he'd throw out the damn shirt tomorrow.

Apparently, he was a glutton for punishment.

Mia wiped her mouth with a napkin. "What did she say? Did you get all awkward and quiet?"

"I don't get awkward and quiet."

Mia laughed. "You're joking, right?"

Noah leaned back a little and turned his torso toward her. "No."

"There's a picture of your face in the dictionary next to the word *reticent*."

His brow furrowed, but he remained silent.

Her lips quirked in a satisfied grin, probably because he was proving her point this very minute. He didn't care. He and Mia had been having silences since they were seven years old. Not having to force himself to make conversation was one reason he loved spending time with her.

One of many.

Finally, he wiped his hands and sat back. "She asked if I was single."

"Straight out? Ballsy for a client."

"No, she tried to be smooth about it. Said something like 'I heard architects work long hours, I bet your wife doesn't like that.'"

Mia laughed, and the sound washed over him. His chest expanded several inches every time she laughed.

"What did you say?" she asked.

Noah rubbed the back of his neck. "You know what a terrible liar I am."

"You said you didn't have a wife."

He nodded.

"Then what?"

"It was almost five by the time we finished up. She asked if I wanted to get a drink."

Mia smacked his arm. "You should have gone!"

He stared at her. "I had plans."

"What, with these chicken wings? Plans with me don't count."

His frown deepened. "Yes they do."

"No they don't. And stop frowning like that. You're gonna have the worst wrinkles when you're old." She took a sip of her beer and faced the television. "Surely you know you can always cancel with me if you have the chance to go on a date."

He didn't dignify that with a response.

Like a dog with a bone, she wouldn't let it go. "You should say yes next time."

"No."

"Why not?"

"I'm not going out with some stranger. And I'm not dating a client."

"Why not?" she said again. "People do it all the time. The stranger thing, I mean. Aren't we all strangers these days?" She pointedly glanced at her cell phone. "It sort of feels that way, sometimes."

He couldn't help but let his gaze rest on her familiar face. "We're not strangers."

"No, but you're not gonna date *me*."

As soon as the words were out of her mouth, Noah's stomach tightened. He thought about that night back in college—and the split second when he thought they might become more than friends.

Her face paled, and he'd bet she was thinking about the same thing. "Anyway, all I'm saying is you can't keep turning women down. You're hot and you're sweet, and women adore you. But eventually they'll stop asking. I've never understood what you're waiting for."

Over the years he'd turned deflection into an art form. He didn't want to answer that, but neither would she. "What are *you* waiting for?"

She frowned. "That's different. I'm not being picky, I just refuse to burden someone with my situation."

"A one-hour drug infusion every week isn't 'a situation.'"

"You know that's not all it is."

Yeah, he knew her excuses. Her disease couldn't be cured, and a few years ago she'd been put on the kidney transplant list. He wasn't trying to downplay it, but it was ridiculous to think those things would stop a man from wanting her.

"If they ever find a match for me, I'll have to go through the transplant process, and even then, at my age, I'll probably need another one eventually. This will affect my entire life, and it's not fair to put that on another person. I don't even let my parents help me. There's no way I'm asking a man to."

"What if someone thought you were worth it?"

She huffed out a breath. "Stop trying to turn this around. We were talking about you, and why you don't date."

Noah fixed his eyes on the television. "I'm seeing how some things pan out."

"Like what?"

Damn, he was such an idiot. "Just some things."

He could practically hear her teeth grinding. "You drive me crazy," she said. "For the person I know best in the world, sometimes I feel like there's a whole part of you I've never seen."

Her dark brown eyes locked on his, and he kept his expression carefully neutral. "Same."

She watched him for a moment and then dropped her gaze. When she spoke again, her voice was so quiet he barely heard her. "Would you rather be able to fly, or read minds?"

How many times had they started sentences to each other with those three words? Dozens, at least.

"Fly."

"Really?"

"Yeah. People talk too much as it is. I'm not sure I want to know the things people don't want to say out loud."

"I talk a lot," she said.

He grinned. "I know."

She laughed. "Jerk."

"What about you? Read minds or fly?"

"Read minds." Her eyes met his again. "Especially yours."

He was glad as hell that wasn't possible. If she knew what he was thinking every time they were together, she'd probably run for the hills.

He shook his head as if she were crazy. "You don't want to know what's going on in here." He tapped his temple with his index finger. "It's a lot of design details. Planning my next climbing trip. Some guilt and a lot of what-ifs."

He wasn't sure why he said that last part. It just sort of came out, and her expression turned downcast, and a little sad. She glanced at the console table behind them, to the frame he knew contained an image of him and his late brother. In the photo they were eight and ten, sitting on the edge of the tree house in the backyard of their childhood home. Even though Nathan had been two years older, Noah had always been big for his age, and they could have passed for twins, if it weren't for the hair. When meeting new people it was always Noah's ginger coloring that grabbed people's eye first, but it had been Nathan's outgoing personality that captured their attention.

Noah had liked it that way.

As if she sensed he didn't want to pursue that topic, Mia surveyed the table and pointed at the two pieces left on his plate. "You gonna finish that?"

"Nah, I'm done."

"I'll take the rest to Claire." She slid the wings into the container where she had three pieces remaining.

Claire, the third member of their childhood trio from the street where they'd all grown up, was the polar opposite of Mia. She'd joined the crew last—moving into a house across the street from Mia's and Noah's—and had brought a new level of excitement to the group. Where Mia and Noah had been pretty straitlaced, Claire added a layer of mischief that hadn't faded as they'd gotten older.

"What's she up to tonight?"

"Working. She won't be home until late, but she likes a snack when she comes in."

"What about the new girl?"

"Reagan? She's a vegetarian. I met her at that vegan grocery store in Capitol Hill, remember?"

"That's right. I was shocked as hell when Claire told me."

Mia tilted her head curiously. "That I picked up a new roommate in the kombucha aisle?"

He grinned. "No, I stopped being surprised at your ability to make friends with anyone who breathes a long time ago. I mean that you, the girl who loves meat and cheese more than anyone I know, were shopping at a vegan store."

She shrugged. "I wanted to try making vegan cupcakes. It's harder than it sounds."

"Doubtful, since it sounds impossible." Mia was constantly experimenting in the kitchen, something Noah often benefited from. Ever since putting her nutrition degree on hold, she said baking was her outlet to keep that passion present in some facet of her life. "How'd they turn out?"

"Terrible." She grinned and stood, clearing the empty food containers from the table. She took everything to the kitchen, then came back to the living room and resumed her seat. She let out a heavy sigh. "So, I have something I want to talk to you about. I need advice."

"Okay."

She rubbed her hands along her thighs and didn't meet his eyes, almost as if she were embarrassed by what she was about to say.

"Don't laugh, but I sort of applied for a college scholarship."

He blinked. "Why would I laugh at that?"

She scrunched her nose. "I don't know. It's like, a second chance scholarship. For adults who either didn't go to college right away, or who started and didn't finish their degree for one reason or another. Basically, it's for duds and dropouts like me," she said with a self-deprecating smile.

He didn't find it humorous. "You're not a dud or a dropout. You got sick and needed to focus on your health."

She gave him a soft smile. "I know. But still."

"Let me guess. You got it?"

She nodded and looked so forlorn he almost did laugh.

"Mia, that's incredible," he said. "Why do you look like someone just told you Wings To Go was closing its doors forever?"

"Because I can't accept it. I don't even know why I applied. Never in a million years would I have thought they'd pick me." She tucked a long strand of silky black hair behind her ear. "No one ever picks me."

I'd pick you.

He ignored the thought, along with the painful squeeze beneath his rib cage. "Clearly they saw something in you. Why can't you accept it?"

"It's for full-time students. It's a two-year scholarship, and I have sixty hours needed to get my degree. I'd have to take fifteen hours each semester to finish under their financial assistance, plus my dietetic internship. There's no way I could do that while working full-time."

"So, work part-time." Surely his dad would be okay with that, and they could hire another administrative assistant to fill in the gaps.

She shook her head and looked at him, her eyes sad. "I can't. I need the health insurance."

"Oh." He looked away. He should have thought of that.

"When I applied, this small part of me thought maybe I'd have been up for a kidney by now. With a transplant, I'd automatically qualify for Medicare." She rubbed a hand up her forearm and shrugged. "But obviously that hasn't happened."

"It still could," Noah offered. "You could get the call next week."

She pursed her full lips. "Or next year. At which point this opportunity would have passed me by."

"What if you found a part-time job that offered benefits?"

"I thought about that, but I don't think many places do that," she said. "And even if they did, I haven't been in school for more than a decade. I'm a little worried about my ability to maintain the GPA needed for the scholarship if I had to work even that much with a full course load."

"You're smart and hardworking. You absolutely could."

She shook her head. "Plus, my class hours would change every semester. And it's risky with my disease. If I had a flare while trying to work part-time and study… I just don't see it working."

He leaned forward. "What if you didn't have insurance at all? Don't those drug companies have assistance programs for that?" The medication for her kidney condition was unbelievably expensive. "Maybe you could get the drug for free."

"Sure, Kinrovi would probably be free," she said. "But I'd still have doctor visits, lab tests, and other bills. I know it hasn't happened in a while, but when my blood pressure goes out of whack or the cysts mess with my electrolytes and I land in the hospital, it's expensive. I need the insurance for everything."

He deflated. "Oh." He ran a hand through his hair, feeling that stubborn piece in the back stick up again. He sort of loved it though, because it drove Mia nuts, and her fingers smoothing it back down was the best part of his day.

"It's probably for the best," she said. "I have a good job, and I'm happy. I like the client interaction, and I love working with you."

He loved that, too. "But it's not your passion."

"It's good enough."

"Is that really what you want? Good enough?"

"Don't most people feel that way about work? How many people truly do what they're passionate about as a career?"

"I do."

"You're lucky."

"It wasn't just luck. I worked toward that dream. You could, too."

"I get to do it as a side hustle. I'm always cooking new things with a healthy twist, proving good nutrition can still taste good."

"Except vegan cupcakes."

One corner of her mouth quirked. "I'll try again."

"Didn't you want to work in pediatrics? You need to find someone with kids so they can be your taste testers."

Mia waved a dismissive hand. "Surely you'll be married with kids in the next few years. Claire, too. I'll be the cool aunt who's always bringing treats by for my godchildren to try."

Noah completely ignored her suggestion he'd be married with kids anytime soon and studied her, trying to decide why she was making excuses. Was it because she didn't really want to do it, or because she was scared? An idea was slowly forming in his mind, but there was no way in hell he'd put it out there if he thought going back to school wasn't something she really wanted.

"Let me ask you this," he said. "If there was a way for you to keep your current insurance without working, would you take the scholarship and go back to school?"

She laughed humorlessly. "That's impossible. I know your dad loves me, but not that much."

"Humor me. Don't worry about the logistics and answer the question."

She sat there for a moment, a mere foot away, but he knew her mind was miles from his living room. Slowly, her head moved up and down. "Yes."

At that single syllable, the tiny idea bloomed into possibility. It grew even more at her next words.

"If there was a way for me to stop working, keep my insurance, and go back to school, I'd do it in a heartbeat." Her slumped posture indicated she found the entire premise hopeless.

"Maybe there is," he said.

She looked at him, confusion marring her forehead.

His heart pounded, and it suddenly felt as if his lungs couldn't get enough air. A strange sense of excitement filled him, even as his brain rained down rational thoughts to reverse his decision.

Don't.

It's a terrible idea.

It's fraud.

He ignored them all. "What if we got married?"

3

Mia stilled as her mouth dropped open. "What if we what?"

Noah's throat worked as he swallowed. His hands gripped his knees, but his ice-blue gaze remained steady on hers. "We could get married." He said it in the same way he might say "next week let's get tacos instead of chicken wings."

Her pulse tripled, and she frowned at her body's reaction. She just stared at him.

"I could put you on my insurance, and you could accept the scholarship. Go back to school."

"As your *wife*?" she squeaked.

"Yeah."

She remained frozen for a split second, then blinked several times, shaking her head slowly. She'd been confident Noah would come up with a plan, but never in a million years would she have come up with *that*. "Noah."

"Mia."

"You can't be serious." She knew he was, though. He'd one hundred percent do that for her, because that's the kind of friend he was.

He just looked at her. He knew she knew he was serious, too.

"I would never ask you to do that."

"You didn't."

She groaned. "Okay, I couldn't let you do that."

"What's the big deal? It would just be on paper, and it's not like it would be forever. You said yourself you could get a kidney any day. Then you wouldn't need the company's coverage anymore, and we could get a divorce. Or an annulment, I don't really know how that works. And either way, it's only for two years max, right? Once you have your degree and license, you'll get a job as a dietician somewhere and have your own insurance again. We'd separate then."

"Two years, Noah? We can't do that. You can't."

"Why not?"

"What if you meet someone you want to date between now and then? You run into a nice girl at a bar and want to ask her out, but oh, wait." She smacked the side of her head with her palm. "Can't. You're already married."

He shot her a look eerily similar to the one he gave her whenever she said an outfit didn't look good on her. Full of disbelief and borderline annoyed. "I care more about you than I do a few potential dates. What's two years? This is your dream, Mia. Your career. Being a dietician is always what you've wanted to do. If I'd known you were considering going back to school, I'd have suggested it a long time ago. An opportunity like this won't come around again. You have to take it."

She pressed the heels of her palms to her eyes. How could he be so blasé about this? "I… No, Noah. It's too much. You're so sweet, but—"

He held up a hand. "Stop. Just think about it, okay? I mean this. It's not an empty offer."

She laughed a little. "Right. You've clearly given the idea of marrying me a lot of thought. Five whole minutes of it."

"I—" he began, then seemed to think better of it. He clenched his teeth together, a muscle in his jaw flexing. He leaned forward and rested his forearms on his knees. "I know I caught you off guard." Something about the way he said it made her think it didn't feel the same for him. "But just consider it. Please."

"You're insane." She stood and gathered her things. "You're my best friend and I love you, but you're insane."

He remained where he was and let out a frustrated breath. "I'll give you some time to work through the idea. Are we still on for Claire's birthday tomorrow?"

Mia wanted to laugh at the routine question, slid into the ridiculous conversation they were having. "Yeah. Claire has to work, but she still wanted to go out. She'll meet us there at eight."

"I'll come by your place at seven thirty to pick you up," he said. He rose and walked to the door, opening it for her. "I mean it, Mia. Just think about it, and be ready to give me an answer."

That night, Mia dreamed about Noah.

She'd had the dream before…several times. In reality, it wasn't so much a dream as a memory of that night in college.

She did her best not to think about it and did a pretty good job avoiding it while awake. But when she fell into unconsciousness all bets were off, and it seemed to be one of her brain's favorite scenes to replay, sending her back in time to that party at the Sigma Chi house.

Claire had that look in her eye. The one that landed them in detention no less than five times in high school and almost got them arrested last year. "Never have I ever wanted to kiss my best friend."

Mia quickly focused on the rules of the game…everyone who wanted to do that had to drink.

She froze. Without thinking, her gaze jerked across the table to Noah, and her stomach flipped when she locked eyes with him.

He maintained steady eye contact as he calmly took a drink.

Her heart jumped into a sprint and heat spread up her neck. She tore her gaze away and blinked, turning her attention back to Claire.

Her friend's perfectly arched brow raised in question.

Mia's head spun, both from the alcohol and from the way Noah had looked at her. Did that mean he wanted to kiss *her*? Maybe he had another best friend.

Don't be an idiot.

She dropped her eyes to the table and lifted her own beer. She took such a big gulp she coughed, bringing more attention on herself.

Claire laughed and patted her on the back. "Well, then." She stood, planting her hands flat on the table. "I'll just leave you two to talk. Come on, Brad. Let's dance."

Brad, one of Noah's fraternity brothers, complied, shooting Mia a wink before he set off after Claire.

Mia pulled her lips between her teeth and bobbed her knee up and down below the table. She kept her lids lowered and rotated the beer bottle between her fingers.

"Will you ever look at me again?" came Noah's quiet voice.

Only if I know you'll look at me like you just did.

Her voice shook. "It's hard to say."

A chair scraped across the floor, and the familiar scent of pine and spearmint flooded her senses. Noah's large form settled beside her and his hand landed on her bouncing knee. She stilled and lifted her face.

She found everything she wanted in his eyes. His blue irises were soft and kind, and the tiniest hint of a smile played around his lips. And yet, something about his expression was uncertain. She slid her hand down her thigh to his hand, touching his skin with the tips of her fingers.

He swallowed. "Can we go somewhere? To talk, or…?"

She nodded.

"I—"

A set of beefy hands grasping Noah's shoulders cut him off. "Agnew!"

Noah's body faced Mia, and he didn't move his torso so much as a millimeter. He craned his head back to regard the bear of a man behind him. "Yates. What can I do for you?"

"We need more beer. Your turn to buy."

"I can't drive."

"I've got a freshman DD. Let's go."

Noah sighed heavily. He faced forward again and regarded Mia with apology deep in his gaze.

His fraternity was hosting the party, and she knew how these things worked. He didn't have a choice. She gave him a small smile. "It's fine. Go."

He hesitated before turning back to his fraternity brother. "I'll be right there."

"Good man." With a pat on Noah's back that forced him several inches forward, Yates ambled off.

Noah lifted one hand and gripped the back of his neck. "Will you stay? Until I get back? It won't be more than half an hour."

She nodded.

His eyes filled with hope. "Meet me in my room?"

She opened her mouth to answer with words this time, but he suddenly held up a hand.

"No, wait. My roommate's girlfriend is in from out of town and he, um…sort of claimed the room." He scrunched his nose, appearing deep in thought for a second. "Mick's gone all weekend, and he has his own room, the lucky bastard. We'll have privacy." He checked the time on his phone. "Can you meet me there? At twelve thirty?"

Holy shit. "Okay. Which room is his?"

"It's—"

"Agnew!" someone boomed. "Move!"

"Calm the fuck down," Noah called over his shoulder as he stood.

"Just go," she said. "I'll ask someone."

"It's on the second floor," he began, and someone turned the music up, sending bass pounding through the walls. "Anyone can direct you," he shouted, walking backward, but still facing her. "You'll be there? Twelve thirty?"

"Twelve thirty. I'll be there."

Mia startled awake, heart pounding. Her eyelids fluttered and she pressed her hands into the sheets, awareness setting in.

The dream always ended in that moment, never continuing on to the disaster that set in shortly thereafter.

It was almost as if fate wanted a do-over.

She stared up at the ceiling, her eyes adjusting to the darkness. *A do-over.* What would she do with a second chance with Noah, if such a thing were possible? What if things had turned out different and they'd been able to meet that night like they'd planned?

She covered her face with her hands. Thinking about it was pointless. She couldn't go back in time, and couldn't change what happened that night, or shortly after.

Even if Noah's proposal could be seen as a second chance (which it shouldn't, because he was just doing it to help her out), and even if she wanted a second chance with him (which she didn't, because their friendship was perfect), her reasons for staying out of a real relationship were still valid. Even if it were Noah, someone who loved her (like a *friend*) and cared about her well-being, he still didn't deserve the burden of her illness. It was time-consuming, costly, and stressful. It came with a lot of unknowns, and that was something she was determined to shoulder alone.

It was bad enough her parents had to foot the early medical bills. She'd never be able to repay them.

Her hands slid down her face a little, as a new realization set in. She'd have a better chance of giving them some money back, if she had a better paying job. She wouldn't become rich as a dietician, but she'd probably double her current salary as an administrative assistant. She could keep her current expenses and put aside a little every month for them.

They wouldn't accept it, a voice in the back of her mind argued.

That was beside the point. It was the principle—the fact that she tried. Even that would lessen her guilt, if only a fraction.

She'd barely spoken to her parents in two years, and couldn't put her finger on exactly why she felt she owed them so much after learning of their deception. Her conscience argued it was probably because they were so good to her for the first twenty-eight years of her life, but she wasn't quite ready to make peace yet.

She missed them more every day, so maybe she was getting there.

She glanced at the clock—ten minutes before her alarm. There was no point in closing her eyes again, so she got out of bed and got ready for work.

When she arrived at her desk, she found two things.

One, her entire computer was covered in plastic wrap. Tower, screen, keyboard, mouse. All of it. And thick, too—her computer could survive an explosion with the multilayered protection around it.

Two, a steaming cup of coffee from her favorite coffee shop.

She hadn't even looked up yet, but she knew she'd find Noah's light on. She was often the first one in, and when his car was in the lot before hers, it was usually because he'd arrived early to mess with her workspace. She grabbed the warm drink that smelled like caramel heaven and walked to his office.

She stopped in the doorway, fixing him with her best glare, trying to pretend he hadn't completely thrown her for a loop last night.

He didn't even look up. "Morning." He said it like nothing was out of the ordinary.

And in a way, it wasn't. This was standard operating procedure. Last Friday she'd covered everything on his desk with Post-it notes.

It was that pesky proposal that had her stomach turning over itself, but she wasn't going to be the one to bring it up.

"Your use of plastic isn't good for the environment," Mia said.

"Recycle it." He still hadn't looked away from his computer screen. A single pink Post-it remained on the back, and she wondered if he'd missed it.

"You gonna help me get it off?"

"Did you help me the time you put cups of water around my desk like a castle moat?"

She had not.

She took a sip of her coffee, savoring the sweet flavor. He knew exactly how she liked it. Without conscious thought, she let out a little sigh.

She lowered the cup to find his gaze on her face.

A few seconds of silence passed and he leaned back in his leather chair. "Stop thinking so hard and just marry me already."

She nearly dropped hot coffee all over her shoes. Her eyes darted to the open doorway.

"No one else is here," he said, guessing what she was thinking.

Still, she turned and closed his door before sitting across from him. She cupped the warm drink between her palms, unsure how to begin.

"Mia." His voice was low and even.

"Noah." Hers came out unusually high-pitched.

She kept her eyes on his immaculate desk.

"Look at me."

Something in his voice forced her eyes to his. He looked at her the same way he always did—with focus, friendly affection…maybe a hint more intensity than usual. But overall, he just looked at her like he was Noah and she was Mia.

So what was it about this moment that had her breath trapped in her lungs?

"Don't make this a bigger deal than it is," he finally said.

That sent an exhale between her lips. "Marriage isn't a big deal? Insurance fraud isn't a big deal?"

He pursed his lips and glanced around briefly, as if to confirm his earlier assertion they were alone. "Insurance fraud isn't why you're hesitating."

Dammit, why did he know her so well?

He just watched her for a few seconds. "I usually don't have to ask what you're thinking."

Funny, she felt the exact opposite about him.

"Noah, it's too much."

"It's not. It's signing a piece of paper. I'll even let you pay the court fees if it would make you feel better." He leaned forward and rested his forearms on his desk. His sleeves were rolled up, revealing the dark ink covering the inside of his left forearm.

Her eye caught on the words *the sun will rise and we will try again* less than two inches above his wrist. If he slid his sleeve a little higher, she'd see a mountain.

"Don't focus on the short term. Think about what it could mean in the long run. We do this, what—for a few months, a year? *Maybe* two? Until your time comes and you get a transplant? Then it's over, and what did we lose? Nothing. What did we gain? You took a chance on an opportunity that could lead to the career you've always wanted."

"What did *you* gain?"

"The knowledge that I helped my friend achieve her dream. Lifelong happiness."

"What if you meet someone—"

"I won't."

"Noah."

"Mia. I don't care about that." His eyes dropped to his

hands for a second before he looked back at her. His next words were so quiet she almost didn't catch them. "You mean more to me."

Her mind skipped back to that night in college, and a tiny part of her wondered if they'd made a mistake. *What if…?*

She swallowed and glanced away. "What if we got caught?"

"We wouldn't. We've been friends for decades. It's completely plausible we've been pining after each other all these years and finally decided to do something about it. No one else needs to know the situation."

"Don't you think your dad would know? If I quit, we got married, you put me on your insurance…he'd know something was up."

"Let me deal with my dad."

Her face must have revealed her doubt, because he kept going.

"My dad loves you like you're his daughter. Even if he suspected something, he'd never say anything."

Was she actually considering this? "I'd leave him in a lurch." She waved a hand in the direction of the lobby.

"Don't take this the wrong way, but we can find another administrative assistant. Maybe even one who doesn't pry the letters off my keyboard once a week."

She grinned at that. "You'd probably move offices if I left." He hated being so close to the lobby.

"Probably."

She leaned back, slumping against the cushion. "I—I can't, Noah." She closed her eyes, wishing… For what, she didn't know. Just…wishing.

"Can't or won't?"

"Both."

"Because you don't want to marry me? Or because you don't want to put me out?"

She sat up and frowned. "Both, I guess."

"Wow. Okay."

"Noah, you're my best friend. I love you, you know that. But I don't want to marry you because it's not fair to you. And because it would be too much of a burden."

"So, it's all because of how you think it affects me? It has nothing to do with hating the idea of being married to me? Or because you'd be embarrassed to introduce me as your husband?"

"Of course not," she said, surprised he'd even think that. "I'd be proud to call you that. But we're friends. We're not in a relationship. It's...weird."

"Lots of people get married in name only."

"Is that the marriage you've always envisioned for yourself? A fake one?"

"Is this the life you've always envisioned for yourself? In a job with no potential for growth, while your dream of improving childhood nutrition passes you by?"

"I hate it when you do that."

He stilled. "Do what?"

"Answer a question with a question."

"Well," he said with a shrug. "This is about you, not me."

"It's about both of us!"

"It's really not." He stood and walked around his desk, then sat in the chair beside her. He took her free hand, and she dropped her eyes to his large warm fingers encompassing hers. A tingling sensation traveled up her arm. "My mind is made up. I want to do this for you. You just have to let me."

She stared at their hands for a moment, then lifted her eyes to his face. His ice-blue gaze was concentrated, but gentle. He pulled the corner of his lower lip between white teeth, waiting.

His desk phone rang, the tone piercing through the air. Noah released her hand and leaned over to look at the caller ID. "I need to get that."

Mia leapt to her feet. "Sure. We'll talk later." She went for the door.

"Mia."

She stopped with her fingers on the handle and kept her back to him.

"Do one thing for me." The phone kept ringing.

"What is it?" Her voice wavered like it always did when she was uneasy.

She rarely felt that way around Noah.

"Do me a favor and consider both options. One, be my wife for a little while so you can start your career as Colorado's best registered dietician. Two, don't be my wife and stay in a job you think is just okay, forever. It's your choice." He paused for a second. "You always say you value my opinion, and that's why you tell me everything. So here it is: if I were you, I'd think about the one I'd regret less, and pick that one."

4

Mia avoided him for the rest of the day. Which was a feat in and of itself, since they worked mere feet from each other. But somehow she managed, and Noah didn't find himself near her again until that evening at dinner.

Noah, Mia, Claire, and Graham were at Claire's favorite pub, seated in a leather booth laughing over beers. Well, everyone else was… Noah laughed over water.

His tongue loosened way too much when he drank, so he kept himself on a pretty short leash when he knew Mia would be there.

It felt like old times when the four of them were together. With their schedules, it didn't happen as often as they'd like. Claire's and Graham's especially—she was a nurse and he was a firefighter—and Noah had never been able to keep their shifts straight. But maybe once a month they made it work, and it was like college all over again.

Noah, Mia, and Claire kept their neighborhood gang intact in college, but branched out as they met new people. Graham was a little older and had been a friend of Nathan's, but Noah had gotten to know him well on climbing trips he took with his brother. When Nathan died, Graham and Noah's shared grief brought their friendship closer, and Mia and Claire were happy to absorb him into their group.

Claire set down her bottle with gusto and clapped her hands, her blond curls bouncing with the movement. "So," she began. "This dinner actually worked out really well, because I've got something I want to talk to you guys about."

Graham shook his head. "I'm not into foursomes."

Claire didn't even spare him a glance. "I watched that episode of *Friends* last night where they all set up their 'backups.' I thought about it all day, and I decided we should do that."

Noah had seen that episode. He quickly brought his glass to his lips.

"What does that even mean? 'Set up their backups'?" Graham asked.

"You know. Like, if they aren't married by a certain age they'll all marry each other."

Mia, who sat next to Noah, jerked her head in his direction. Her eyes went wide and held slight accusation.

He shot her a look that said *I didn't say anything*, and she relaxed marginally.

"Why do we have to get married at all?" Mia asked. She never had been fond of the idea and, far as he knew, she'd never dated the same guy for more than a few weeks. It was one reason Noah wasn't completely offended that she hadn't accepted him yet.

"I don't know." Claire shrugged. "It just sounds nice. Guaranteed companionship. Someone to have dinner with."

"A penis at your fingertips," Graham added, and Noah choked on his water.

Claire looked at Graham. "That's not the prize you think it is."

Graham grinned and raked a hand through his dark wavy hair. "Oh, but it is."

Claire pointed at Noah. "This is why I want Noah to be my backup."

"Me?" he said, at the same time Mia said, "Noah?"

"Sure," Claire said. "Why not?"

Before he knew what was happening, Mia had leaned forward and put her palm flat on the table, as if she were placing a bet at a craps table. "If anyone gets Noah, it should be me."

It was Noah's turn to give Mia a surprised look. God knows what would have shown on his face if he'd been two beers deep like Graham—as it was, it took effort to keep the warm surge of pleasure out of his expression.

"But you just knocked the whole idea of getting married," Claire pointed out mildly. She didn't sound surprised.

Mia frowned. "That was before you tried to take my best friend and marry him out from under me."

Noah kept his mouth shut, wanting to see how this panned out.

"He's my friend, too," Claire said.

"It's not the same." No one argued with Mia because everyone knew it was true.

Graham put his arm around Claire. "Guess that leaves you and me, Claire Bear."

She ducked out of his embrace. "Don't call me that."

"Fine. What nickname do you want when you're my wife?"

Claire sighed heavily. "I should have picked Mia."

Noah chuckled, but she was right. Mia was the best choice out of the four of them.

Graham held out his hands. "If not me, who? Noah's off the table. Am I so bad?"

Claire regarded him like she was inspecting a melon at the farmer's market. "You're hot and all, but… I don't know. I just always hoped for someone more…romantic. I want a man who looks at me the way Mia looks at chicken wings."

Noah wanted Mia to look at him the way Mia looked at chicken wings.

"If you're at the point where you're calling in backup, I think it's safe to say that's never gonna happen," Graham said.

Claire gave him an adoring look. "You say the sweetest things."

Noah held up a hand, halting their bickering. "When is all this happening? What's your age cutoff that requires we in-state the backup plan?"

"Fifty?" Graham suggested.

"Hell no." Claire looked at him as if he were crazy. "That's way too old. I'd say thirty if we hadn't all hit it already."

"Forty?" Mia offered.

Claire considered. "That works."

"That's only five years away," Graham said.

"Speak for yourself, old man," Claire said. "The rest of us are thirty."

Noah held up his index finger.

Claire rolled her eyes. "Fine. Thirty or thirty-one. Either way, forty works."

"So it's Mia and Noah, Claire and me?" Graham confirmed.

Claire scowled. "This didn't work out like I planned." She

turned eyes on Noah. "You haven't given any input. Who do you want as your backup?"

He stilled.

"We all know he'd pick Mia," Graham said. "Face it, my dear. I'm your man." He winked. "And what a lucky woman you are."

Claire scrunched her nose. "I have to know all my options. Come on, Noah. Between Mia and me, who do you want as your backup?"

He hesitated, unsure how to proceed, especially with the question hanging between him and Mia. But after a few seconds passed, Mia angled her torso toward him and one dark eyebrow lifted. She looked incredulous. Irritated, almost.

He stifled a laugh.

That one look settled his nerves, and it was like everything fell into place. He met her dark gaze and kept his voice as nonchalant as possible.

"I pick Mia, if she'll have me."

Between the two of them, Mia had always been the talker. In a group or on their own, she carried the conversation.

She was so sweet and genuine, people never seemed to mind. Noah certainly never had.

Even when he'd disappear into the tree house in his backyard to read in peace, she'd often find him there. Unlike Nathan, who would interrupt without so much of a *you busy?*, she'd at least wait until he'd finished his chapter, peeking over his shoulder to make sure before she started rambling.

Then they'd gotten old enough for cell phones and the text messages never stopped. He could probably count on one hand the days that had gone by where they hadn't conversed at least once that way.

Which was why today had felt so weird. He hadn't heard from her at all since Claire's birthday dinner Friday night, and he still had no idea what was going through her mind. He'd been more tense today than the day he started the series of tests that were part of the Architect Registration Exam. He hadn't wanted to push her, so he just let her think.

But he'd thought of little else.

He settled onto his couch Sunday evening and was seconds away from popping the top off a beer when his phone lit up.

Mia: Okay.

He closed his eyes and his shoulders relaxed.

Noah: Did you just agree to marry me via text message?

Mia: I'll do it in person if you open the door.

The knock sounded two seconds later.

He moved the cold beer to one of the Frank Lloyd Wright coasters Mia had gotten him for graduation, stood, and walked the several feet to the front door. Mia stood on his porch looking familiar and beautiful in a white V-neck and jeans. Her black hair was pulled up into a messy ponytail, as if she hadn't had the patience to deal with it today.

"Hey." Her voice was soft and a little hesitant, but her dark eyes met his in a steady gaze.

He'd planned to ask if she was sure, but now, having seen her face, he didn't have to. She might be scared and a little freaked out, but she was sure.

He felt the same.

He stepped to the side. "Come on in."

They sat side by side on the couch like they always did. She tilted her head when she noticed the beer, but didn't comment.

"Wanna know what convinced me?" she asked, slipping off her shoes and tucking one foot underneath her thigh.

He lifted his eyes to her face. "Was it because according to Claire, we'll just end up married at forty, anyway?"

She laughed lightly. "No, but it seemed a little like fate she asked that question that night. It was actually today when I stopped at Target to grab a few things. It wasn't busy at all, and no one was in line behind me, so I ended up chatting with the cashier for a while."

He grinned and shook his head. Mia could make friends with the royal guard at Buckingham Palace if given the chance.

"I said something about how I'd probably spend my entire paycheck in the store if I was there every day working."

"You are there every day."

Her eyes narrowed. "Not *every* day."

He'd put money on twice a week. At least.

"Anyway," she continued. "The lady was probably in her fifties, and she said she liked her job, but it wasn't where she'd thought she'd end up. Turns out she'd always dreamed of opening up her own quilting store, but never made it happen. Said she's regretted it ever since. I don't want to end up in the same situation, even if it means accepting some help."

Noah heard the struggle in those final words.

He extended his arm along the back of the couch. "I'm glad you're letting me."

"Also, I got another one of those stupid affirmation messages today. It said *I will make the most of every opportunity.*" She quirked her brow at him and he laughed.

Their pranks were usually limited to desk or computer manipulation, but he had to admit—he'd been proud of himself for coming up with that one.

"My first request as your wife will be that you cancel that. And the animal one."

"Really? That one seemed kind of cool."

"I mean, now I know that a shrimp's heart is located in its head. And every time a bat exits the cave it turns left. But that's not exactly useful information to me and I need it to stop."

He processed the fact about shrimps (fascinating) and focused on the matter at hand. "Fine. I'll cancel them."

"Thank you." She pressed her lips together and pushed them out a little, something she often did when considering what to say next. "So…how are we doing this? What happens next?"

Three days ago, Noah never would have guessed he'd be sitting here discussing marriage to his best friend. "What's your timeline? With the scholarship stuff?"

She scrunched her nose. "Well, that's the thing. The first full semester won't start until the fall, but because it's a program for adults returning to school, there's a one credit hour course they want me to take this summer. It's not required, but it sounds cool—it's about finding your passions and pursuing them. I'd need to enroll pretty soon. But we don't necessarily have to do our thing, yet. I think I could keep working at Agnew until August—"

Noah interrupted. "I say we just do it now. Get it done, so that way everything is consistent with your paperwork and we've worked out any insurance kinks before you start school full-time. You can take the summer to get back into the groove of being a student." He shuddered internally at the memories of long hours struggling to stay awake in class and staying up all night in the studio working on design projects.

"I can't imagine going back to school. I'm proud of you for doing this."

"I wouldn't be doing it if it weren't for you."

"I'm proud of us, then," he offered.

Mia released a long exhale. "So, by 'now' you meant..."

He shrugged. "Next week?"

Her eyes widened.

"What?"

"I don't know...it's just so soon. Is that even possible?"

"I looked into it a little this afternoon, just in case you... you know. Decided you wanted to go for it. We just have to go together to purchase the marriage license, and there's no waiting period in the state of Colorado. We could get the license and get married that day, if we wanted."

"Oh." Her eyes darted around the room before meeting his again. "Are we, um. Telling anyone? The truth?"

He'd thought about that, too. "Claire's gonna know something's up. She's the only one I think we should be honest with. Graham's great and all, but..."

"He can't keep his mouth shut."

"Exactly." He paused. "Do you want to tell your parents the truth?"

"No," she said. "I'm still worried about your dad, though."

"I said I'd handle him, didn't I?"

"You did. But I've worked for him for a long time, and I know he pays attention to every little detail. I don't think he'll believe it."

"I'll convince him it's real," Noah said. His parents knew him pretty well, and he had a hunch it wouldn't take much for them to believe he was in love with Mia. "Don't you trust me?"

"You know I do," she said, almost grudgingly. "What about

the other principals at work? Will they be suspicious? What about Julia? David? Especially him—I never got the impression he liked me much."

"What? Why do you say that?"

She shrugged and looked down. "I don't know. I just don't get a good vibe from him."

"Mia." He heard the hard edge in his voice, but couldn't stop it.

She sighed. "It's not a big deal."

Why was this the first he was hearing of this? He attempted to soften his tone. "It is to me."

"When I was first hired on, I messed up some of his appointments. I felt terrible and apologized—but not before he said your dad hired me out of pity and that I didn't deserve the job. It's always stuck with me, and I get nervous around him. Any time I mess something up, it feels like it always involves him. A few years ago, I failed to get an important message to him and he's never let me forget it. Last week I misplaced a client contract, and naturally it was his client. I get all flustered and just mess stuff up, and he makes sure I know it."

Noah's short fingernails dug into the skin of his palms. David had been at the firm a few years before Noah started his internship, and Mia was already a fixture at the front desk. He'd had no idea she'd felt that way. And for so long. "You're great at your job. Everyone makes mistakes sometimes."

"According to him it's more than that."

Noah had never cared much for David, and now he really didn't like the guy. "Why haven't you said something before?"

She arched an eyebrow. "What would you do? Defend my honor?"

Hell yes. "Maybe."

She gave a rueful smile. "It's not that big of a deal. But I guess he's the one I'm most worried about finding out. If he knew I was committing insurance fraud through the company..."

"Stop saying that," Noah said, firming his tone again. He lowered his chin and looked at her pointedly. "We've been secretly dating for months, and tonight I popped the question. We don't see any point in waiting for a fancy ceremony, and we decided to get married next week. Now that you'll be a kept woman, you decided to go back to school like you've always wanted. I don't mean this to come out wrong, but I don't think anyone at the office cares enough about you or me to think otherwise. People are concerned about their own business. They'll believe what we want them to believe."

She closed her eyes and took a deep breath, as if convincing herself his words were true. Slowly, she nodded. "Right. Okay."

"Want me to get down on one knee?"

Her eyes went wide. "No!"

He gave her a few seconds to process before asking his next question. "What about living arrangements?"

Her mouth opened and closed, and she stilled. "Wow, I really didn't think this through." Her eyes darted around the room as if she hadn't been there a thousand times. "If we want everyone to think this is real, we have to live together, don't we?"

Had she not considered that part? He sure as hell had. The idea of her being around all the time was equal parts thrilling and terrifying. They hung out enough that he was used to daytime Mia, going-out Mia, and lazy, let's-stay-in-tonight Mia. It was the thought of first-thing-in-the-morning Mia that had made his heart lurch. It was the only side of her he didn't know. The side reserved for roommates and lovers.

What was she like in those quiet, intimate moments just

after she woke up, before makeup touched her skin or a stray thought made her anxious? Did she listen to music while she got ready or turn on the TV when she made coffee? Or did she, like him, enjoy starting her day in silence?

Would that version of her become his favorite?

He swallowed. "We probably should."

She nodded, though she seemed a little dazed. "You have a house, so it would make sense that I'd move in here." Suddenly she frowned. "But what's Claire going to do? Our condo is too expensive for just two people. And Reagan *just* moved in. I'm not even sure Claire likes her yet." She buried her face in her hands and groaned. "Maybe we shouldn't do this."

Noah squeezed her shoulder. "We don't have to," he said. "This is a choice, and you can back out anytime until we sign the papers. But don't let things like living arrangements stop you. We'll figure all that out. It won't cost you anything to live here, and we could keep paying your share of rent at the condo until Claire finds another roommate. Hell, Graham might want to move in with them. He's been complaining about his place and talking about looking for something else."

She shifted and peeked up at him, a small grin on her face. "Claire, Graham, and the vegetarian living together? I'd love to see that."

He slid his palm down her back, enjoying the soft brush of her ponytail along the back of his hand, before pulling it back into his lap.

"How am I ever going to repay you for doing this for me?" she asked.

"You probably can't," he said, smiling a little. At her dejected expression, he changed tactics. "Don't do that. I don't want anything."

"Too bad. The guilt will be unbearable." She squinted, tilting her face to the ceiling. "I'll make you homemade breakfast every morning. And I'll make carrot cake every weekend."

His mouth watered at the mention of his favorite dessert. "Wow, I'm gonna gain like fifty pounds, aren't I?" It would totally be worth it.

"I'd say I have ulterior motives to stop other women from checking you out, but it wouldn't matter. They'd want you no matter your size."

He grinned at that, flattered and far too pleased at the thought of Mia feeling possessive of him. Her face simultaneously transformed to a frown.

"What?" he asked.

"What about—" She stopped short, her cheeks flushing. Her eyes flashed to his waist and quickly away.

Oh, shit.

He wanted to tell her not to say another word, but his tongue was suddenly glued to the roof of his mouth. Could they just ignore this part? Not talk about it, like normal adults?

"I, um. I don't want to hinder your sex life..." she started, pressing her balled fists together near her stomach. "But I'm not sure how that could work. I mean, it's probably not a good idea to bring anyone back here, but going elsewhere would just require discretion, you know? It could look bad if—"

This was so fucking uncomfortable. "Don't worry about that," he interrupted.

She nodded, neck flushed. "Yeah, you get it. Sorry."

"No, I meant don't worry as in it won't be an issue. I'm not going to sleep with someone else while I'm married to you."

"It could be two years, though."

He just stared at her.

"Noah—"

He held up a hand. "Stop. Don't bring that up again, okay?" She opened her mouth, but he added, "I mean it."

She clamped her mouth shut, apparently registering his tone.

Unless... Why had he assumed that issue referred only to him? "What about you?" The words burned as they came up his throat. He tried to think as little as possible about Mia being anywhere close to naked with another man, but he had no claim on her. Even in a marriage like this one.

She shook her head. "I wouldn't. I mean, I won't. I know this isn't real, but it wouldn't feel right. For me."

He could remind her, as she had for him, how long a time frame they were talking about. But he liked her answer too much, and besides, she knew.

They both did.

Two years would be a long damn time. But if his choices were meaningless sex with a stranger while the woman he loved was waiting at home, or nothing?

Nothing it would be.

5

"I can't believe I agreed to this."

"I think this is the best idea you've ever had."

Mia looked at Claire, who was sitting in the passenger seat. "Even though you wanted Noah as your backup?"

Claire snorted. "Please. I'd never do that to you. I've always wanted you two to get together and I was just trying to get the conversation going. I didn't know Noah had already popped the question by that point."

Mia dropped her forehead to the steering wheel. "You're talking about it like it was a real proposal."

If he'd actually gotten down on one knee like he offered to, she might have legitimately swooned.

"Real proposal, real marriage," Claire said. She pointed to

her retro blue-and-white polka-dot dress. "Thank you for not making me wear a real bridesmaid dress, though."

"That's because this is a *temporary* marriage," Mia corrected. She straightened and pinned Claire with as stern a stare as she could muster. "That part's secret, though." Adding that had been more for her benefit... She knew Claire would run down I-70 naked before ratting them out.

Claire pulled down the visor to fluff her blond curls. "Keep telling yourself that."

"I will." Little else had been on her mind over the last week.

Butterflies filled her stomach. She swept her eyes across the brick building, CITY HALL displayed in large letters above the door. The parking lot seemed empty for a Friday morning. Mia took the day off, but Noah planned to head to the office after. "Do you think he's in there already?"

"Probably."

Mia's phone buzzed.

Noah: Stop thinking so hard. Get in here and marry me.

A laugh escaped her lips. It was humorous because their roles were reversed—Noah was usually the thinker—and it was exactly what she needed. "Okay. I'm ready."

Claire met her at the front of the car and they took a few steps before Mia gasped and doubled back, flinging open the rear door. "I almost forgot the license."

Claire snorted. "Get yourself together, Adrian." She paused. "Wait, should I call you Agnew from now on?"

"No." Mia slammed the door, paper in hand. She waited until she was next to Claire again, and whisper-yelled, "This isn't real! I'm not changing my name."

Claire shrugged. "Okay. Lots of people keep their names these days."

They entered the courthouse and found Noah sitting on an old wooden bench along the wall, one ankle propped on the opposite knee. He was the picture of comfort, like marrying women by judge was something he did every other Friday.

He looked up as they entered, his red hair swept to the side in a style more polished than usual. He wore a tailored navy suit, white dress shirt, and a tie.

A tie.

Mia slowed to a stop a few feet away. She looked down at her simple pink dress, feeling her lips turn down at the corners. "I feel underdressed."

He stood, his expression serious. "You're beautiful."

Her stomach dipped at the look in his eye as he said that. She had no idea why—Noah looked like he always did. Like some quiet, brooding hero from an angsty film.

But her reaction was different in that moment. Nerves, probably.

She supposed there was nothing wrong with a little flattery on her wedding day.

It's Noah, she told herself. *Your best friend*. She put her hand on his arm, and he was hard and firm, just like always. Just like she needed. He'd been her rock through so many trials over the years, and she needed his calm presence. She went up on her toes. "Are you sure about this? Last chance to back out."

His voice was as steady as his words. "I'm sure."

The next ten minutes went by in a blur. They'd made an appointment with a particular judge and were called back immediately. The ceremony took place in a nondescript office that looked nothing like some of the grandiose churches where Mia had previously attended weddings. Claire hovered in the background, a witness and a friend, taking photos for the friends and family that would no doubt ask to see them.

Mia's parents were gonna flip out when they found out.

"Mia?" Noah said, his brow furrowing.

She blinked. "Huh?"

He tipped his head toward the judge, who repeated what Mia had apparently missed.

"Noah and Mia, I pronounce you man and wife."

Her eyes widened with realization, and she gripped his warm hand tighter, suddenly feeling light-headed.

It was over already? They were married?

Had she done everything she was supposed to? Said everything she was supposed to?

The judge, an older man with thinning gray hair, gave her a strange look, and Mia belatedly realized this was supposed to be the happiest moment of her life. She took a deep breath and pasted a smile on her face.

She must have looked convincing, because the judge happily returned her smile and said, "You may kiss your bride."

Mia turned back toward Noah, and at his expression, her smile slowly faded.

His blue eyes were on her face, roaming across her cheeks, forehead, her lips, like he was memorizing her. His brows were together, a tiny wrinkle between them, almost as if he were concentrating on something difficult.

Was he already regretting this? It was on the tip of her tongue to ask if he was okay, but nothing came out. Her heart had stopped, and she seemed unable to do anything but stand there and stare at him.

He still held her hands in his, and tugged gently at the same time he took a single step forward. He released her left hand

and put his on the back of her head, swallowing thickly before he bent to her.

Her eyes fluttered closed the moment he kissed her. His lips were warm and soft, his mouth slightly open. Her free hand lay flat against his firm abdomen, and the other trembled in his grip. He pressed closer, his fingers gentle in her hair, their clasped hands disappearing between their bodies, and an unexpected warmth coiled deep in her belly.

Hot damn, Noah knew how to kiss.

Then he pulled back, his gaze never wavering as he took his hands from her. Her fingers shook, worse now that she didn't have him to hold her steady.

"Congratulations," the judge said.

Mia startled, having forgotten all about the man.

Claire clapped and bounded up to them, a smile on her face and her eyes wide. "I can't believe you guys just did that."

Noah said nothing, and Mia knew the second his gaze slid away from her, like she'd been standing in the sun and a cloud had rolled in to block the soothing warmth.

The three of them walked out together, passing another couple on the way out. The woman was practically sitting on the man's lap, and they looked on top of the world.

Mia glanced over at Noah walking beside her. His eyes were straight ahead, his hands loose by his sides.

Not touching her.

Why did that suddenly feel disappointing? Did she want him to hold her hand, or something?

The wedding—that *kiss*—had knocked her off balance. *Get it together, Adrian.*

Noah barely looked at her as he headed for his car. "See you tonight?" he called over his shoulder. When she didn't reply immediately, he stopped and turned, his eyes meeting hers, a question in his gaze.

"Yeah," she said. "See you tonight."

"Let me get this straight."

Mia kept her back to her new, now ex-roommate, Reagan, who lounged on her bed while Mia did some last-minute packing. She'd been too nervous about the wedding—wondering if they'd really go through with it—to get everything done beforehand.

But they had gone through with it.

They were married, and tonight she'd move into his house as his wife. His house was fully furnished, so all she needed to take were clothes, toiletries, and most important, her KitchenAid mixer.

"You and this guy Noah have been secretly dating for months, decided on a whim to get married at the courthouse, and now you're moving out?"

"Yep." Mia thought it best to give as little information as possible. It helped that she and Reagan had only known each other for a month—she could say almost anything about her and Noah's history and Reagan wouldn't know any better. But she had spent enough time with her new roommate that before last week, Reagan thought Mia was single. She was glad she and Noah had gone with the "secretly dating" thing. It seemed the most plausible.

The thing that would make things look less plausible would be getting married and *not* spending her wedding night with her husband. Without thinking, she'd suggested she make the move over the weekend, but he'd pointed out how odd that would appear.

He was right. The safest way to go about it was to treat this like the real deal from the outside.

What will it be like on the inside?

She had no idea what it was like to live with a man. With her firm "not looking for anything serious" outlook on dating, she'd never gotten that far. And while she enjoyed meeting new guys and casually dating some of them for a few weeks, she'd never been tempted to amend her rule.

It had never been hard to walk away.

Something told her it wouldn't be so easy to leave Noah at the end of this ruse, but she would.

She had to.

She finished cleaning out the drawer and her gaze snagged on the sealed envelope sitting there. On the front was her name, printed in her mother's neat handwriting. She should have read it well before now, but some mixture of fear, guilt, and anger had so far kept the letter unopened, contents unknown. She hesitated for a beat and considered leaving it, but grabbed it and stuffed it in with her socks.

"I heard you talk about him a few times. Did I ever even meet him?" Reagan wondered aloud.

Mia thought back. "I'm not sure he's come over since you moved in," she said. Noah had always been more comfortable in his own space. "But he and I work together. And we've been friends since we were seven."

"That's adorable. It's like it was meant to be."

She glanced back at Reagan, who had a wistful look on her face. Mia forced herself to smile like a newlywed should. "It was."

"I wish I had a man." Reagan tucked her feet underneath her. "What's he like?"

Mia zipped the duffel bag and turned around. She put

her hands on the edge of the dresser behind her and leaned against it.

There were so many words to describe Noah.

Protective.

Observant.

Gentle.

Disciplined.

Intense.

All things she loved about him, but for reasons that were hard to explain to someone she barely knew.

"Noah is...wonderful. He's the definition of kind. Thoughtful. He does everything with intention and purpose. He's a gentleman. Intelligent, and even though he doesn't show it much, he's funny."

She thought back to the years before his brother died. He'd always been reserved, but there was a noticeable difference in his personality from that point on. Noah had a before and an after. One wasn't better than the other, but "before" Noah had been a little more carefree and easygoing. "After" Noah took a little coaxing to relax and let loose. "He's adventurous. Loves to go rock climbing. He used to go all over the country with his brother to climb mountains."

"Used to?"

Mia dropped her gaze, wishing she hadn't mentioned that. *As little information as possible.* "He doesn't travel as much anymore. He still climbs, but mostly around here." She grabbed the bag and slung it over her shoulder, frowning a little.

She hadn't thought about that in a while, but occasionally wondered—why didn't he go on climbing expeditions anymore? At first, she figured it was just because he missed Nathan, and didn't like the idea of going without his brother.

But that was a long time ago. Graham still went out of state, sometimes on multiweek trips to Canada or Wyoming. Noah never went unless it was nearby and was never gone for more than a few days.

"I guess that's a good thing," Reagan said, jumping off the bed to follow Mia out of the room. "He's a married man now. Can't be going out of town every weekend and leaving you alone."

It took a few seconds for those words to settle into Mia's brain, but when they did, she stumbled a little.

Reagan steadied her. "You okay?"

"Yeah," Mia said distractedly.

Leaving you alone.

Noah's brother had died the same weekend Mia was diagnosed...but no. Surely that—surely *she* had nothing to do with his change in his lifestyle.

She shook off the thought as they entered the kitchen.

Claire stood near the counter, her hand deep in a bag of chips. "Ready?" she asked, mouth full.

"I think so."

Claire brushed her hands off and grabbed the KitchenAid box from the counter. "Damn, this is heavy."

Mia had set two suitcases by the door, and she rolled one behind her while Reagan took the other. Her friends helped load the items into the car, which was already packed with hanging clothes.

"See ya later," Reagan said, giving her a quick hug and heading back inside.

Mia turned to Claire, who leaned against the Subaru with a satisfied grin on her face.

"Are you not even a little sad to see me go?" Mia asked.

"Of course I am."

"Your creepy, clown-sized smile says otherwise."

"Okay fine, I'm not." Claire laughed and stepped forward to hug her. "But only because I know I'll still see you all the time, and because Noah's house is where you should be."

Mia chose not to respond to that. "Dinner at least once a week?"

"Probably more."

"Deal. At least until the fall semester starts. After that I might be studying a lot."

"Studying, having wild sex with Noah…po-tay-to, po-tah-to."

Mia pulled back with a sharp inhale. "Claire! It's not going to be like that."

"Okay."

"I'm serious."

"Sure."

Mia closed her eyes and inhaled deeply. "I'm leaving now."

"'Kay. Love you."

"Love you, too."

When they first visited CU's campus as high-school seniors, Mia had been uncommonly nervous. It hadn't made any sense, because she'd been so excited for college. So *ready.* Still, the sweeping campus, with all the buildings separated by lush lawns and mazes of walkways, had felt overwhelming. After the formal tour, Mia's and Noah's parents had left, but Mia wasn't ready. Noah had walked with her around every inch of that place, ever patient as she explored and found her bearings.

That same feeling of uncertainty filled her just twenty minutes later, as Mia stood frozen in Noah's entryway.

"Why are you looking around like it's your first time here?"

She swallowed. "It sort of feels like that."

"Nothing has changed." He stood beside her, letting her have her tiny freak-out moment.

"Marriage is a pretty big change."

"Nothing else has to change."

"Promise?"

He paused. "No."

She frowned, keeping her gaze on his couch. *Their* couch. Her eyes settled on the right side, where she usually sat while she was here. Did she want that to be her permanent spot? It was fine when she was here for an hour or two...but every day? Was it really the best seat in the room?

Maybe she'd claim the armchair.

Noah's voice was warm, and closer to her ear than before. "Hey."

She looked up to find his blue eyes assessing her face.

"Would you rather be a ninja or a pirate?"

She grinned. "I'm pretty sure you've asked me that one before."

"When?"

"High school, maybe."

"You're different from the person you were in high school. What do you say now?"

She pushed her lips out as she thought. "Ninja."

"Why?"

"I'd rather be a stealth fighter than someone who goes around stealing other people's stuff."

Noah grinned. "Remember when you stole Claire's diary to confirm her crush on Damien Harris?"

"She didn't talk to me for a week after she found out."

"But you discovered her crush was actually on Bobby Buskins, which made it all worth it. That reminds me, we haven't teased her about that in a while."

"It's been at least two weeks."

"Let's remedy that next time we see her." He slid one hand into his pocket. "You also stole my favorite coffee mug last year. I had to use Styrofoam from the break room that day," he said with a shudder.

"But it spurred you to convince the office manager to start ordering biodegradable coffee cups."

"Man, she was hard to break. She really didn't want to switch."

She grinned at the memory, already relaxing, which she suspected was Noah's intent. She was lucky to have him as a friend.

No, as a husband.

And just like that, it was weird again.

"Mia."

"Noah."

"Stop."

"What?"

"Stop making it awkward. This is fine. It's us."

She met his gaze. His expression was serious. Steady. Comforting.

"You're right. It's us."

He smiled at that and grabbed a suitcase in each hand. "Stay there as long as you like. I'll put these in your room."

That triggered something in her mind, and she frowned. "My room?"

He stopped and turned, the luggage dangling by his sides. "Yeah. I figured you'd take the guest room…?"

She nodded. "Oh, okay. That's fine."

He didn't move. "Were you thinking of being in my room?" His voice sounded a little rough when he added, "With me?"

"I don't know. I guess I just thought… Graham comes over

sometimes. What if your parents stopped by? Would they see all my stuff in another room and wonder what was going on?"

One corner of Noah's lip disappeared between his teeth. "I didn't think about that. We'll already be sharing the bathroom and I just assumed you'd want your own space."

"I do. But I'm also afraid someone will figure this all out, and we'll find ourselves in a mess. I can barely pay my medical bills—I definitely can't pay fines. Or your salary if you get fired. I just want to be careful, I guess."

He nodded. "How about we put your stuff in my room, but you can sleep in the guest room?"

She thought about that for a moment. "Okay, yeah. That works. I mean…if you have space in your closet."

His gaze passed over her, and he started down the hallway again. "Don't worry. I've got room for you, Mia."

6

Noah was eighteen when he realized he was in love with Mia. They, along with a group of friends, had bought tickets to a concert of a popular rock group. It wasn't until they arrived at the venue that she pulled him to the side, pointing to a different entrance than where their friends were headed.

"Our seats are over here."

He'd hesitated, not because he wouldn't follow her anywhere, but just because he was confused.

"They wanted to be on the floor," she'd explained. "It's not our scene. Everyone will be wasted and it will be crowded and loud. We won't be able to enjoy the show."

He'd have *hated* to be stuck on his feet in the middle of a pulsing crowd for three hours. It would have embarrassed him if she'd bought separate seats just out of consideration for him, like he was the killjoy who didn't like to have fun, but she'd done it because she didn't want to be down there, either. She loved music, loved the band, and she had stood in their front-row seats in the bleachers, swaying and singing along with the most beautiful, content smile on her face.

It had been perfect for both of them, and he'd realized if he could choose just one person to experience these moments with—a concert, a school dance, or even just hanging out on a Friday night—it was her.

His affection for her had only deepened with time. And today, he'd married her.

What have I done?

He lay in bed staring at the dark ceiling, wishing back everything he'd said to her over the last week and a half.

He wanted to help her, sure. He'd cut off his right arm if he thought it might make her happy. Not the left, though. He glanced down to his left forearm and the outline of the dark tattoo there.

Most days he would have said her happiness came before any hesitations he might have. But that was before he saw her KitchenAid mixer on the counter next to the refrigerator. Before her dresses and silky shirts hung in his closet beside his starched oxfords. Before he glimpsed her in a tank top and shorts as she padded down the hall to the guest room.

They'd snuck into her parent's hot tub all the time as kids. He'd seen her in a swimsuit a million times, for fuck's sake. She was more than covered up in what she was wearing, but he'd nearly tripped over his feet when he caught sight of her tan legs as she walked past his doorway, her forever-long midnight hair trailing down her back like a waterfall.

This idea was stupid. It was torture.

He'd realized it during the wedding, the second his lips

met hers. It should have been a quick peck. She wasn't in love with him, this wasn't real, and Claire and a ninety-year-old judge had been watching them. But he hadn't been able to stop himself from pressing just a little closer, just for one second more. Her palm had gently touched his abdomen, and it had taken everything in him not to haul her up against him, wrap her legs around his waist, and take her to the nearest room where they could be alone.

The things he would do to her...

He'd known living with her would be difficult. But now that he knew the softness of her lips, the feel of her breath against his skin?

He wouldn't survive it.

A low groan escaped his throat and he rubbed a hand down his face just as his phone lit up on his bedside table.

Mia: You up?

Noah: Are you texting me from the next room?

Mia: Yeah. Is this weird?

Yes. It shouldn't have been, though. How many nights had they spent texting for hours from their next-door bedrooms mere yards away, because it was too cold to meet in the tree house?

Noah: Nope. Feels like high school.

Noah: You okay?

She didn't reply for several minutes. What was going through her mind? When she'd asked him the other day if he'd rather fly or read minds, he'd said fly, and meant it. Mia was open with her thoughts, and honest to a fault. He didn't think she hid anything deep inside.

Not like he did.

Plus, he figured it might just bring him down to find out she didn't think about him as much as he did her.

But right now? He sort of wanted to change his answer. Today had been weird, and they hadn't spoken much, and he needed to know what she was thinking. He hoped like hell she didn't regret this.

He heard a crash in the next room and was on his feet in a flash, ice-cold fear shooting through him. Did she fall? Was she sick? She'd looked kind of pale when they'd finished unpacking—had she pushed too hard?

He tore into her dark room, eyes searching. He found her hunched form on the floor next to the desk.

Noah lurched forward and knelt beside her. "Mia? What's wrong? Are you okay?"

She swept the mane of dark hair back from her face, sending the sweetest scent of vanilla in his direction.

"I'm fine," she grunted. "I thought it was stupid to be texting you and got out of bed to come talk to you. I'm not familiar with the room yet and walked right into the chair."

Relief whooshed out of him on an exhale. "You scared the shit out of me."

"Sorry." She looked up at him, and he realized his hand was spanning her back. Touching the soft, warm skin at the base of her neck. He pulled his hand away and she made to stand, wobbling a little.

He rose with her. "Are you hurt?"

She shook her head as she straightened all the way. "I just hit my knee."

Her eyes did a slow sweep of his body, and he was keenly aware he was shirtless. He'd kept shorts on because it felt weird to sleep in only his boxer briefs with her there, and in that moment, he'd never been more thankful for the foresight.

His skin felt hot and he fisted his hands at his sides, trying not to notice the curve of her shoulder or the delicate outline of her collarbone.

"What did you want to talk about?" he managed to get out.

Her eyes snapped to his face. "Oh. I, um, I just wanted to say thank you. For everything. It kind of hit me all at once that we actually went through with it. What you did for me." Her brown irises appeared almost black as they bounced back and forth between his. "I'll never be able to repay you for this."

"Stop saying that. I told you, it's enough for me to see you happy."

"That's ridiculous."

"Why?"

"I want you to be happy, too," she said.

"And?"

"Doesn't mean I'd have offered to break the law to do it."

The muscles around his lips twitched. "I think you would have."

She grinned. "Yeah, you're probably right."

"Plus, you're making me homemade cinnamon rolls in the morning."

"Cinnamon rolls? I don't think I was so specific…"

He shrugged. "I heard it."

"Like, with yeast and two rises and everything? That's a lot of work."

"You promised."

She laughed, and he relished the sound. "Fine. Cinnamon rolls it is."

"Good."

She lowered her gaze a little, looking straight ahead, level with his chest. She frowned and her finger touched his left pectoral. Goose bumps erupted across his skin. "Is that a new one?"

"Yeah." He cleared his throat. "I mean, I've had it a few months."

She nodded. "I guess I just haven't seen you lately without..." She waved a hand across his midsection. "Like this. It's beautiful. Is it finished?"

The tattoo was a single feathered wing spread across that side of his chest and onto his shoulder. "Yeah."

"Just one?"

He wasn't in the mood to talk about it, so he simply nodded.

She didn't push. Probably because she understood him so well and knew when to leave things be.

"Well," she said. "I'll let you get back to bed. I'm sorry I made you get up."

"It's no problem."

She just watched him for a beat, then stepped forward and wrapped her arms around him, laying her cool cheek against the tattoo.

"Thank you, Noah."

He slid one arm around her back, then the other. Standing in the dark with her lush body pressed up against him caused his heart to stutter to life, beating erratically inside his rib cage. His eyes slid closed and his throat closed up, a mixture of pleasure and guilt swirling inside him like a tornado. The guilt, an ever-present ache deep in his gut, clawed itself free and rose up to destroy the joy in his heart.

The pain made it difficult to breathe, his chest filling with pressure. He released her and headed back to his room without a word, his earlier assertion disturbingly clear.

He definitely wouldn't survive this.

Breakfast had always been Mia's favorite meal of the day. Well, before she discovered chicken wings, anyway.

Noah's mom had always loved making a big thing out of Sunday brunch, and when they were younger, Mia had usually drifted over to his house those mornings. It became such a regular occurrence that his mom started cooking for five, and Mia still showed up even when he and Nathan were away in the mountains.

He'd missed it since leaving home, though he now realized it might not be remorse or unrequited love that would do him in; he'd definitely die of a heart attack if Mia kept feeding him like this.

"Want another?"

"Don't ask ridiculous questions, wife."

She laughed and slid another warm cinnamon roll onto his plate. She refilled her coffee mug and sat across from him.

He let his eyelids drift down as he closed his lips around a forkful. "You're definitely making these every weekend."

She snorted.

He opened one eye.

"You'll get pancakes," she said.

He opened his other eye and grinned. "I'm okay with that. You can take next weekend off, though. I'm climbing with Graham."

"Yeah? Where?"

"Eldo."

"Of course."

Eldorado Canyon was his favorite place to climb, even

though it could get busy with tourists in the summer. His brother had always preferred Flatirons, and in high school they'd hit that area every chance they got for climbing and camping.

Noah hadn't been back to that particular spot since Nathan died.

He swallowed another bite and leaned back in his chair. "So. Are we gonna tell people we're married today?"

Her eyes widened a fraction. "Like our parents?"

"Yeah. Graham, too, probably."

She nodded. "I guess we should. I'll just call mine."

"You don't want to stop by and tell them in person?"

She winced. "Not really."

He wondered if she might say more, and just regarded her for a few moments. Her strained relationship with her parents was hard on her, and for her sake, he wished they could figure things out. They used to be so close. But no one seemed to know how to overcome what happened, and he wasn't sure they ever would.

"Do you think they'll be upset?" he finally asked.

"Only surprised, I think. Besides, they have no room to get upset. They're no strangers to keeping secrets." She looked down at her lap, then back up at him. "They've always loved you."

She didn't know, but after their big fight, Noah had promised her dad he'd look after her, especially during those months when they weren't on speaking terms. Noah's allegiance was to Mia first. Always. But every day he'd passed her parents in the waiting room of that hospital, Mia having put them on the unapproved visitor list, and the pain and worry etched on their faces had been more than he could bear.

He'd simply stopped in front of them one day and said, "I've got her."

Her mom had started crying, and her dad had hugged him, while Noah stood stiffly with his arms at his sides. That was two years ago, and as far as he knew Mia had only spoken to them a handful of times since.

"Your mom's gonna be pissed we didn't have a real wedding," Mia was saying. "And that she wasn't invited to the courthouse." She glanced behind her. "Think I can take the rest of those cinnamon rolls over as a peace offering?"

He straightened. "No. Those are mine."

"I made two dozen."

He locked eyes with her. "I don't like to share."

Her gaze held his for a beat, and he had no idea if she caught his double meaning. "Fine. But if she starts crying, that's on you."

"Of course she'll cry. It's my mom. But it'll be because she's so happy. I think she was losing hope for me."

Mia's face contorted and she put her elbows on the table, dropping her head in her hands. "Noah."

"What?"

Her words came out muffled. "I'm going to break your mom's heart." She lifted her head and let her arms fall across each other on the wood. "When we eventually break up. It's going to kill her."

He sighed. "Yeah. It will."

Mia looked so forlorn he almost laughed.

"Let me worry about that," he said. "For now, think about how happy you're about to make her. Isn't a little temporary happiness better?"

She frowned. "Not always."

Yeah, true.

Mia twisted around to look at the clock. "My parents will be up by now. I'm just gonna get this over with."

She picked up her phone and tapped the screen before she put the phone up to her ear.

"Want to put them on speaker?" he asked. "Do it together?"

She looked at the ceiling as if in thought, then shook her head with a little scrunch of her nose. Suddenly her face cleared. "Hey, Dad. Is Mom around, too? I have some news." She paused. "No, I'm fine. It's nothing like that."

Noah knew exactly how her dad felt in that moment. He constantly worried about her health, too.

"Hey, Mom. I'm fine. I, um, called to tell you both that... well, Noah and I got married yesterday." She met his eyes and tucked her lips between her teeth as she listened.

What were they saying? He couldn't hear yelling or screaming from where he sat, so that was good, right?

"I know. It was a spur-of-the-moment thing for us, too. The marriage, I mean. We've been, um, dating for a while now." She widened her eyes and held up her free hand, fingers spread, as if asking if she was doing this right. He shrugged, and she kept going. "But we've just been friends for so long we weren't sure how it was gonna go, and wanted to keep it between us for a while. Turns out I've never been happier, and when Noah suggested we get married, I said yes."

"Oh sure, put it all on me," he muttered.

She pursed her lips to hide a smile. Then, her face suddenly went pale. She locked eyes with him, and he tilted his head to the side, mouthing, "What?"

She swallowed. "Yes. I do. I love him." Her voice got quieter with each word. "More than I ever thought possible."

Noah stood, his chair scraping across the floor, and took his plate to the sink. His hands shook as he rinsed it and put it in the dishwasher. Mia continued talking, doing a damn good job convincing her parents she'd fallen for him and knew he was the man she wanted to spend the rest of her life with.

They'd said *I love you* to each other before, but only in the context of *I've known you forever and you're one of my closest friends,* not the *I'm about to go out of my mind because I'm so crazy in love with you* kind of way.

When it came to her, he'd felt both.

But he'd only ever shown her one. It was important it stayed that way.

And for the hundredth time in twenty-four hours, he wondered just what he'd gotten himself into.

On Sunday, they had lunch with his parents and told them the news.

His mom cried for a half hour.

His dad was pretty quiet about it, especially when they also mentioned Mia planned to quit her job at the firm to go back to school. Unease had spread down Noah's spine, so he pulled his dad aside while his mom fussed over Mia.

"I know the timing is weird, but this is real, Dad. We've been talking about it for a while, and it made the most sense to get it done before she got caught up in school again."

When his dad didn't immediately reply, Noah quietly added, "I've always loved her."

His dad looked at him silently for a few more seconds, then gave him a nod. "Then I'm happy for you."

On Monday morning, they rode together to work. When she met him at the front of his car, she stopped and opened her palm.

"Should we…?"

"Yeah." He took her hand and enjoyed the feel of her fingers curved around his entirely too much. He shouldn't get used to this. Couldn't.

When they reached her desk, she looked up at him with a small frown. "Coming to work together will make it difficult for me to mess with your office."

"Guess you'll have to get more creative, then."

She arched an eyebrow, and he knew she'd definitely accept that challenge.

He disappeared into his office for a few hours, completely lost in a new shopping center design when a knock at his door startled him.

"Sorry," came Julia's amused voice.

He waved her in. "Don't be."

"You always lost all sense of time and place when designing." She closed the door and walked forward. "Even in school."

"I haven't changed much."

"I don't know if I'd say that."

She sat in the same chair as Mia had less than two weeks ago while they discussed the possibility of getting married. She stretched to eye his computer screen. "Whatcha working on?"

He didn't like people looking at his work before he finished, something he was pretty sure she remembered from the many hours they'd spent working on projects together in architecture school. But he kept his expression neutral. "The extension for Spring Creek Shoppes."

Thankfully, she didn't keep her eyes on the screen for long and dropped her gaze to her lap.

He scooted his chair back a few inches. "Did you need something?"

"Is the rumor true?"

"What rumor?"

"You and Mia got married?"

He knew Julia pretty well. Had even gone on a few dates with her when they were in school, though she was more into it than he was, and he wasn't one for stringing women along. She'd always been easygoing and they remained friends after, and when his dad hired them both after graduation they'd become colleagues. They worked well together and complemented each other's professional strengths.

It was this degree of familiarity with her that alerted him to the need to tread lightly here. He didn't quite understand why he felt that way, but the sensation was there all the same.

"Yes."

"I didn't know you two had been dating."

"We didn't tell many people. Especially here at the office. We thought it was best to keep our personal lives separate."

"Hmm." She inspected her bright red nails. "Where's your ring?"

Shit. He hadn't even thought about rings. But why did she care? "We haven't shopped for rings yet. It was kind of a sudden decision and we just went to the courthouse."

"I see." Her green eyes met his. "You know David's office is on the other side of that wall, right?"

What did that have to do with anything? The question seemed rhetorical, so he kept silent, discomfort clamping his jaw together.

"He came to my desk this morning, bursting with gossip I didn't believe at first," she said. "But you just confirmed it."

Noah resisted the urge to do something with his hands, like run them through his hair or grip the armrests. He realized where she might go with this, yet somehow hoped he was wrong. "I'm not sure I like hearing my marriage referred to as rumor, and I definitely don't like it being called gossip."

Julia's expression bordered on sympathetic. "Excuse my word choice, but that's not the important part. David's convinced he heard you and Mia talking a couple weeks ago. Said he came in early that day, and you two showed up and clearly thought you were alone. He claims you only got married so she can keep her insurance."

Was the storm raging inside him visible? "What? That's not true—"

She held up a hand. "I don't need to know, Noah. I really don't. I consider you a friend, and I've seen how you look at her. It's why I gave up on you within weeks of meeting her. I believe you wanted to marry her. But David doesn't, and we both know he can be kind of an asshole. I wanted to warn you and tell you to be careful. With your dad's retirement announcement, everyone knows positions will shift. If he thinks he found something to use against you..."

"Thank you. But I—we—have nothing to hide."

Her mouth flattened into a line, but she nodded and stood. "Congratulations, then." She walked to the door and tossed one more comment over her shoulder before she left. "Can I give you one word of advice?"

He gave a terse nod.

"David is ruthless when he wants something. Do yourself a favor and don't underestimate him."

7

On Tuesday, Mia had to wait until Noah stepped out for lunch before she could hide printed photos of Nicolas Cage in every drawer of his desk. He'd seemed quiet last night—which for Noah, essentially meant silent—and she figured their whole situation was putting him out of sorts. It certainly was for her. It would take time for them to settle into a new routine, but in an attempt to keep things as normal as possible, she resorted to their usual antics.

Hopefully it would make him smile.

She was closing the filing drawer to the left of his chair when she looked up and nearly dropped the pile of papers.

Straight ahead, angled just right to be visible from his desk chair, was a photo of her and Noah.

On their wedding day.

Where had that come from? Claire must have given it to him, but when? She hadn't offered one to Mia.

Mia straightened and picked up the frame. It was taken mere seconds before their kiss. She and Noah were facing each other, her right hand in his left, his other hand hidden in her hair. The longer Mia stared at the photo, the harder it was to breathe.

They looked…into each other. In love. Enamored, even. Mia remembered how nervous she'd felt in that moment—but you wouldn't know it. Her eyes locked on his and the way her lips were parted just so—she looked desperate for him to close the distance between them.

And Noah? A tingle spread along the nape of her neck. His expression, normally restrained and serious, was bare and exposed, the longing on his face so apparent it was almost uncomfortable to look at.

Mia set the photo down and took a step back, though her gaze remained on the image. Was it real?

Or was he just a good actor?

His words from nine years ago echoed in her brain, so clear it was like he stood behind her now. *I was drunk. It was a mistake. I just want to stay friends.*

Of course he was acting.

He'd known Claire was taking photos. Knew they'd show them to people, and that they needed to convince others their marriage was authentic.

He'd always been one to plan ahead and consider everything. Handle things with poise and intentionality. Surely that's what happened here—he'd made sure their secret would be safe.

He was just protecting her, like he always had.

She let out a shaky breath, nodding to herself. She finished her task and snuck back to her desk, giving him a bright smile when he passed by twenty minutes later.

On Wednesday morning, instead of finding everything on her desk turned upside down or a foghorn mounted underneath her seat, she was greeted by the most beautiful bouquet of flowers she'd ever seen. The architects had a group meeting every Wednesday, so she waited until she knew Noah would be back in his office before going to him.

He was at his desk, looking at his phone screen. He looked up when she came in, but didn't smile.

She stopped a few feet from his desk. "Thank you for the flowers. They're beautiful."

He tipped his head to the side. "Why are you nervous?"

"I'm not."

"You're fidgeting."

She stilled her hands and forced her knee to stop moving. He didn't say more, and her eyes dropped to the floor.

"I guess I just wasn't expecting that," she said.

He stood and walked toward her, stopping right in front of her. "Would you have preferred I fill your drawers with packing peanuts?"

"Yes."

One corner of his mouth inched up.

"I was trying to keep things as normal as possible," she added.

His teeth sawed across his bottom lip. "But they're not. Everything's different." He lowered his voice. "At least, it needs to seem that way."

She glanced out the window behind him and sighed. He was right. Even at home, he'd been more intentional about considering her. That first morning she'd assumed she'd be forcing black coffee down her throat, because that's how Noah drank it. But when she'd opened the fridge to start the cinnamon rolls, right there in the door was an unopened container of her favorite coffee creamer.

She'd stared at it for so long he asked what she was looking for, and she'd almost burst into tears right then and there. He'd also arranged their electric toothbrushes just so on the bathroom counter, positioning the chargers at a perfect angle so they lined up side by side like little husband and wife appliances.

She needed to up her game, it seemed. She pointed to the frame on his desk. "I saw the new photo. Nice touch."

"Yeah," he said, running a hand through his hair. "I thought they turned out pretty good."

She pursed her lips and put her hand on his shoulder for balance, going up on her toes to fix his rogue lock of hair. "They? You have more?"

"I asked Claire to email them to me."

"Oh."

"I thought people might ask."

"Right. Good idea."

He looked over her shoulder and straightened, his jaw going taut. She frowned, and just as she turned to look behind her, a masculine voice came from the doorway.

"Noah—whoops, sorry."

David smiled at them—wait, David was smiling at her?—and gestured between them. "I haven't had the chance to congratulate you two. What a sweet surprise."

Mia turned back to Noah, and his eyes were strangely hard. It didn't appear he intended to reply, so Mia smiled back at David. "Thank you. We're really happy."

"I can see that," David said.

"Did you need something?" Noah asked. His voice was as

cold as the pint of ice cream Claire always kept in the freezer for emergencies.

"Nothing important," he said. "You're busy, I'll come by later."

David left, and when Mia turned back to Noah, he was walking back to his desk. He sat down and rubbed a hand across his jaw.

"Is everything okay?"

He nodded.

Now was one of those times she wished she could read his mind. "You sure?"

"Yep."

His phone rang, startling her. She checked the time and backed out of his office. "That's probably your conference call. Talk to you later?"

He watched her as she went and she closed the door behind her. She returned to her desk, and gingerly rubbed a soft, pink flower petal between her fingers.

As she leaned forward to inhale the pleasant scent, she hoped this whole thing got easier as time went on. Feeling awkward around Noah wasn't something she was used to, and she didn't like it one bit.

Thursday was Mia's favorite day of the week. It was probably weird to look forward to an appointment at an infusion center, but she got to relax in a comfortable chair, have snacks brought to her, and visit with interesting people. And she always, *always* stopped for chicken wings afterward.

She was scheduled in Natasha's section, and sat in her usual recliner. The office had a few secluded chairs along the wall with curtains patients could pull together for privacy, and they were always occupied. Even if they weren't, Mia would have stuck with this one. She preferred the middle section where the chairs were a little closer together, and she could chat with the other patients.

She supposed she'd earned Noah's title as "the most social person he'd ever met."

The downside was there was only one television in this area, and they usually kept it on the Travel Channel. Natasha once explained that the manager thought it was soothing for the patients to see beaches and beautiful landscapes while they got their treatment.

Probably true for most people, but for Mia, those ocean scenes brought waves of guilt. Today was no different as the screen displayed an hour-long special on New Zealand, one of the many destinations her parents had talked about when she was a kid. They'd had a huge map hanging on the wall in the living room with little pushpins marking each place they wanted to visit someday.

Ireland. Japan. Greece.

Brazil. Fiji. Switzerland.

Would they have hit all of them even if she hadn't gotten sick? Probably not. They'd have tried for as many as possible, though. But now? The financial burden of those first few years of her illness had sent those dreams down the drain.

Mia tried to keep her attention elsewhere, and ten minutes into her infusion, the medical assistant brought an older woman to the chair on Mia's left side. After taking her vital signs the assistant left, and Mia smiled at the newcomer. Her gray hair was in a long braid down to her waist, and she wore bright red glasses. She looked nervous.

Mia reached into her bag and pulled out a wrapped brownie. She held it out. "Brownie?"

The woman gingerly took the offering. "Oh. Thank you."

"They're gluten-free, but you'd never know it," Mia said with a smile.

"Are you my chair mate for the day?" the woman asked.

"Yep. Best seat in the house. Best nurse, too."

"I heard that!" Natasha called from her computer, a grin on her face.

Mia leaned over. "Flattery gets you everywhere with Natasha."

"Noted," the woman said with a smile. She held out her hand. "I'm Barbara."

"Mia. Nice to meet you."

"What are you in for?"

She said it like they were in prison, and Mia laughed. "Kinrovi."

"Never heard of it. What's it for?"

"I have a rare kidney disease. I'll need a transplant at some point, but until they find a match, this keeps things under control."

"A kidney transplant, huh? My cousin had one of those. Got it from his dad, if I remember right."

Mia looked down at her hands. "Yeah, family members are usually the easiest way to go." She tucked a piece of hair behind her ear. "I'm adopted, so it's not an option for me."

Mia looked up to see the slight wince on the other woman's face, probably from the way Mia had said it. "Ah."

"What about you?" Mia asked, changing the subject. "I haven't seen you here before."

"First time. My doctor's been wanting me to try this new drug for my Crohn's disease for a while now, but I held out as long as I could." She eyed Mia's arm and shuddered. "I hate needles."

"I understand. I did too, at first. But Natasha's so good you'll barely feel it."

Barbara took a deep breath. "I hope you're right."

Natasha approached and introduced herself to her new patient. While they chatted, Mia sent Noah a text message.

Mia: Wings?

Noah: Sure.

Mia: They have a new flavor. Orange ginger. Wanna try it?

Noah: Nope.

Mia: Come on.

Noah: Why can't you accept the fact I like them plain?

Mia: Because it's weird.

Noah: Some might call it loyal.

Mia: That's a good quality in a husband, I guess.

Noah: You guess?

Mia: Okay, it's definitely a good quality.

Noah: Meanwhile, my wife's out there trying a new flavor every chance she gets.

Mia: Guess you'll have to find a way to keep our marriage spicy then, huh?

As soon as she hit Send, she regretted it. She scrambled to find something else to say, to explain she hadn't meant it *that* way. But everything she typed out seemed ridiculous, and she kept erasing it to start over. Finally, another message from Noah came through.

Noah: We're so different.

They were. As she considered how to respond, Barbara said, "Mia?"

Mia looked up. Natasha had placed the tourniquet on the older woman's arm and stood at the ready with the needle.

Barbara's eyes were wide, her lips quivering. "Would you talk to me? To distract me?"

Forgetting all about her conversation with Noah, Mia dropped the phone in her lap. "Of course." She launched into a monologue about going back to school, and what prompted her interest in pediatric dietetics. She talked about her own issues with eating growing up, and told Barbara that the brownie she'd handed over was one of her many attempts to have perfected recipes at the ready for future patients with allergies or food aversions. Natasha expertly started the IV and left, while Barbara and Mia kept chatting. They spent the rest of the time discussing their favorite recipes and baking techniques, and before Mia knew it, her pump beeped to indicate her infusion was complete.

Natasha disconnected the empty bag and pulled the IV from Mia's arm.

"See you next week," Natasha said with a smile.

"I'll be here." Mia stood and turned to Barbara. "Will you be back?"

Barbara nodded. "As long as this works, I'll be here every other week."

"If you didn't mind me talking your ear off, ask for Natasha again."

"I thoroughly enjoyed it. It was lovely meeting you, Mia."

Mia gathered her things, and as she made her way to her car, she realized she'd left off in the middle of a conversation with Noah. She opened her messages to type out an apology, and found another message from him she hadn't seen. She slowed her steps, reading it twice, unsure what to make of it.

I guess it's a good thing opposites attract.

After dinner that night, Noah said he had something for her and disappeared to his room. She cleaned up the table and out of habit separated the extra wings for Claire before realizing she wouldn't be going back home to take them to her.

She *was* home.

Instead, she wrapped them up and put them in the fridge, wondering if she'd have time to take them to Claire tomorrow.

Noah reentered the living room and sat beside her. She'd kept her original spot on the couch, and it felt like every other Thursday night.

Except this time, he offered her a ring.

She stared at his open palm and the two circles there. They were silicone, the larger one black and the small one a dark purple.

He took the purple one between his thumb and forefinger. "I'm sorry I didn't think about rings before. But someone asked me, and I realized we should probably wear them."

She nodded, her throat strangely tight. She took the band, bending it between her fingers.

"They're nothing fancy. It seemed silly to spend a lot of money. You know, since…" he trailed off.

Why did her heart feel so fluttery, bouncing around inside her chest? This was for appearances, plain and simple. Still, she couldn't hide the emotion in her voice. "Purple's my favorite."

"I know."

She slid the ring on her fourth finger and watched as he slowly did the same with his. She looked up to find his ice-blue gaze on her.

"Thank you," she whispered. "Not just for the ring."

"I swear, Mia. If I hear those words from your mouth one more time…"

She grinned. "You'll what?"

He paused. "I—I'll think of something."

She settled back and picked up the remote. "Let me know when you do. It's *Bachelorette* time."

He stood. "You're on your own with those fake relationships tonight. I still need to pack for Eldo."

She sidestepped the opportunity to point out a "fake relationship" was exactly what they were doing. "You took off work tomorrow, right?"

"Yeah. We're gone Friday through Sunday morning. My parents are having a little get-together for my mom's birthday on Sunday, so I wanted to be back for that. Would you mind coming with me?"

"Of course I'll come."

He started toward the hallway, then stopped and faced her again. He gripped the back of his neck, worry marring his brow. "Will you be okay? Here? While I'm gone?"

She laughed. "Why wouldn't I be?"

His expression didn't change. "I don't know. It's just…you

were always with Claire before. I feel sort of weird leaving you alone."

"You think I can't handle living by myself? I have roommates because Denver is expensive, not because I'm incapable of being alone."

He shook his head, wincing. "No, I just meant…what if something happens and you need a doctor or something?"

Oh.

She frowned a little, still unsure how she felt about that. Part of her appreciated his concern while another rebelled at the thought of him feeling responsible for her. "I feel fine."

He must have noticed her tone, because he opened his mouth like he might say more, but clamped it shut. He swallowed and nodded, leaving her alone.

8

"Go on, get out of here." Graham put the car in Park, his glare belied by the wide grin on his face. "We're not doing this again until you're out of the honeymoon phase."

Noah grunted something in response and grabbed his backpack. He'd been a shitty companion the last two days, it was true. He'd worried about Mia the whole time, and hadn't been able to shut off his thoughts. Service was sketchy at the campsite, and the inability to text her and check in anytime he wanted made it worse. Being around her constantly these last few weeks had put her on his mind more than usual, and not just with the usual thoughts of whether she was happy or if she was feeling well. Now he wondered if she felt at home at his place—and what his electric bill would be. The woman left every light in the house on, and without him trailing behind her turning them off, his house probably sat like a neighborhood homing beacon all weekend.

He was also concerned about what Julia had said about David, and the fact David likely knew what he and Mia were doing. David had yet to say anything, and Noah had decided not to tell Mia. It would only stress her out, and maybe nothing would come of it. But just knowing that David knew… It still made him uneasy.

He should have canceled the trip altogether. Climbing while distracted was a recipe for disaster, but thankfully nothing had gone wrong.

He got out of the car, and when he was halfway up the driveway Graham yelled through the window.

"Think about Banff, okay?"

Noah didn't even look back. That was another reason this weekend had sucked—Graham had brought up ice climbing. They'd avoided the subject for nine years, and Noah had been stupid enough to believe it was an unspoken understanding to leave it that way.

"Nathan would want you to go."

Noah stopped in his tracks. He slowly turned.

Graham leaned across the passenger seat, his face clear as day through the window. His cocked brow was unapologetic.

"You don't know what a dead man wants."

Graham's stone face slipped a little. "I know that much."

"No." Noah turned his back on his friend and went inside.

He dropped his bag by the door, his eyes immediately searching the room. Mia was on the couch, smiling at him.

"Hey. You're back."

He took her in, the coiled tension in his chest slowly releasing like a pressure valve.

The pink in her cheeks—she was here and healthy.

The smile on her face—she was happy to see him, and he reveled in the intoxicating satisfaction that brought him. Even if he had no right to it.

The cascade of dark hair around her shoulders, framing her face and neck—she was the most beautiful thing he'd ever seen. He'd give anything to be able to lay her down on that couch and make her as breathless as he felt just looking at her.

The pressure spread lower, doing the opposite of relaxing, and he dragged his eyes away from her. "Yeah."

"How was it?"

"Good." He glanced at his watch. "I'm gonna grab a shower, then we can head over to my parents'. Sound okay?"

"Sure."

He went to the bathroom and smiled when he found the light on. He shut the door and turned on the water as cold as it would go.

The party at his mom's went okay at first. The May weather was perfect, and people spilled from the house onto the large back patio. His parents had spent years perfecting the outdoor entertainment space and used it at every opportunity.

When Mia's parents lived next door it had been nothing but a concrete square with an aged iron table and chairs, but it hadn't stopped them from spending summer evenings out here. His mom's penchant to chat for hours had driven him crazy most of the time, but those nights? It meant he and Mia could hang out in the tree house well after curfew while their parents talked for hours about travel and politics.

Those nights were long gone, though. Her parents had downsized several years ago and moved across town, and if his parents had kept in touch with them, he didn't know about it.

Tonight the space was filled with aunts, uncles, and several of his parents' friends and colleagues, and he and Mia mingled among them, repeating their rehearsed story of their impromptu marriage several times over. A few of the principals from the firm were there as well, and Noah either held Mia's hand or had his arm around her most of the party, conscious of the eyes watching them.

Especially his dad's.

He hoped the other men's gazes were simply curious about his new, unexpected wife, and had nothing to do with how gorgeous she was in a white tank top and long blue skirt wrapped around her slender waist. That may have been another reason he didn't stop touching her, possessive bastard that he apparently was. At times he worried his touch might burn her, hot as he felt. But she didn't seem to notice, or mind his hands on her.

He wasn't stupid enough to read anything into it. She knew what was necessary here.

About an hour after they arrived, his mom tapped her glass. The conversation died down and everyone turned their attention to her.

"I just wanted to thank everyone for coming. Twenty-five is such a big birthday—" chuckles went around the yard "—and I'm so blessed to have you all here to celebrate it with me. I also want to extend congratulations to my son, Noah, on his recent marriage. Even if they didn't invite me to the ceremony."

Noah forced a wide smile as everyone looked at him and Mia, clapping and whistling.

His mom smiled and pressed her fingers to her lips, tears welling in her eyes. "I'm just so happy you two ended up together. I always hoped for it."

The lump in Noah's throat tripled in size. Mia's hand felt

warm in his, and she blinked up at him, smiling belatedly, like she remembered performance was required here.

"Me too," Mia said. She leaned into him, her face tilted up, and Noah acted on impulse.

He lowered his head and pressed his lips to hers. The second he made contact, he pressed closer, unable to stop himself. Her grip on his hand tightened, and his eyes popped open to find her dark eyes looking right at him. He fought the urge to jerk back and separated from her mouth slowly. He cleared his throat.

"Clearly, I'm in agreement," he croaked out.

Everyone laughed, shattering the external tension he felt pressing against them, though the turmoil roiling in his abdomen didn't abate. Not even a little.

Everyone eventually drifted to the kitchen for the catered dinner and dessert. Noah excused himself and slipped outside, his long silent strides taking him through the grass to the tree house in the corner of the yard.

He climbed inside, thankful for his father's foresight to build something sturdy enough for adults. He and Mia had spent hours here through middle and high school. Hours, days, years.

A lifetime.

Settling his back along the exposed tree trunk, he stretched his legs out and slid his phone from his pocket. He searched his music library for Snow Patrol, found "Chasing Cars," and put it on repeat.

He leaned his head back against the bark and closed his eyes, letting the familiar song—and the feelings that came with it—surround him in the darkness.

He'd just kissed Mia in front of his entire family. In truth, he'd thought of little else since that day in the courthouse.

He'd been dying inside, hoping for the chance to have his lips back on hers. But fulfilling that desire had done nothing but plunge him deeper into his constant state of misery.

Not to mention the blue balls—another state he lived in on the daily.

What had he been thinking, marrying her? What on earth had he thought he'd accomplish? He could tell himself all day long he wanted to help her pursue her dreams, and it would be one hundred percent true. But there was more to it, much as he tried to deny it.

He'd wanted to be closer to her. Because apparently seeing her every day at work, and at least three times a week after work, wasn't enough. He'd denied himself for so long, knowing he didn't deserve her. Didn't deserve to be happy after what he'd done. He'd kept his distance for years—almost a decade—and put Mia firmly in the friend category.

Then she'd given him the opportunity for more, and under the guise of doing it for her benefit, he'd jumped on it like a ravenous lion on an injured gazelle.

Well, now she's close, you idiot. Living with her was like standing next to a fire, feeling the pleasure and warmth, but knowing he didn't dare put his hand inside the flames.

"Fuck me," he muttered.

A low creak alerted him that someone was climbing up the ladder. Mia's dark hair was the first thing he saw, and she climbed on all fours until she was beside him. She tilted her head, listening.

"Snow Patrol, huh?"

"Yeah."

"Reminiscing?"

"Something like that."

"We must have listened to this song a thousand times."

"At least."

The sun was setting and it was dim inside the tree house, but his eyes had adjusted. She smoothed out her skirt and crossed her legs at the ankles, absently picking at her thumbnail. Her dark hair slid forward, a curtain hiding her features. He ached to slide his fingers through the strands and push them back.

To see her face. To touch her lips again.

He looked away. "Was that okay? What I did out there? It just seemed like the believable thing to do."

"The kiss?"

"Yeah. If you could even call it that." Maybe minimizing it would force his own feelings to take the hint.

"It wasn't a kiss?"

His shoulders tensed, and he was thankful for the darkness. "Not really."

"Felt like it. Your lips were right here." She tilted her face and touched her bottom lip with her thumb.

It took a mountain of strength not to let his eyes linger there. "I may have put my mouth there," he managed to get out. "But I didn't kiss you."

"I'm pretty sure that's the exact definition."

He shifted his gaze to the wood planks at his feet, unable to look at her when he said, "If you and I ever kissed for real, you'd know the difference."

She shivered, and he wished he had a jacket to offer her.

"Hmm," she murmured. "Now you've got me curious. What would a real kiss from Noah Agnew entail?"

The words came without thought, his number one fantasy one of the clearest scenes in his mind. He'd thought about it so often it was embarrassing. "You know that feeling in your stomach when you know something good's about to happen? A lot of that. Anticipation, excitement, and maybe a little bit of nerves. When our lips touched, it would be one of two things. Soft and sweet, or deep and intense. Either way, there would definitely be tongue involved. My hands would be in your hair—" He suddenly stopped and coughed, noticing her wide eyes. *Shit.* "I mean, hypothetically."

The song ended and silence surrounded them for a few beats before it started back up again.

"Well," she finally said, and he couldn't help but notice she seemed a little breathless. "Sounds like it would be quite an experience."

He forced a quiet laugh, trying to lighten the tension. "I'd like to think so." He pulled his knees up and extended his arms, resting his forearms there.

They didn't speak for some time, and he wondered what memories this song conjured up for Mia. He was too chickenshit to ask that, so he asked a different question.

"Would you rather kiss me every once in a while to make sure our relationship seems believable, or find some other way to convince them?"

"Real kisses, or what you did in there?"

Real ones. "What I did in there."

"That seems easier, don't you think?"

"I guess." He nudged her with his shoulder, hating how awkward he felt. "Is this too weird?"

She bumped him back and grinned. "It's a little weird. But it's you and me. We'll figure it out."

"When? It's been more than a week." He didn't know which was worse—before this whole ruse, where he'd been pretending to only think of her as a friend or now, pretending to be her husband.

The only difference between the scenarios was who he was lying to.

"I don't know," she said. "Do you think…"

She trailed off, and he looked over at her. "What?"

She rubbed her hands up and down her thighs, the blue fabric of her skirt rippling under the movement. "Um, do you think maybe we should kiss again? Maybe we just need to get used to it. Make it less of an ordeal."

He almost choked on his tongue. "Here? Now?"

"Yeah. While we're alone. It feels so much worse with an audience, and maybe that's the problem."

He shook his head at the same time his heart screamed the affirmative. "I don't think—"

"You're always thinking," she said, shifting to her knees. "We both are. Let's just stop for a minute."

She took his face in her small hands, angled his head toward her, and pressed her lips to his. Like before, her eyes were open, brown and wide and beautiful. His hands shook with the effort to keep them to himself.

"Noah," she murmured against his mouth. "Don't think."

Don't think.

He gave in to his body, allowing his arm to rise up and his fingers to slide across her cool cheek. Her eyes slid closed and a small murmur escaped her throat, and at that tiny sound his control snapped. He grabbed her by the waist and hauled her onto his lap. She let out a little yelp but kept her lips against his, settling her thighs down to frame his waist, her hands still on either side of his face.

One of his arms clamped around her back, pressing her against him, while the other slid up the back of her head, gripping her hair in a frenzy. She arched her back—fuck, he couldn't get her close enough—and opened her mouth to him.

Deep and intense, it is.

Her tongue was in his mouth and he was completely lost.

Dying and drowning in her breath, her scent, her touch. He never wanted to come up for air. Ever. Her hands were under his shirt, scorching his skin as they slid up his stomach to his chest.

He lifted his hips a little, unable to stop himself, and she pressed down against him, causing the most beautiful and painful friction. When she said his name on a breathless moan, he was seconds away from flipping her onto her back.

That's when he came back to himself.

It took the strength of every single cell in his body to take his lips from hers. He dropped his head against the tree, anchoring himself there. Her eyes slowly opened, taking him in.

"Wow. Noah, I—"

He shook his head, his eyes dropping to her swollen lips. *Dammit.*

"I'm sorry." His voice sounded raw, like he'd been screaming for hours. "I shouldn't have done that."

She slowly climbed off his lap. "Actually, I think I did that."

"I took it too far."

She looked at him curiously. "I was okay with it."

"We can't do that."

"Okay," she said. Her eyes dropped to his lips, then lower. Her eyes went wide. "But, um, why not?"

He shifted a little. "Because. You're my best friend. We got caught up in the acting. And even though we're doing this thing, it's not forever, right?"

Right?

Mia had been anti-relationship and anti-marriage for the last nine years. Vehemently so. He wasn't naive enough to think one kiss would change her mind, but he wanted to hear it from her.

"Right." Her tone was all the confirmation he needed.

“Then it’s not worth it to risk our friendship,” he said. “It could mess everything up.”

“Maybe,” she said thoughtfully. “But…what if it makes everything better?”

How could it, if it wasn’t real? “It could ruin us.”

“Maybe it already has.”

He shook his head. “Don’t say that. That was just practice for our public performances. Nothing more. And you were right, it will definitely be easier to kiss you in front of other people now.” When had he become such a good liar? He didn’t know if he was proud or ashamed of himself. Either way, if he allowed things to go further, this wouldn’t end well. “I won’t be weird about it if you won’t.”

She wiped her hand across her lips and he wanted her to take it back. Or to kiss her again, to put *him* back on her. “Okay. I won’t be weird.”

There was nothing for it. The silence that fell inside that tree house was ten shades of awkward.

“Quick, tell me the thing that’s annoyed you most since I moved in,” she said.

“What?”

“I must do something that drives you crazy.”

She was attempting to lighten the mood, and it worked. “I’ve had to triple the amount of toilet paper I buy.”

Her mouth dropped open. “Excuse me? I have to use it no matter what I’m in there for, you know.”

He laughed. “I know. I guess I just didn’t realize how much faster women go through it. Also, you refold my towels.”

“It’s not my fault you do it wrong.”

“Why don’t you show me the right way, then?”

She shrugged. “Just seems easier to fix it.”

“Every time I wash them?”

"Yep."

He laughed. "Okay, what about me?"

"You leave dishes in the sink."

"For like, a day. I do them in the evening."

"True, but in the morning you just set your coffee cup in there and move on." She gestured to the right as if she were standing at his sink this very moment. "The dishwasher is *right there.* You just pivot and put it in there instead of the sink."

"Could be worse," he pointed out. "Have you ever seen the state of Graham's kitchen?"

She shuddered. "No, and I think I'm better off not knowing."

They climbed down shortly after, though not before Mia peeked through the other side of the tree house at the redbrick home next door. He saw the sadness in her eyes and his own gaze passed over the window that had been her bedroom as a kid.

Her parents had sold the house shortly after the medical bills started rolling in.

They made rounds to say goodbye to everyone, and when they came to his parents, his mom pulled him into a hug. "I'm so proud of you," she said.

"Thanks, Mom."

"Nathan would have been so happy," she continued, tears welling in her eyes again. "He'd have loved to see you and Mia together."

He stepped away and put his hands in his pockets, suddenly wanting to be anywhere but here. His mother's words reminded him he'd just kissed the woman he loved, while somewhere in this town his brother's fiancée was alone, no longer able to kiss the man she loved. A hollow sensation spread through him, as if all his organs had been removed.

He was bones and skin, nothing else, in his childhood home without his brother here beside him.

David finally sauntered into Noah's office a week later. Noah had been expecting him, and quite frankly felt relieved David would finally bring up his accusations. The time that had lapsed since Julia gave her warning had only increased Noah's concern, which was probably David's intention.

David left the door open and settled in across from Noah, relaxing casually against the chair. He folded his fingers across his abdomen and smiled.

Noah did his best to appear relaxed despite being wound tighter than a public school budget. "What can I do for you?"

"Julia spoke to you, I presume? I told her not to mention it, but I don't expect she listened. She always had a soft spot for you."

Noah wasn't interested in dancing around the subject. Or talking about Julia. He stood and walked to the door, swinging it shut before resuming his seat. "Why don't you save us both time and say what you came here to say?"

He let out a low whistle. "Someone's in a bad mood. What, the wife didn't put out last night?"

Noah was out of his chair instantly, bent forward with his palms flat on the desk. "Don't talk about her like that. Ever," he warned. "I wouldn't put up with it anywhere, but don't think just because we're at work I won't break your jaw."

David appeared delighted. "Sure would make things easier for me if you did. Then I wouldn't have to use the fact that you're committing insurance fraud against you."

Noah schooled his features, still on his feet. "I don't know what you're talking about."

"Come on, Noah. Let's not do that. I heard you and Mia talking."

Noah hated hearing her name come out of this asshole's mouth. "Whatever you think you heard, it's not true."

"You didn't marry her so she could quit her job and keep medical insurance? The timeline of events suggests otherwise. Seems a little too good to be true that two friends who have never had a public relationship up and get married within weeks of one quitting their job. Especially when that person has a costly medical condition."

Noah straightened and slid his hands into his pockets. "Regardless of how it looks, that's what happened. We've known each other forever and have been dating for months. I don't give a shit that you weren't aware. Your head is too focused on your own business to care about other people. Had we planned on getting married so soon? No. I'll give you that little piece of honesty. She had an opportunity that required her to quit, and yes, we moved up the wedding for logistical reasons. But it was happening either way."

"The conversation you two had doesn't jive with that. Nice try, though. It almost sounds plausible." He paused. "Almost."

"Why do you care?" Noah asked. "What is it you want?"

"Sure, I'll cut to the chase." He checked his watch. "I have an appointment that started…five minutes ago, anyway."

Noah's back teeth snapped together.

"We both know your dad's retiring, and the string of promotions will open up an associate position."

Noah's spine straightened. He'd meant what he said to Mia—he didn't expect an automatic promotion and he'd worked his ass off to prove his worth at the firm independent of his role as the boss's son. Either way, Noah was ten times the architect David was. Between the two, Noah was unquestionably the better fit.

"I'm the better candidate," he said. It may not be the best decision to outline David's professional shortcomings, but it was the only objective way he knew to explain why he deserved it. "Everyone knows you've made some questionable decisions on your projects. Code violations, accessibility issues related to ADA regulations, and vague notations. It's no secret they've required you to have drawings reviewed by a more experienced architect before they're passed to the engineers."

David's cocksure expression slipped a fraction. "That only happened twice, and it was years ago."

"That's not what I heard."

"I guess we're both eavesdropping on conversations we shouldn't, huh?" David propped his elbow on the armrest and rubbed his thumb and forefinger together. "I've put everything I have into my career and I deserve a shot at the top. I've been here longer and have more experience. You shouldn't assume it's yours based on nepotism alone."

"I never assumed that."

"No?"

"No."

James McKinley, one of the principals, who would become CEO after the senior Agnew left, had been a key mentor in Noah's growth and development as an architect. He hadn't cut Noah any slack. If anything, he'd made him work harder because he was an Agnew.

Did Noah hope to carry on the legacy? Of course. It was far in the future, but he'd always hoped the company might be passed down to him one day. A dream his father shared, especially after Nathan had planned on a completely different career path in Public Relations. The only means to keep the company in the family was through Noah, but even so, he'd never assumed it a foregone conclusion.

Noah resumed his seat, suddenly exhausted with the conversation. "Someone who does their job well doesn't need to resort to blackmail to move up. It takes hard work and dedication, plain and simple."

"Things I've demonstrated, but people seem so focused on the boss's son they overlook it."

"The other principals are in their sixties. Another position will come along."

"If you're so sure, it won't matter if I'm promoted this time, will it? You can wait."

Noah met David's stare head-on. "It's not my decision."

"No, but your dad listens to you. So does James." David stood, evidently deciding to honor the time of the client he'd kept waiting. "It would probably be a good idea for you to tell them both you're not ready, or you think I'm the best fit. You've noticed my success and...dedication to the company, as you put it. I don't care how you do it, but if you want your secret to stay safe, you'll figure something out."

David left, and Noah put his elbows on his desk and dropped his head into his hands.

Things just got a lot more complicated.

9

Mia couldn't stop thinking about that kiss in the tree house. Sure, she'd made progress, thinking about it only when she got into bed at night rather than every hour on the hour.

But seriously, what had it meant, if anything?

And what should she do about it?

She'd been sitting firmly in the "do nothing" camp for the last several weeks by not bringing it up. Still, she thought about it with alarming frequency.

She couldn't quite believe she'd initiated it, but with the way he'd described his kiss to her? There was no way she could have let that pass her by. It had sounded thrilling and scandalous, and turned out to be both. The way her body—and heart—had responded, it was as if she was meant to be in his arms with her lips on his, all day and all night and forever.

Stupid, stupid, stupid woman.

She'd worked damn hard to keep her thoughts about Noah platonic all these years. Had convinced herself she didn't want more, and never would. She'd always encouraged him to see other women, despite knowing when he finally settled down with someone else it would hurt. A lot.

It did, in fact. He'd had a few girlfriends over the years, and even if none had gotten superserious, her days were darker when he wasn't around, like someone had put a black-and-white filter on her life. She'd never let him see it, though, and made sure she seemed supportive on the outside.

It was for the best.

She was more certain of that than ever, now that she'd kissed him. *Really* kissed him. Noah Agnew was the one person who'd tempted her to amend her stance on relationships, but he was also the biggest reason she'd built her walls so high. He'd already adjusted his life so much for her. More than she should have allowed. She couldn't live with herself if she saddled him with her illness forever.

It had only been five weeks since they got married and already she was feeling things. Dangerous things. And not only was that not in her plan, he wasn't into her that way. He'd made his feelings toward her clear all those years ago, and they'd had a lovely, fulfilling friendship since.

He was a man, after all, and had simply gotten carried away that night. She'd basically jumped on him, for goodness' sake. Few guys would put a stop to that.

She had to be more careful.

Stop. Thinking. About. It.

She shook her head and looked around, taking in the beauty around her. It was the first week of June and her summer class had started today. It was only one credit hour and geared toward reintroducing scholarship recipients to life as a college student. But she was just so happy to be back on a college campus that she hung around after class to share coffee with some new friends. They'd left the Student Union a half hour ago, but she wasn't quite ready to go home. She leisurely wandered the campus, taking in the sophisticated redbrick buildings and perfectly manicured green lawns, feeling excited and energized.

But then she remembered the last time she'd done this, and who had been with her. Once again she was back to Noah.

Her last day at Agnew Design Group had been yesterday, and she'd cried when Noah carried the box of her things to her car. Worse, that evening when they got home, she had a little breakdown, freaking out about school and quitting her job, and everything changing. Noah had sat beside her the entire time, soothing her with his presence and calmly talking through her fears without dismissing them.

The woman who snagged him one day would be lucky. *Damn* lucky, in fact, now that Mia knew what it was like to kiss him.

No, wait, not thinking about that. Focusing on school.

Moving on.

No problem whatsoever.

When she got home that evening, Noah took her to Wings To Go to celebrate, even though it seemed silly to make a big deal of it. She was thirty and it was a one-hour summer school course. But he'd insisted, and as he held the door open for her to enter the restaurant, she couldn't wipe the smile from her face.

"Hey, Mia!" Steve called from behind the counter.

Noah chuckled and whispered, "First name basis?"

She elbowed him in the ribs. Weekly visits had ensured she'd become good friends with the adorable older couple who owned the restaurant. "How's it going, Steve?"

"Good, good." The man's smile was happy and familiar, but his brow furrowed a little when he took in Noah beside her. He looked pointedly at him, then back at her.

Yeah, she usually came by herself. Did they have to make a big deal of it?

Steve cleared his throat. Looked at Noah again.

Mia pursed her lips. "Steve, this is my fr—uh. I mean, this is Noah. He's, um. My husband."

She loved Steve, but he was gonna embarrass her for sure.

"Your *what*?"

She sighed. "You heard me."

"Paula!" Steve yelled. "Get out here. Mia's here and she brought a husband with her."

She leaned into Noah's shoulder. "Maybe we should just go."

His arm shook beneath her forehead as he laughed.

Steve's wife was beside him in seconds. "What? Whose husband did she bring?" Her eyes alighted on Noah and she immediately smoothed the graying auburn hair around her face.

Mia looked to Noah for help, but he just watched her with amusement.

Her face heated. "Mine."

Paula grabbed Steve's arm. "Steve, did you hear that? Mia's husband!" She leaned across the counter and grabbed Noah's hand. "How wonderful to meet you."

"Likewise," Noah said.

Steve gently pulled his wife's hand back. "You've got quite the lady here, Noah. She's everyone's favorite around this place."

"I don't doubt that for a second."

"Oh look, Steve," Paula said. "She's blushing."

"Don't call attention to it, dear."

"You never say things that make me blush."

Steve leaned over and whispered something in his wife's ear, and her face did indeed turn a deep shade of red.

Mia giggled.

Noah took her hand, and she immediately stopped, her breath catching in her throat.

"So is this recent?" Paula asked. "Or have you been keeping this handsome man a secret from us?"

"It's been a little over a month," Mia said. Noah's fingers were large and warm, and his thumb shifted across her skin, sending a shiver up her arm.

"Newlyweds," Paula cried. "Congratulations!"

"Dinner's on us," Steve said. "We insist. What can we get for you?"

"I can't decide. Pick something for me, Paula."

"What about you, Noah?" Steve asked.

"Plain for me, please."

An identical knowing look settled on Steve's and Paula's faces.

"Of course. You're the ten-piece plain." Paula pinched her husband. "I told you Mia wasn't eating all those wings. You never believed me."

Mia laughed. "This entire time you thought they were all for me?"

Steve shrugged. "I'm here to sell chicken, not pass judgment."

"Well. Even if the marriage is new, you two have been together a long time, then." Paula's smile was wide as she waggled her eyebrows up and down. "And he sure is handsome.

Well done, my girl. How come you never brought him in before?"

"She probably didn't want you flirting with him," Steve muttered good-naturedly.

"Oh, stop." Paula made her way back to the kitchen. "I'm a happily married woman. Just like Mia."

Noah pulled his wallet from his back pocket. "Are you sure I can't…?"

Steve shook his head. "No, sir, put that away. Congratulations from us to you."

"Thank you."

"We'll bring it out when it's ready."

Noah squeezed her hand and as they headed to the small dining area, a man who looked to be in his fifties walked in.

"Hi, Mia!"

"Hi, Tom," she said with a smile.

The man kept moving to the counter and Noah leaned down. "Another regular?"

"Sort of. I was behind him in line at Trader Joe's a few weeks ago," she said as they found a table. "We bonded over our mutual love of oat milk. He said he'd just moved to town and wanted to know good places to get takeout. I've seen him here a few times since."

They sat across from one another and he met her gaze, his blue eyes even more striking next to the bright window. "You charm everyone you meet, don't you?"

"Pretty much."

He grinned. "Humility looks good on you."

"Oh wait," she said, holding up a finger. "One person doesn't like me."

"Who?"

"David."

His expression hardened. "I really wish you'd said something to me about that sooner."

"I don't need you to protect me, Noah."

His jaw went taut and he fixed his eyes on something through the window.

A ringtone came from his pocket, and he pulled his phone from his jeans. He looked at the screen and then his gaze flicked to hers, returning to his phone almost immediately. He silenced the call and slid it back into his pocket. He looked… guilty?

"A lady friend?"

"Don't be ridiculous," he snapped.

She settled back in her chair, then frowned as something dawned on her. "You know, I've always tried so hard not to get in the way of your love life. I know it's hard for someone new to come along when a man and a woman are as close as we are. I always wanted to make sure I didn't hinder you." She laughed, even though nothing about it was funny. "Then I went and did it, anyway. Put a ring on it and everything."

Noah just looked at her for a few seconds, a muscle flexing in his cheek. "Actually, I bought the rings."

Did he regret what they'd done?

"I'm sorry, Noah."

He leaned forward a little, his voice low. "*Don't.* Don't say you're sorry, don't thank me. Stop all of it. I mean it."

She blinked, surprised by his tone.

He closed his eyes for a beat and sighed, maintaining his forward posture. "Mia, no matter what you call us—spouse, roommate, best friend—you're one of the most important people in my life. End of story."

Heat spread up her neck as his blue eyes roamed her face.

"You're blushing again."

"Yeah, when did that start?" she said, trying to sound flippant. "I think the ring went to my head."

He chuckled, and the tension seemed to lighten a fraction. "Thirty bucks well spent."

"Promise me when you find a real wife, you'll find a girl who's okay with me still being in your life. I know it will be different, but I can't give you up completely."

"I will if you will."

She rolled her eyes. "I'm never getting married. You know this."

He cocked a brow and lifted his left hand, the black ring a contrast against his skin.

"You know what I mean," she said.

He shrugged. "Maybe you'll change your mind. Think of this like a trial run. I'll give you a report at the end on what it's like being your husband. Maybe you'll realize how ridiculous you're being."

"Are we talking about this again?"

"You brought it up."

Mia kicked his shoe. "You drive me crazy."

"Same." Something about the look in his eyes when he said it sent a tingle down her spine.

She dropped her eyes to the table and brushed it off. "So how was work today? Without me?"

"Quiet. And safe."

Mia laughed. "I should have taught the new girl how to put tape on the bottom of your mouse and remove the handles from your desk drawers."

"A missed opportunity, for sure."

"You're gonna be so bored."

"Or more productive."

Another couple passed their table, and Mia briefly broke eye contact. "True. You'll get that promotion for sure. They'll be blown away by the work you can get done without me distracting you." She grinned. "Hey, I feel a little less guilty now."

Noah frowned a little. "James mentioned the position the other day. He said he's looking forward to discussing it more after my dad retires."

"What? Noah, that's incredible. Why aren't you more excited?"

"It's not guaranteed to be mine. David's gonna go hard for it, too."

She waved a hand. "You definitely deserve the position over him. You managed twice the number of projects he did last year." Plus, she'd overheard several of the other architects comment on David's propensity for laziness and lack of attention to detail.

"He had a few extensive projects that turned out really well."

"So did you."

He shrugged and folded his arms across his chest. "So how was class today?"

The excitement that rushed through her was the only reason she allowed the blatant subject change. "Good. There are fifteen of us. We went around the room and talked a little about ourselves. Why we're coming back to school and the degrees we're pursuing, that kind of thing. I had coffee with some classmates and walked around campus afterward." *And thought about you.* Did he remember walking the campus with her when they were eighteen? "It was fun."

"That's awesome." His hands dropped to his lap. "I'm happy for you."

"Me too."

Paula appeared at the table with their food, directing a megawatt smile in Noah's direction. He smiled back.

"Thank you. I hope you'll forgive me for being so unadventurous when it comes to food."

"Oh pish." Paula flicked her wrist. "Consistency in a man is one of the best qualities."

Noah raised his brows and looked at Mia. "Did you hear that, honey? One of the *best* qualities."

Mia crossed her eyes at him and couldn't help but grin. "How long have you and Steve been married?"

Paula beamed with pride. "Thirty-five years this spring."

"Wow," Noah said.

"That's awesome. Good for you two."

"He drives me crazy sometimes," Paula said dryly. "Especially since we work together. But I love that man to the moon and back."

Mia glanced at Noah and found his eyes on her face, soft and contemplative. He didn't look away when he said, "Hey, Paula. If you could give us newlyweds once piece of advice for a long, happy marriage, what would it be?"

"That's easy. Never stop showing affection." She winked. "You'd be surprised how much a simple touch can mean to someone you love."

10

"Get a room."

Noah tightened his hold on Mia and leveled his gaze at Graham. "Maybe we will."

Graham snorted and went to the kitchen, probably in search of another beer. Claire and Reagan had just left, the group having spent the evening playing Cards Against Humanity.

Mia tilted her head up a little and whispered, "How are you so good at this?"

Noah barely moved when he responded. Close as she was with his arm wrapped around her, if he so much as turned his head, their faces—*their lips*—would be centimeters apart. That kind of temptation might just push him over the edge. "Good at what? The game?"

"That, too. But I meant with us. Graham has no clue this isn't real."

He couldn't respond without lying, and he sure as hell wouldn't tell her the truth: that he'd taken the words Paula spoke to them several weeks ago to heart and had constantly been looking for excuses to touch her. He said nothing, and soon Graham was back in the armchair to his left. "Man, I'm glad you invited me tonight. Free beer, good times, and I scored a new place to live."

"Yeah, are you sure about that decision?" Mia asked. "Claire's not the easiest person to live with. She comes and goes at all hours, leaves bags of chips everywhere, and will definitely cut you if you turn the thermostat below seventy-two."

"Seventy-two?" Graham cried. "It's a condo, not a sauna!"

"Try telling her that." Mia paused. "But when you do, can I watch?"

"Me too," Noah added. Claire was feisty as hell, and he'd love to see Graham go toe-to-toe with her.

Graham waved his bottle in the air. "It's gonna be fine. We'll get along great. You'll see."

"This will be fun to watch," Noah murmured.

Mia laughed. "Totally."

Graham took a swig. "So what time are we heading out tomorrow, man?"

Noah eyed his friend. "You know I like to head up early. But I don't know if you're gonna make it. What is that, number five?"

"Dude. I'm good. I'll finish this one and crash here, if that's okay. I'll be good to go by eight."

"Here?" Mia asked.

"I probably shouldn't drive. I've stayed in the guest room

plenty of times," Graham said. He looked between the two of them. "But I guess that was before you two...is that still okay?"

Mia went still against his ribs.

"Sure, that's no problem," Noah said. Graham had no clue this was all fake, and it needed to stay that way. He gently squeezed Mia's arm, and she relaxed marginally.

"You sure? Mia, you don't mind? I guess I still think of this as Noah's bachelor pad."

Mia's pitch was a little higher than normal, but her voice was steady. "Of course you can stay. You're always welcome here."

Boy, was Noah glad they'd decided to keep all her stuff in his room. It was probably annoying for her, but she'd been good about not leaving personal things in the guest room and making the bed every morning. No one would know that's where she'd been sleeping. That they'd never shared a bed.

Until tonight.

His stomach clenched, and he resisted the urge to drop his chin to his chest. Tonight Mia would share his bed. Sleep beside him, her soft skin inches from his, her hair spread across the pillow next to his face.

He swallowed thickly, one hundred percent unprepared for this.

Half an hour later, Noah lay in his bed, trying and failing to focus on the book in his lap. He wasn't even sure which book he was holding.

He didn't look at her as she slid in beside him. Her vanilla scent immediately enveloped him, and dammit, why hadn't he gotten a king-size bed? The queen felt way too small for the two of them.

She may as well have been on top of him.

"Whatcha reading?"

She'd piled her hair on top of her head and her skin looked freshly scrubbed. She was so beautiful his chest ached.

He held up the cover.

"Is it good?"

"I don't know," he said without thinking.

She laughed.

"Keep it down in there," Graham called from the next room. "And if you get it on, for the love of God, don't let me hear you."

Mia covered her face with her hands, her face beet red.

"No promises," Noah yelled back.

She smacked his bicep.

"What?" He grinned, feeling a little more himself.

She smiled back, then her eyes dropped to his bare chest.

His smile faded. "Do you want me to put a shirt on?"

She shook her head.

Okay…

"How many tattoos do you have now?" she asked softly, her gaze on the wing on his chest.

"Five."

She nodded slowly, her dark eyes connecting with his. "Will you tell me about them?"

"Which ones?"

"All of them."

"Aren't we supposed to be going to sleep?"

"Not according to Graham," she quipped, and her cheeks flushed again.

He cleared his throat. "You know about this one," he said, pointing to the one on his forearm. The mountain with the words *the sun will rise and we will try again* was the one he and his brother had gotten together after summiting Mt. Rainier for the first time.

"I know about most of them," she agreed. "But I still like hearing you talk about them." She touched the compass on his right shoulder. "Remind me when you got this one?"

He tried not to focus on the small pad of her fingertip against his skin. "That was my third. I've had it for a few years."

"What does it mean?"

"Guidance and protection."

She made a little *hmm* noise and his chest tightened. It was too quiet in the dim room and she was so damn *close*.

"The mountain was your first and this was your third. Which was your second?"

He held up his left arm, his muscles flexing as he bent his elbow to display the roman numerals on the inside of his bicep.

"Oh," she said quietly. She definitely remembered that one.

Nathan's birthday.

Her eyes dropped to the new one on his chest again. Before she could ask about it, Noah set his book down and flipped off the lamp next to his side of the bed. "That's enough for tonight."

He lay down flat on his back, his eyes on the dark ceiling. She shifted beside him, her arm brushing his as she moved.

"Good night, Noah."

"Good night, Mia."

When Noah woke up the next morning, he knew immediately something wasn't right. Mia was still beside him, but she was curled up in a ball, the covers thrown off, her hands in tight fists.

"Mia?" He leapt out of bed and went to her side, crouching down by her face. "Are you okay?"

She winced. "I—I'm fine. I'm just having some pain."

"What do you need? Medicine? Do you need to go to the doctor?"

"I took medicine a few hours ago. It hasn't helped much. But sometimes it just takes time."

He'd only seen her like this twice—once when she was first diagnosed and then again when she was put on the transplant list. But he'd also never lived with her, so he wasn't sure how bad it was. "Is this normal?"

She swallowed. "No. I mean, it happens sometimes, when I have a flare. But not often."

"What can I do?"

A tear slipped from her eye and he went rigid, his own eyes burning. His breath became shallow as a vise closed around his chest, and he stood. "I'm taking you to the emergency room."

Her hand shot out to grab his wrist. "No, you're going climbing today. I'll call Claire."

"The hell you will." He gently pulled her hand away and leaned down to kiss the side of her head. "I'll be right back."

"Noah…"

He ignored her and went to the guest room, taking barely two steps inside the room.

"Graham," he barked.

Some sort of questionable sound came from his friend's form sprawled across the bed.

"Mia's sick and I'm taking her to the hospital. Stay here as long as you want."

Graham's head popped up. "Is she okay?"

"I think so. But she's in pain and we need to go now."

"Want me to come?"

"No. I'll call you later."

In seconds Noah was back in his room, slipping on jeans and a T-shirt. He grabbed one of his own T-shirts and brought it to where Mia still lay on the bed. She hadn't moved at all, her eyes squeezed shut.

He brushed her thick, dark hair away from her face. "Let me help you put this on."

He helped her sit up and slid the shirt over her tank top. The shorts she had on would work.

"Can you walk?"

She nodded, but a sound of pain slipped from her throat when she straightened.

A chunk of Noah's heart chipped away, lodging in his throat. He scooped her in his arms, cradling her close to his chest. She immediately buried her face into his shirt, and he struggled to keep himself composed.

In minutes he'd settled her in the passenger seat, her legs tucked up and her head resting against the window. He drove her to Saint Luke's, where she'd gone the few other times she'd required hospitalization.

It took them forty-five minutes to get her back to a room, and Mia's body curved into his side was the only thing that kept him from causing a scene at the desk, demanding a doctor to come see her.

To help her, fix this, take her pain away. *Now.*

As it was, he brushed his hand up and down her arm, alternating between staring at her wearing his gray CU shirt and glaring at the man in scrubs who took their information, but who clearly had no sense of urgency when it came to people who needed medical attention.

Noah didn't breathe again until she was in a bed, an IV in her arm, and watched the pain medication take effect. Her countenance relaxed, color returned to her cheeks, and her breathing evened out.

He pulled a chair next to the bed and sat as close as possible, her hand in his.

"You're staring," she whispered.

He wasn't ready to speak just yet.

"I feel better," she continued when he didn't respond. "I promise."

He nodded, knowing he looked like a complete asshole just watching her, unsmiling. But nothing about this was okay. His mind had gone to a dark place in the last hour, and he couldn't seem to follow the sound of her voice back to the light. Memories of that night, when he, Nathan, and Graham were on the side of a mountain filled his mind, and the text message he'd gotten from Claire.

They were away for Nathan's bachelor party. Instead of a night of drinking and strippers, Nathan had said all he wanted was to get out of town and climb some rocks with his groomsmen. They'd been shooting the shit around the campfire when the text came through.

Mia had a seizure and passed out. She's in the ICU.

Service on the mountain had been complete shit when he tried to call, and he didn't remember much after that.

All he knew was he'd needed to get to her.

On the drive down the mountain, a deer had leapt out of the darkness in front of the car. Nathan had reacted and tried to swerve, sending them into a thick patch of trees.

Noah knew the second he looked at his brother, still strapped into the driver's seat, that he was gone.

After dealing with his own injuries, he'd attended his

brother's funeral. Then he'd gone straight to the hospital and barely left Mia's bedside for a week.

He'd never felt so lost. Losing his brother had been a shock, not to mention devastating. Losing both Nathan and Mia would have killed him.

Lucky for Mia, when they finally figured out what was causing her symptoms, it turned out her disease was manageable, and could even be cured with a transplant. As she improved, he'd leaned heavily on her as he dealt with the grief of losing Nathan. She did the same with him as she adjusted to life with a chronic illness.

"Noah." Mia's voice brought him back, and he squeezed her hand tighter. "I can't tell if you're playing the part of worried, doting husband, or if you've had a stroke."

He huffed out a breath. "Neither. You scared me."

"I know. I'm sorry."

"What would have happened if I hadn't been there?"

"Claire would have brought me. She'd sit here with me like you are right now. She'd have left the chair over in the corner, though."

He didn't find that funny.

"I should have come sooner," she said. "I know it's better to catch it early, but I just hoped the pain would pass."

"What happens now?"

"We wait for my blood work to come back. Usually when the cysts act up like this, other things are off, too. I'll probably need a few more medications."

He ran his free hand through his hair. She tugged at his hand and when he looked at her, she nodded to the top of his head. He lowered it and leaned forward, and her fingers smoothed the back of his hair.

"I'll be fine. You know that, right?"

He kept his head bowed. "That's what I'm telling myself."

"Trust me. I've been here before. A few times. I know the drill."

He lifted his head and met her gaze. "I hate this for you."

"I hate it for *you*."

Anger flared like a bottle of whisky poured on a flame. "Don't."

"Why? You shouldn't be here. You should be on your way to Clear Creek Canyon with Graham right now." She pulled her hand away. "As a matter of fact, you should still go. There's nothing to do now but wait."

He didn't reach for her hand. He didn't move at all. "I'm not going anywhere."

She glared at him, which was almost laughable. Mia didn't do angry well.

Cheerful? Yes.

Welcoming? Always.

Mischievous? Definitely.

Angry? Didn't suit her.

He lowered his voice. "What kind of husband would leave their wife while she's in the hospital?"

She pursed her lips.

"You know I'm right," he added.

"This is exactly why I never wanted to be married," she muttered.

Noah straightened and pulled the ring from his finger. He held up the band between them. "You really think this is what's keeping me here? I'd be here, with or without it. The quicker you get that through your head, the better."

She folded her arms across her chest, careful not to pull on the IV line in her hand. They stared each other down for a long moment.

Finally, her face fell, and she dropped her arms. She closed her eyes. "I just..." she whispered.

"What?" he urged.

"I don't want you—or anyone—to disrupt their life for me."

"Why? Why is it so terrible to have people that care about you? Who would put your needs before their own? Most people would count it as a blessing."

"Most people haven't watched their parents lose their house and go into debt to pay their medical bills." Her eyes filled with hurt. "And I'm not even their real daughter."

It was unusual for him, but Noah spoke on behalf of her parents. "In their eyes, you are."

She shook her head. "It doesn't matter." She brushed a hand across the white blanket covering her legs. "If I'd known when I was young and had time to process it before, maybe I'd see it differently. But I found out I was adopted when I was *twenty-eight*, Noah. And only because during the transplant workup I found out I had a completely different blood type. Do you have any idea what that felt like?"

"No." He only knew how much it had hurt to be a bystander to her emotional turmoil.

"How could they have kept something like that from me?"

He wished he had the answers for her. "I don't know."

"Isn't it my right to know where I came from?"

He thought so, but what did he know?

"Not only did they lie to me my entire life, but I ended up with a genetic condition that came from someone else, and they took the financial hit for it. I'll never be able to repay them, or give them back the world-traveling life they wanted. I'll carry that forever and I don't want to add more to it."

Nothing he said would be the right thing, so he kept silent. After her parents came clean and the initial shock wore off, Mia had responded in anger, and essentially cut herself off from them. Things had improved only marginally since.

After a few moments, Mia picked up the remote attached to her bed and turned on the television mounted in the corner of the room. Noah turned his eyes to the screen, but couldn't have said what he was watching.

When the doctor came in, he confirmed what Mia suspected. Several values from her labs were out of range, and they wanted to admit her until they normalized. They moved her to a room on the sixth floor, and once they were alone, they argued about Noah staying. He finally gave up and left, letting her win this round.

He figured if she had enough energy to get that worked up, she was probably okay. Once he was home and settled on the couch, several popping sounds from the street caught his attention, followed by echoing booms from farther away. He'd completely forgotten it was the Fourth of July. He stood and peeled back the curtains—ones Mia had hung after declaring his house needed a more "homey" feel—and spotted the bright fireworks in the sky.

He wished he and Mia were there, sitting on a blanket, his arms around her while they watched in wonder. In reality, he stood alone in his dark house, hoping she was watching the same breathtaking show from the window of her hospital room.

Mia was discharged two days later. Noah took the day off on Monday when she came home.

She made homemade lasagna for dinner even though he told her not to. She was probably trying to make a point, but it was entirely possible she'd just missed cooking. He kept an eye on her while she moved around the kitchen—a hardship he was willing to endure—making sure she seemed steady and the color remained in her cheeks.

Damn if it wasn't delicious. He didn't know how he'd ever go back to frozen dinners and sandwiches when this was all over.

On Tuesday evening she had plans at a local bookstore coffee shop with her new friends from the summer school course. He suggested she reschedule for the following week, but she gave him a look and said she was fine.

"Mind if I tag along?" he asked.

She arched a brow. "Why?"

Because he still had the image of her usually smiling face devoid of color and contorted in pain burned in his brain. He wasn't quite ready to let her out of his sight yet.

"I finished my book. I thought maybe I could browse around the store."

After a beat she shrugged and muttered her assent, and they rode to the bookstore together in silence.

In the parking lot he took her hand, which had become second nature. The fact that she didn't pull away told him she wasn't too upset with his obvious ploy to remain close to her. He briefly dropped her hand when he opened the door for her, but she waited for him to follow her inside and he took it once more.

The café was in the front corner of the store, and Mia led him to a table where two women sat. One was probably in her early fifties, with graying hair and a kind smile, and the other looked closer to his and Mia's ages.

Mia's face lit up when she saw them. "Bridget, Anita, this is my husband, Noah."

Noah exchanged pleasantries with them and slid his hand

down to Mia's lower back. It was well beyond keeping up the act at this point, but he couldn't stop himself.

The smile she turned on him was the first real one he'd seen in days, and his breath seized in his lungs. She looked so happy to be there, completely in her element. Making new friends had never been his strong suit, and her warm, welcoming nature was one of his favorite things about her. Being around her was the definition of experiencing joy and light.

Without thinking, he leaned forward and kissed her forehead, letting his lips linger a second longer than necessary. "Have fun," he murmured, and exited the café, stepping away into the shadows.

11

Mia watched Noah's back as he walked away and turned the corner, moving out of view. He moved with confidence and purpose, and her eyes trailed down his body, butterflies rising with each step he took.

Stop. What are you doing?

The forehead kiss had disarmed her, and she shook her head a little. She sat between her new friends, ready to talk about class and whatever else, but they both stared at her, mouths hanging open.

"What?"

"Girl," Bridget said.

"That's your husband?" Anita asked.

Mia smiled, suddenly unsure what to do with her hands. "Oh. Um, yeah, that's my husband."

"Well done. Very well done," Anita said. "Very."

Mia laughed and her cheeks heated.

"I almost burst into flame just watching him look at you," Bridget said, wafting air toward her face.

"What do you mean?" Mia asked.

Bridget cocked a brow. "That man is head over heels for you."

"Um." Mia glanced back to where he'd turned the corner. "I mean, he's into me the normal amount. That a husband is for a wife." She sucked so bad at this.

Anita laughed. "No. My husband is into me the normal amount. That?" She waved a hand in the general direction where they'd been standing. "That was not normal."

Mia didn't know what to say to that.

"How long have you been married?" Bridget asked.

"It's almost been three months. But we've known each other since we were kids."

Anita sighed. "That's so sweet."

Bridget propped her elbow on the table and rested her chin in her hand. "I can't wait to find a guy who looks at me like that."

Mia kept her face carefully arranged into a smile while her brain whirred to process their words.

Noah had done nothing different tonight. He'd always looked at her like that.

"How is that, exactly?" she heard herself ask.

Bridget chuckled. "Like you're the only thing in the room that matters. Like he wants to worship you and give you everything he has to offer, while at the same time throw you over his shoulder and carry you to bed."

Mia's eyes went wide.

"You're right—we don't know each other that well yet. Too much?" Bridget asked with a grin.

"No. You remind me of my best friend Claire," Mia said.

Bridget nodded. "Sounds like my kind of woman."

"We already ordered," Anita said, and Mia could have hugged her for changing the subject. "Did you want a drink?"

Mia got up to order a latte, and when she returned they talked for an hour and a half about everything from their favorite places in town to get their nails done to how they planned to integrate themselves back into a full college course schedule. Bridget was pursuing a degree in early childhood education while Anita's path was in communications, but despite their varied paths they shared a similar excitement of what was to come.

It was nice to know she wasn't the only one.

After saying goodbye, Mia wove her way to the back of the store to find Noah in a chair in the fiction section, engrossed in a mystery novel. He looked up when she approached.

"Whatcha reading?"

He held up the book just like he had that night when they'd shared his bed.

"Is it good?"

He grinned. "I don't know."

She couldn't stop the smile that spread across her face. Sometimes he surprised her, like now—bringing up the awkwardness of that night. He'd seemed a little dazed that night, but she hadn't wanted to call attention to it. She'd been nervous, too. Of all the nights to get sick, it had to be the one where she'd slept inches away from his warm body.

The mental image of him propped up against the headboard, all that skin and muscle and ink on display…there was no denying she'd felt…things. The attraction she felt for him had smacked her across the face like a harsh wind during a snowstorm, sending her heart fluttering around her chest in search for an escape.

He looked just as sexy now, in a leather wingback chair, wearing chinos and a navy V-neck T-shirt, one ankle propped on the opposite knee. His red hair was in slight disarray but his blue eyes were sharp, regarding her with interest.

That man is head over heels for you.

Her eyes dropped to his left hand and the ring circling his fourth finger. She swallowed. "Ready to go?" she managed to get out, her voice a little uneven.

He stood. "Sure. Let me just put this back."

"I thought you said you needed a new book?"

He shrugged, and she waited for him to put the book back in its proper place. They walked side by side past the rows of books, and she kept her hand available by her side, feeling strangely bereft. Had he only held her hand as a show when they were meeting her friends?

But then his fingers slid across her palm, linking their fingers, and a tiny piece of the wall she'd built broke off and crashed to the ground.

"I need advice."

Claire set down her cocktail glass and threw her hands in the air with a flourish. "Finally! I've been waiting weeks for this. Tell me." She leaned forward, nodding sagely. "What happened?"

Mia put her elbows on the table and pressed her fingers to her forehead. "I—I don't know how to say this."

"Boned? Had sex? Rocked each other's worlds? Take your pick and let's talk *details* already."

"Jeez, Claire," Mia exclaimed. "Noah and I didn't have sex."

"You didn't?"

"No."

Claire looked bored. "What's this about, then?"

Mia shook her head, getting her thoughts back on track. "It's like… I don't know. I've been feeling things. And I sort of get the feeling Noah has, too."

"Feelings," Claire deadpanned. "That's all you've had?"

Mia pushed her lips out a little. "Well, we made out in the old tree house."

"*Excuse* me? When was this?"

"A few months ago."

"And you didn't tell me?" Claire pulled the bowl of edamame they'd been sharing to her side of the table, curving her arm around it protectively.

"Are you punishing me by withholding the appetizer?"

"Yep." She put a bean between her teeth and pulled the shell back out. "Talk."

"I don't know. I didn't think it was a big deal at the time. Noah said it was a mistake, and I believed him. We just did it because we knew we'd have to kiss in front of other people every once in a while to keep up appearances, and wanted to get past the weirdness."

"Did it work?"

"I'm not sure. It wasn't weird. Not during, anyway. It was pretty hot, actually. I don't think I would have stopped if he hadn't pulled away."

Claire pumped her fist. "Fucking finally."

"Claire!"

"What?"

"What's that supposed to mean?"

"Don't play dumb with me. You and Noah have the most messed-up dynamic I've ever seen. You both want each other but you pretend not to, and it's the most exhausting and delightful thing to watch. You're a train wreck of epic proportions."

"I can't believe you just called us a train wreck."

"It's true."

"We don't want each other."

"Lies. When you walk away, he always watches you go. And you always look back."

A flush traveled across her skin and she wanted to sit with those words and analyze them (he always watched her go?), but she ignored temptation and shook her head. "He told me he didn't want me. Point-blank, to my face."

"You misinterpreted. Or were high on pain meds. Or something. And it was nine years ago, so. Who cares?"

"I care," Mia maintained. "Don't you remember how everything went down?"

"Not really. I was pretty worried about you when you first got sick. It's kind of a blur, to be honest."

How had Mia ended up with such wonderful people surrounding her all these years? "I know. I'm sorry."

"You have nothing to be sorry for."

She disagreed, but arguing with Claire was rarely worth it, so she let that part go. "Well, let me refresh your memory." Seemed like her own heart could use the reminder, too. "After you tried to set us up that night in college—"

"Because it was so obvious you wanted each other," Claire interrupted.

Mia continued as if she hadn't spoken. "—we never met up because I felt sick and went home. He left for Nathan's bachelor party camping trip, and while he was gone I got diagnosed. When he got back, do you remember how he stayed in my room for like, a week straight?"

"Yeah. Every time I came by, he was there."

"He even slept there. It was like two in the morning one night but neither of us could sleep. I don't know why, but I brought it up. God knows we had enough on our minds, but I'd realized in those few days I'd be saddled with this illness for the rest of my life, and what it would mean to everyone around me. I had to tell him I couldn't do it. It was eating at me, wondering if he'd been thinking about it too, and if he was hoping we'd pick up where we left off that night at the fraternity house. I told him I wanted to talk about it. Right away he told me he hadn't meant any of it. That he just wanted to be friends, and he was sorry he led me on like that."

Mia paused, letting those words hang in the air. Claire looked at her thoughtfully. She took a drink and set her glass back down.

"Tell me something," Claire began. "You wanted to put a stop to things because of your diagnosis. Not because you didn't have feelings for him. Right?"

Mia tucked her hair behind her ear. "Yes. I guess that's true."

"What if Noah did the same?"

"What do you mean?"

"Noah cared for you back then. I knew it. Everyone knew it. What if something about the stress of losing his brother and your illness made him have the same reaction? What if he said those things, but just like you, he said them *despite* his true feelings? What if he wanted to be with you, but felt like it wasn't the right time?"

"Why wouldn't he just say that?"

"Why didn't you?"

Mia frowned, feeling defensive. "He'd just said it was a mistake. I followed his lead and said I wanted to stay friends, too." It would have led to the same result either way.

"But you didn't tell him you had feelings for him. You just said you wanted to be friends."

"Yeah…"

"I think that's what Noah did, too."

The space between Mia's brows became even smaller. "I don't. That conversation is burned in my brain like it was yesterday. When he called it a mistake, he definitely meant it." She'd worked hard in the weeks following to dispel any deeper feelings she had for Noah, and focus on their friendship. She'd known they would need each other after everything they'd been through.

It had taken several months, but she'd finally arrived at a place where she didn't think of him as *more*. He was her best friend, and she was thankful for that. It had been that way ever since.

Until that damn kiss.

"Well," Claire said, pushing the edamame bowl back to the middle. "I still say you talk to him about it."

"Why?"

"Because something's changing. You just said something feels different. And you're confused and don't know what's going on in his head. Noah doesn't deny you anything. All you have to do is ask."

"Then what? What if he says he wants more, and what happens if I want more? It's just going to muddle everything even more because my stance hasn't changed. I won't put my baggage on someone else."

"Even someone who loves you?"

An image of her parents flashed through her mind, and her resistance flared stronger than ever.

"Especially someone who loves me."

12

"Noah, come in."

Noah stepped into the office of James McKinley, senior principal and part owner of Agnew Design Group. The man who'd mentored him, supported his dad's decision to hire him, and treated him the same as any intern right out of school. Noah respected the hell out of him, which made what he was about to do all the more distasteful. There was only one reason James would have called him into his office today.

He closed the door and sat in the available chair. James's office was twice the size of his, with two walls of floor-to-ceiling windows. An old-school drafting table was in one corner and a large bookcase took up another wall, full of model cars and airplanes, one of James's favorite hobbies. A bright red sports car caught Noah's eye.

"Is the Charger new?"

James leaned back in his burgundy leather chair. "Just put the finishing touches on her this weekend."

Noah nodded slowly, drawing out the mindless conversation. "Ever drive one of those?"

"I wish. Closest I ever got was a 1963 Corvette when I was in my forties." He let out a low whistle. "She was a Stingray with three-sixty horsepower and fuel injection. Handled like a dream."

"You've got a Corvette up there somewhere, don't you?"

"I do." James crossed his arms over his chest and regarded Noah steadily. "Let's stop talking about my toys and get down to business. I'll be announcing Tanya's promotion tomorrow, which means a junior principal position will be opening. I wanted to personally say I hope you'll consider the position."

Noah flicked his gaze to the bookcase once more, psyching himself up.

This is for Mia.

Noah turned his attention to James. "I'm honored you thought to discuss it with me. I sort of thought David might be a shoo-in for it, though."

James's eyebrows rose. "You did?"

Noah nodded. "Don't you agree he's a good candidate?"

"Are you telling me you're not interested in the position yourself?"

Noah tightened his jaw. Mia was right. It was annoying when someone answered a question with another question.

"I haven't decided," he hedged.

James leaned forward and steepled his fingers. "I see." He said nothing more, and Noah felt his neck prickle with sweat. His dad taught him the skills of patience and silence, and the art of managing a conversation with aplomb. *You won't believe how much people say if you just give them time to say it.* Noah was naturally quiet and had taken well to the advice, while Nathan had always struggled with it, jumping in and interrupting others in excitement and impatience.

The only person who did the silent stare better than Noah's dad was James. Noah broke under the weight of his intelligent gaze.

"I'm not sure I'm ready. I've only been out of school for eight years. David has been around longer, and it only makes sense he should be a top contender."

"You were paired with David on a couple of projects last year. After working with him, you have no concerns about his workmanship? Attention to detail or ability to meet deadlines?"

They'd worked on two projects together, to be exact. Both times Noah had been required to redo several of David's designs because he hadn't paid attention to what the client wanted, and they'd been unable to finish either of them on time.

"I'm not saying he won't need some coaching," Noah said, acid burning his throat. It felt unethical, not only to lie to James, but also to pretend David was a strong professional candidate who deserved the position. "But I think with your leadership he could get there. He has potential."

"Potential," James repeated.

"Yes."

James tilted his head, his styled gray hair not moving an inch. "I wish you could hear yourself. It sounded the same as if you were predicting the Denver Wildcats will win the Stanley Cup."

The Wildcats had ended last season dead last.

You're not selling it. Mia's face appeared in his mind, her beautiful eyes lit up with joy as she'd floated through the front door after her first day of class. She deserved this, and he'd do everything he could to give it to her.

"Did you see the museum he finished last month? That project was complicated with the lighting and exhibit designs. It turned out great."

Julia had had a heavy hand in that project.

James nodded slightly. "It was impressive."

"The nontraditional window panels were David's idea." That part was actually true. The guy wasn't completely worthless, or else his dad would have never hired him. "And he's currently working on a high school field house and press box that sounds cool. It's a bigger challenge than anything I've worked on to date." Also true, much as he hated to admit it.

James stroked his chin with his thumb and forefinger. "I see. Maybe I should wait and see how that project turns out."

Unease prickled down Noah's spine. Something told him a delay in the promotion would raise David's ire. "Why wait? My dad's gone in two months."

"Are you telling me you're not interested in the position at all?" James asked. "Or are you just asking me to consider my options?"

Noah swallowed. "It's been suggested I've received special treatment since I'm an Agnew."

James straightened. "I haven't cut you any slack, Noah."

"Believe me, I know," Noah said with a humorless laugh. "But this company is important to me, and I intend to be here for the long haul. It doesn't look good for me to be promoted before someone with more experience. I don't want to create an environment where I—or you—lose the respect of other employees. Some might say seniority is more important than productivity—"

"I'm not one of those people."

"But it's not unreasonable to consider."

"I get the feeling there's something you're not telling me," James said. "But I'll make you a deal. I'll consider David, and I mean seriously consider him, as long as you put in for the position, too."

Noah released a long exhale, unsure how that would go over, but he didn't think he had a choice.

"Okay. It's a deal."

Noah left work in a terrible mood, and Mia picked up on it immediately.

"What's wrong?"

She sat in the passenger seat of his Subaru as they wove through traffic to meet Graham and Claire for dinner. Coming home to Mia had been one of the best ways to bring him back to himself after a hard day, but her calming presence hadn't had the usual effect today. He could usually talk through what had upset him, but that wasn't an option this time and he'd been on edge waiting for her to ask.

He kept his eyes trained on the road. "Nothing serious. Just thinking about a deadline."

"I wish I was there to pull a prank on you and brighten your day."

He chuckled. "I don't think that would help. Remember the time you put duct tape around my chair? It took me an hour to get it off before I could get any work done."

"Bet it made you smile, though."

"Yeah, but mostly because I started planning my revenge."

"What was your revenge that time?"

He squinted. "I honestly don't know. I lost track over the years." He glanced over at her and found her smiling. "I really loved working with you."

Her eyes were uncertain as she tucked her thick hair behind one ear. "Me too. So much that sometimes I want to forget this whole thing and come back."

He slowed to a stop at a red light and kept his gaze on her.

"It's not so bad because we're living together, but what about when I finish school and move out? When will I see you?"

He didn't like thinking about that. He was shit at distancing himself from her, as evidenced by the failure rate of his attempts at dating other women. So far none had been comfortable with his and Mia's friendship long-term, and he couldn't blame them.

"We'll always be in each other's lives," he said.

"We'd better be," she said. "I refuse to accept anything different."

"Good."

The light turned green and they continued on, remaining silent until they arrived at the restaurant.

Noah ordered a beer, knowing it would be the only one he drank but wanting something to take the edge off.

After they'd placed their food order, conversation flowed easily around the table. Graham relived scoring a date when he went with the fire crew for a grocery store run; Claire told a story about a patient who came to the hospital with a glass beer bottle somewhere one should never go.

Noah let his own beer sit for a few minutes after that, eyeing the bottle critically. He zoned out and missed the next few minutes of conversation, not realizing until Mia pointed it out. She was in a great mood, laughing and commenting animatedly. Occasionally she gestured with her arms and it sent a stream of her vanilla scent his way.

Just as he was considering the pros and cons of sitting beside her rather than across from her (pros: the incredible way she smelled and the occasional brush of their arms or thighs; con: he couldn't stare at her without looking like an imbecile), she asked how it had been going since Graham moved in with Claire and Reagan last week.

"Awesome," Graham said.

"Terrible," Claire said.

Both looked at the other.

"How has it been terrible?" Graham asked. "I'm an excellent roommate."

"I'm not talking about *you.* When we agreed on this arrangement, you failed to mention you were bringing Satan's minion with you."

Graham gasped. "Are you talking about Gertrude?"

Noah couldn't help but interject. He shot Graham an incredulous look. "You didn't tell her you had a dog?"

"It's not a dog," Claire disputed.

"How did you not know about Gertrude?" Mia asked. "Graham talks about her all the time."

Claire waved a dismissive hand. "I knew about her, but he didn't say he was bringing her. I thought maybe he'd get rid of her."

"Get *rid* of her? I'd sooner give up my left testicle."

"That's quite the sacrifice," Noah noted.

Claire made a face. "It's perfect to illustrate his obsession with that little terror. I've never met such a mean dog."

"She's not mean," Graham defended. "She doesn't like change. She'll come around."

"She pooped in my shoe," Claire growled. "She tries to bite me whenever you're not home. And she's torn up two of my throw pillows. So far."

"What does Reagan think of her?" Mia asked, her lips pursed as if struggling to contain a smile.

He'd failed that endeavor as soon as Claire called Graham's dog Satan's minion.

"She loves her," Graham said. "Claire's the only one who has a problem with her."

"That bitch started it."

"Her name is Gertrude. Or Gertie, depending on her mood."

Claire cupped her hands around her mouth and whisper-yelled across the table, "Help me."

Mia grinned. "Speaking of Reagan, did anyone invite her tonight?"

"I did," Graham said. "She had plans."

Claire continued muttering under her breath about the offenses Gertrude had committed in the span of a few days, and Mia laughed quietly.

Their food arrived, and as everyone began eating, Graham looked up. "Hey, Noah, wanna go camping this weekend?"

"Camping?" Noah surreptitiously glanced at Mia sitting beside him in the booth. "Uh, nah. Not this weekend."

"Why not?" Graham asked.

"Do you have something else going on?" Mia asked.

"Uh..." He scrambled to think of a plausible excuse that wasn't *I'm still scarred from your recent trip to the hospital and don't want to leave you right now*, which would no doubt piss her off.

"I have an idea," Claire chimed in, waving her beer bottle excitedly in the air. "Let's all go!"

All three of them turned identical surprised expressions on her.

"What?" she said, clearly affronted. "I can go camping."

"In a tent?" Mia asked.

"Hell no. We can rent a cabin or something."

Graham shook his head. "That's not camping."

"Sure it is."

"No, it's not," Noah agreed.

"Snobs," Mia coughed into her hand.

"Elitist," Graham corrected.

"Okay fine," Claire said. "Instead of *camping*, let's all go *spend the weekend in the mountains*. In a cabin. With a bed and a shower." She leveled a glare at Graham. "And without *Gertie*."

Graham narrowed his eyes, considering, then shrugged and turned to Noah. "Well? How about it?"

He shifted in the booth. "Well, if everyone's gonna go…"

"Yes!" Claire said. "We're all going! This will be so fun. There's hardly ever a weekend when Graham and I are both off work and we can do something as a group."

"Hold on, I didn't agree to this," Mia said.

Noah nudged her foot. "Come on," he urged. "It'll be fun. The fall semester starts next week. When are you gonna have another weekend free from studying?"

"I guess that's true."

"Plus," Graham said with a wag of his eyebrows. "Cabins in the mountains are supersexy. Isn't that right, Claire?"

He leaned toward her and she stiff-armed him. "Nope."

"Fine." He gave Noah a head nod. "Looks like you'll be the only one getting laid up there, man."

"Only Noah?" Mia asked. "If he's getting laid, I'd better be there, too."

Graham barked out a laugh, and Noah smiled down at her. Claire fanned herself.

"True, true," Graham conceded. "So we're doing it then?"

"If we can find a cabin for a decent price," Noah said.

Claire was already pulling out her phone. "I'm on it."

Noah took Mia's hand under the table. She entwined her fingers with his as if it were as natural as breathing. The PDA had been awkward at first, and he'd had to constantly remind himself to touch her. Not because he hadn't wanted to before, but because he'd denied himself for so long.

It was hard to believe he was supposed to now. They'd both settled into it, and it was second nature by this point.

How would he ever go back?

"You sure you want to go?" he asked quietly while Claire and Graham hovered over Claire's phone.

"Sure," she said. "Why not? I don't have anything else going on, and it's been too long since I've been to the mountains. I only went with you once last year, and it was a bust."

"Bringing Claire was our first mistake," he said in a low tone. "She scared all the fish away."

Mia laughed lightly.

"Remember that trip senior year?" he asked, bumping her shoulder with his.

She grinned. "Yeah. It's one of my best memories of high school."

At least a dozen of their high school friends, plus Nathan and several of his friends, had gone to Roosevelt National Forest. They'd spent two days hiking, fishing, enjoying nature, and hanging out around the bonfire. Noah and Mia were about to head off to college, and there had been a sense of excitement and possibility in the air. It wasn't only his favorite high school memory, it was also one of his favorite memories of Nathan.

The familiar rush of guilt rose up like smoke, threatening to choke him. In his mind's eye, he could see Rachel, Nathan's fiancée, and her tear-streaked face as she ran from him at his brother's funeral. His throat tightened and a stab of pain shot through his heart. Just as he was about to stand and excuse himself, Mia squeezed his hand.

He focused on her familiar face, which looked back at him with affection and a hint of concern. "Memories?" she whispered.

"Yeah," he croaked.

She nodded and laid her head on his shoulder, allowing him to collect himself. How he deserved someone like her to be here and alive beside him, while his brother's fiancée was living her life with half a heart was beyond comprehension.

But in this moment, he reveled in the feel of Mia's warm breathing body pressed against him and didn't question it.

13

"Are we there yet?"

Claire's whine rivaled that of any three-year-old, and Mia's patience was wearing thin. She stopped and turned, waiting for Claire to huff her way to where Mia stood on the wooded trail.

She propped a hand on her hip. "How are you so out of shape?"

"I'm...not," Claire panted once she was by Mia's side. She bent over and put her hands on her knees. "The air is...thinner up here."

"We're pretty close to our normal altitude."

"I don't exercise, okay?" Claire wheezed. "You know this." She straightened and sucked down a gulp of water. "Whose idea was this?"

"Yours."

"The hiking part wasn't!"

"Noah said the lake view is worth it," Mia said. "We can do this. We both know Noah wouldn't choose a tough route purely out of concern for me."

Claire's eyes softened. "That's true. He's been superattentive today. It's adorable to watch."

"No more than usual."

"Wrong. He looks at you different now. Take it from someone who's had her eye on you two for almost a decade—he's completely lost over you."

Her skin prickled in a way that wasn't altogether unpleasant.

"The ridiculous blush on your cheeks is awfully telling."

Mia glanced up the path where Noah had stopped to wait for them. Graham was nowhere to be found. Noah wasn't close enough to hear, but still she lowered her voice.

"What should I do?"

A Cheshire cat grin spread across Claire's face. "Take advantage of a romantic mountain getaway."

Mia scrunched her nose. "You and Graham are staying with us in the cabin."

The only decent place they'd found on such short notice was a two-bedroom, one-bath. Claire said she didn't mind sharing with Graham for one night, loudly declaring if he tried anything funny she'd kick his ass to the couch.

"So? We're all adults. We know what happens between married couples. Or what usually happens, anyway." Claire tucked her water bottle back into her backpack. "Besides, I think Graham could use a little convincing."

"What? Why?"

Claire shrugged. "The other day at the condo he said something about you two. Nothing big, just that he thought you seemed awkward around each other sometimes. Made him wonder what was going on."

"You backed us up, right?"

"Yeah, I told him it was just weird for you two to be public with your relationship after keeping it a secret for so long. Still, it couldn't hurt to...you know. Make things a little clearer, if you know what I mean." She leaned in and winked. "Might clear things up for more than just Graham."

Mia pulled her bottom lip between her teeth and once again peeked at Noah, who appeared as if he were about to come back down to see what was going on. He wore a fitted, soft-looking heather-gray shirt that outlined his impressive chest and biceps and left several of his tattoos on display. His hair was messy and his eyes were hidden behind sunglasses, and a huge backpack framed his shoulders. He'd been insistent about Mia not bearing any extra weight and carried everything they both might need on his own back. She was too far away now, but earlier she'd noticed the veins in his forearms, more visible from the heat and exertion. Today, her usually gentle and soft-spoken husband exuded a power and raw masculinity she sometimes forgot about.

"Holy shit, Mia." Claire's voice shook her out of her trance. "You look like you want to eat him alive."

Mia dragged in a ragged breath and took a long drink of her own water before resuming her trek up the trail.

"Yeah," Claire muttered from behind her. "If I had a prize like that waiting for me, I'd get moving, too."

Noah had been right. The lake at the head of the trail was worth the hike, with crystal clear water perfectly reflecting the trees and mountains beyond. They took a break on some rocks and passed around a bag of Mia's homemade granola, chatting and relaxing.

"I swear, Mia. You should open up your own bakery," Claire said.

Mia tossed another chunk of granola in her mouth. "Nah. I'd love to write a cookbook someday, though."

Graham got up and walked near the water while the other three remained seated.

"Excited to start school next week?" Noah asked, even though he had to know the answer. She'd been talking about it nonstop.

"I'm so ready," Mia said.

Claire took the bag from Noah. "What classes are you starting with?"

"Medical Nutrition Therapy, Nutrition and the Life Cycle, and a few food service and management courses."

"Sounds intense," Claire said.

Mia shrugged. "I have a lot of time to make up for. No time to waste."

"You're gonna do great," Noah said with confidence. "Top of the class, you'll see."

A little while later, Mia asked Graham to take a picture of her and Noah and, with Claire's words fresh on her mind, she placed herself in front of Noah's body and pulled his arms around her. He hesitated only briefly before molding his body to her back and hugging her close to rest his chin on her head. She took a few selfies with Claire too, and once Claire stated she'd had enough outside time, they made their way back to the cabin.

While Claire declared a nap to be next on her agenda, Graham took a fishing pole down to the shore of a small lake nearby. A beat-up metal canoe floated in the water, tied to the post of a wooden dock jutting out into the blue-green water.

Noah nodded his head toward the boat. “Wanna check out what’s on the other side?”

His eyes shone with the excitement of even the simplest of adventures, and suddenly Mia was sixteen again, going out on the water with him for the first time. It was in the middle of a lake that day she’d unknowingly started what would become their most cherished ritual. They’d been floating in the middle of the calm waters, the boat gently rocking, and she’d studied the expanse of the lake and looked up at the sky.

“Would you rather be a fish or a bird?” she’d asked, embarrassed immediately at how silly she probably sounded.

Noah hadn’t laughed at her, though. He’d thought on it for a minute, then said, “Fish.”

His answer had surprised her, and she’d glanced back at him. “Why?”

He’d shrugged, dipping the paddle smoothly into the water. “They’re not as visible. People wouldn’t be able to see me unless I wanted them to.”

It was such a Noah answer.

Now, some fourteen years later, she warmed at the memory.

She grinned. “Sure.”

Mia enjoyed the view as he moved them through the water, strong and steady. It had been a long time—too long—since she’d done something like this with him.

“Doing okay up there?” he asked after a few minutes.

“Yes. This is perfect.”

“Thinking about how you’d rather be a bird?”

She twisted around, careful not to jostle the canoe too much. “What?”

His ice-blue gaze met hers. “Bird or fish, right?”

She kept her expression carefully neutral despite the fluttering in her stomach. "I don't think I ever answered that one."

"You'd pick bird, though."

"How do you know?"

"Always moving, flocks to groups, constantly talking? Birds are your people."

She couldn't help but laugh, the fondness in his tone erasing any possibility of taking offense to his words.

They returned an hour later, and after dinner, Noah and Graham started a fire in the pit in a clearing near the cabin. Several Adirondack chairs dotted the area, and they spaced themselves out around the fire, enjoying drinks and conversation. As night fell, Noah pulled his chair close to Mia's.

"Can I see our pictures from today?"

"Sure." She unlocked her phone and handed it to him, leaning over his arm to watch as he swiped through them. Graham had taken several in the pose with Noah standing behind her, the breathtaking expanse of mountains beyond.

Noah passed the phone back to her with an image still up. "Send that one to me?"

Why were her hands shaking? Did he notice? She quickly rested them against her thighs, moving her thumbs across the screen. "Okay."

He draped his arm across her shoulders, a happy smile on his face.

"I forgot how much you love it here," she observed. "In the mountains, I mean."

She thought about the other night at the restaurant, and how tense and stressed he'd seemed. Now, with his relaxed posture and contented features, he was a completely different person.

His blue eyes met hers, the nearby flames casting dancing shadows across his face. "It's one of the only places I feel at home."

"We should come more often," she blurted. "Together, I mean."

A sweet smile spread across his face. "Yeah?"

She rubbed her cheek across her shoulder. "I mean, if you want to. I can't rock climb like you and Graham do, but if you occasionally want a less physical trip—"

He leaned close, his breath tickling the tiny hairs on her neck. "I'll take you wherever you'll let me."

A shiver zipped down her spine at the deep husky tone of his voice.

"Whatcha talking about over there?" Claire called out.

"I was telling Mia I think we should consider getting a dog," Noah said coolly, putting some space between them.

"You can have Gertrude," Claire said.

Graham swiped the beer from Claire's hand.

"Hey, give that back."

"Not until you apologize."

"Do you really think I can't get it back from you?"

"I'd like to see you try."

Mia whispered out of the corner of her mouth. "Would you rather watch them or watch TV?"

Noah laughed softly. "Them, for sure. I can't figure out if they hate each other or secretly like each other."

"Your guess is as good as mine."

"Our rooms share a wall. Maybe we'll find out tonight."

Mia stilled. Claire and Graham were still deep in their argument. "About that..."

Noah regarded her with a slight frown.

"Claire said Graham's a little suspicious about us."

His gaze darted across the bonfire and back to her face. "Suspicious how? He hasn't said anything to me."

"I guess we're coming off a little awkward." She toyed with her phone. "She, um, suggested tonight might be a good opportunity to…you know. Make it sound like…"

"Like I'm getting laid?"

She cocked a brow. "Or like *I* am."

"Right. That would be better."

Mia's lips twisted into a side smile. "Are you teasing me?"

"Nope." He crossed one ankle over the opposite knee. "I think it's a great idea."

Her eyes widened. "You do?"

His lips twitched. "Sure. Let's pretend to have sex tonight. It's the perfect opportunity to prove we're the real thing."

"Right." She smoothed her hands down the armrests, nodding. "Yes. Sure, okay."

He laughed and pressed a fist to his mouth. "Mia. That was the most awkward thing I've ever heard." He gave her a friendly pat on the back. "I know you've got this in you. We can totally do this."

"Are you giving me a pep talk before we have fake sex?"

"Is it working?"

She studied his face. She hadn't seen Noah this carefree and playful in a long time, and she'd do anything to not ruin the mood.

She nodded and stood. She held out her hand and with raised brows he took it and stood. She made a show of confidently pulling him across the yard to the cabin and called over her shoulder, "We're heading to bed. You two have fun out here."

Noah rushed up behind her and swept her up in his arms, forcing a surprised giggle from her.

Claire let out a whoop and Graham whistled, and Mia knew her face was ten shades of red. She covered her face with her hands, and as soon as they were inside he slowly lowered her to her feet. He held up his palm for a high five, and she smacked her hand against his.

By the time they'd changed clothes, taken turns in the bathroom, and shut themselves into the room they were sharing, Claire and Graham had come inside as well, their muffled voices echoing in the rooms beyond.

Mia eyed the king-size bed and thought of the last time she'd slept beside him.

Hopefully this night would be kinder to her.

To both of them.

"Are we really doing this?" she asked quietly.

"You bet we are," he said. "You made a show of wanting me out there. It's cruel to get a man's hopes up like that." His smile faded all of a sudden as he realized what he'd said. "I mean, if you want to. Shit, even if we are just messing around, it's always your choice." He gripped the back of his neck. "I didn't—"

"Noah." She got on the bed, on top of the covers. "I know. With you, I always know that."

"Good." He slowly went around to his side and sat.

A strange sense of excitement filled her. She winked at him, wanting the lighthearted Noah from outside to come back. "How are we doing this?"

Noah turned, pausing thoughtfully before he reached up to grip the headboard. He tried to slam it against the wall, but from his position and as close as the bed was to the wall, it didn't have the desired effect.

"Come on," Mia teased. "That's not how a man moves a headboard."

Cocking a brow, he twisted around and got on his hands and knees, and tried again.

Mia burst out laughing.

"I feel ridiculous."

"Oh my gosh, you're like, humping the air," she said between bursts of laughter. She rolled to the side, clutching her stomach.

Noah shifted onto his knees, gripping his thighs. "A good wife would offer to be embarrassed with me. This usually takes two, you know."

Gauntlet: thrown.

The air thickened between them, and finally she grinned and lowered herself to her back, waving in the space above her. "Come on, then. I'll do my part, too."

His smile slipped a little, as if he hadn't expected her to agree. "You sure?"

"Sure. We're clothed, even if they don't know that."

He moved one limb at a time, climbing over her body to position himself above her. "Well. Claire probably does."

With his face hovering above hers and his muscular arms positioned on either side of her head, her pulse doubled. She had no control over her foolish heart, but tried to keep her brain on track and maintain normal breathing. "Let's plant a seed of doubt in her mind."

"Competitive tonight, are we?" His spearmint breath brushed across her face.

She shrugged. "She's been heckling me all day." She wiggled a little, making a show of settling in. "Ready?"

Something flickered in his eyes, but was gone before she could decipher its meaning. "Yeah."

He drew back slightly, then thrust his pelvis forward again, arching his back. Under his weight and the force of his movement, the bed obediently followed his movement away from, then straight into the wall. The satisfying thump brought a smile to both their faces.

"There it is," she murmured.

He grinned—goodness, he was beautiful—and did it again, his eyes focused a little below hers, on her nose or lips, maybe?

She was strangely disappointed by it. But it would probably be too awkward to look him in the eye while he pretended to pound her into oblivion.

Razor-sharp jealousy slammed into her unbidden, at the thought of another woman seeing Noah this way. Holding himself above her, using his athletic, masculine body to bring them both pleasure.

Mia suddenly hated them all. Any woman who had come before her, and all who would come after.

Another thump, and suddenly he dipped his head to speak into her ear, his voice low. "I thought you were gonna help me out. I'm doing all the work here."

"Right," she whispered, bringing herself to the moment and the task at hand. She was the one beneath him right now, and she might never be here again.

Live it up, honey.

She took a deep breath and collected herself before letting out a loud, and hopefully convincing, moan. She clamped her eyes shut, doing it twice more as Noah continued his efforts above her. She gripped the sheets, wanting something to hold on to, and willed herself to channel her inner actress. She didn't dare look at him, for fear embarrassment would overwhelm her.

His breathing became labored, and when a guttural sound escaped his lips, she opened her eyes to find his blue ones staring at her face, his cheeks flushed and his jaw clenched.

Something in his eyes caught her off guard and she couldn't look away.

It suddenly felt as if the game had ended, and they were locked in an intense, intimate moment. Out of their own volition, her hands came up to grip his waist, following his rhythmic motion. His hips lowered slightly, still not touching her *there*, but the heat of his body and the way his eyes stayed connected with hers as he moved back and forth sent a wave of heat through her.

The thought struck her that they weren't even naked, yet she felt more exposed in this moment than she ever had. He could see everything if he wanted to. If he knew what to look for.

Suddenly he stopped, his breath coming quickly, and he pressed his chin to his chest, breaking the connection when he closed his eyes.

She kept her hands on him, unwilling to let go.

He moved forward, slowly, and pressed his forehead to hers, his eyes still firmly closed. A heavy, pained sigh escaped him, as if every bit of air in his lungs needed out.

They remained that way for several long moments, then a loud bang came from the other side of the wall.

"That didn't take long," Graham called out.

Noah rolled to the side and landed on his back, his forearm across his mouth as he laughed.

Mia quickly recovered. "I'm on top now," she yelled, the breathlessness in her voice giving weight to their charade.

Noah, still chuckling, gave her a thumbs-up.

A pause, then Graham's approving, *"Nice."*

14

Noah stood with his elbows on the kitchen island, waiting for Mia. His dad's retirement party was being held tonight at a fancy hotel downtown, and if they didn't leave in exactly three minutes, they would be late.

Two minutes and forty-seven seconds later, a pair of heels click-clacked down the hallway.

"Sorry, my hair wasn't cooperating. I'm ready."

Noah looked up and straightened. He'd been ready to say something, but no words came out. He just stood there staring at her, his mouth hanging open, his heart in his throat.

She nervously smoothed a hand down her wavy black hair and across the skirt of her dress. "Is this okay? Too dressy? My closet consists mostly of office attire and yoga pants."

The pink dress was the same she'd worn to their wedding,

which brought back memories of how painfully beautiful she'd looked that day. It also reminded him of their first kiss, which gave him tunnel vision straight into the tree house and the way she'd fit perfectly into his lap, her mouth hot and eager against his.

He cleared his throat, thankful the island blocked the lower half of his body. "You look perfect."

Things had felt a little weird between them since the camping trip last month. He couldn't shake the feel of her. Of her hands gripping his waist, or the way she'd tried to hide the tremble in her body when he'd touched his forehead to hers.

He caught her watching him more than usual, when they were doing mundane things like watching TV or getting ready for bed. Graham hadn't stayed over again and she'd resumed sleeping in the guest room, but each night they said good-night and went their separate ways, there was an air of tension between them. A spark of heat he'd always felt, but it seemed bigger because the lingering look in her eyes told him she felt it, too.

A smile lit up her face. "Thank you. You look handsome, but you always do."

He did?

"I need to fix your hair, though..." she trailed off as she came closer.

His heart pounded beneath his ribs, her sweet vanilla scent washing over him. He tucked his lower lip between his teeth and obediently lowered his head, closing his eyes when she touched him.

Her fingers made several passes through the strands, sending a shudder through him. Her other hand pressed flat against his chest, and fuck, how much longer could he do this? Her smell, her touch, that *dress*...he was seconds away from grabbing her waist, setting her on the counter, and moving between her legs to kiss her within an inch of her life.

"There." Did her voice sound a little breathless, or was he imagining it?

"Maybe I should just get my hair cut short. Then you wouldn't have to fix it all the time."

"Don't you *dare.*"

He lifted his head and met her dark gaze, one eyebrow raised. He expected a look of surprise on her face, that she'd said those words aloud. But she didn't back down, and just stared at him with a sort of intensity he didn't know what to do with. She didn't usually say things like that.

Did she usually *think* them?

He swallowed hard and swiped his phone from the counter before taking a step back to regain his sanity. "Okay. I won't. We'd better head out."

They walked to the car in charged silence, and she must have felt it too, because when she settled into the car beside him, she asked, "Would you rather have a pause button or a rewind button?"

He looked over to find her eyes on his, searching. Was she asking about something specific? He couldn't get a good read on her.

There were so, so many things he'd change if he could go back in time. He'd never have left the fraternity party that night. He wouldn't have had that extra beer at his brother's bachelor party. He would have let that kiss in the tree house go just a little longer…

Starting the car, he turned his gaze straight ahead. "Rewind."

She let out a little laugh, though it didn't sound happy. "Yeah. Me too."

★★★

By some miracle they made it to the party on time, and by the time they had drinks in their hands and had filled up on finger foods, both seemed to relax. Being in a room with dozens of other people relieved a fraction of the constant tension surrounding them when they were alone, and after an entertaining argument about whether they'd rather wear only '80s clothes (Noah) or have only '80s hairstyles (Mia), she excused herself to the ladies' room.

He leaned against the bar-height table to wait, leisurely perusing the room. Many were familiar faces from the office, others were friends of his parents and family. He couldn't be happier this event gave him and Mia an excuse to spend the evening together. Her classes had started three weeks ago, and she spent most evenings studying. He was reading a lot more himself, so he could be in the same room but not distract her with the television. But he'd been dying to talk to her.

Laugh with her.

Touch her.

Tonight was a relief and a torment, swirling around him like oil and water.

After a few minutes, he sensed someone approach from behind him, and David set a glass down.

"Noah," he said by way of greeting.

Noah just looked at him.

David chuckled. "Relax, man. James and I had a long discussion about the associate position. He said you'd put in a good word."

Noah gave him a terse nod.

"You did your part. I won't say anything about you and Mia," David said. He seemed sincere, and Noah relaxed a fraction. "As long as things keep going in my favor, that is."

"I did what I could," he bit out. "Like I said, it's not my decision."

David seemed to catch the eye of someone across the room and did a head nod. He picked his glass up again. "Maybe you've done all you need to, maybe you haven't," he said before strolling off. "Guess we'll find out soon."

Noah took a long pull of his beer, wishing he'd ordered something stronger. But he was driving and with Mia, so he'd kept it light. He tried to push the interaction out of his mind, and focused on his parents and their smiles. Their happiness was contagious. Not only because they were celebrating his dad's retirement and telling everyone about an upcoming European vacation, but also because anytime they were together, their devotion was clear as day. Their relationship was one Noah had always hoped for.

Julia appeared in the same spot David had just vacated. "What's got you all worked up?"

He didn't even try to hide it. "David."

Her humorous smile fell. "Oh. I'd sort of hoped my warning wouldn't be necessary. Guess I was wrong, huh?"

"And how. He's convinced Mia's and my marriage isn't real." Noah put his elbow on the bar-height table. "It's not true, but a public accusation would still cause problems."

A thoughtful look crossed Julia's face. "You know, I would have agreed with you a few weeks ago. Especially right after finding out. But after seeing you two tonight? I don't think anyone would question your relationship."

He worked to keep his expression neutral and paused for a few beats. "Why do you say that?"

"Anyone with eyes can see you're into each other."

"I'm into her, that's for sure." He said the words without much thought, and he wished them back into his throat.

He trusted Julia, but he still didn't need to plant any seeds of doubt in her mind.

"No question. And she's got it bad for you."

Noah kept his mouth shut, but something must have shown on his face.

"You don't believe me?" Julia laughed. "Watch."

Just as he was about to ask what she was talking about, she took a step closer, her hand on his arm and her head thrown back in a joyful laugh.

"What—" he started, pulling his arm back, when a throat loudly cleared on his other side.

"Excuse me." Mia stepped between him and Julia, which effectively put her right up against his person.

He was momentarily distracted by the warmth of her body.

"Sorry to interrupt," Mia said curtly. She subtly shifted her backside more firmly against him, and he almost choked on the realization.

She was jealous.

"No apology necessary," Julia said, cool as a cucumber. She'd backed up a step and met Noah's eyes above Mia's head, her eyes twinkling.

He quirked a brow, conceding she may have been right. But what did Mia's reaction mean? Was it just a territorial move?

"I think I need another drink," Julia said with a grin.

She walked off and Mia put a few inches of space between them.

"What was so funny?" she clipped.

"Nothing. Just Julia being Julia. Do you want to hit the photo booth?"

"What?"

Noah pointed to the far corner of the room. "It was my

mom's idea. Said she was trying to appeal to us younger people to get us to show up."

Mia smiled fondly. "Oh. Yeah, okay. Sure."

She grabbed his hand—*she* grabbed *his* hand—as they made their way across the room. He caught Julia's eye from the bar and she tipped her glass in his direction.

"Ooh, are you two taking pictures?" his mom called as they neared the deserted booth. "Get some cute ones for me!"

Noah waved her off and peeled back the black curtain, gesturing for Mia to go in first. He settled in beside her in the small space, their arms and thighs pressed together. The curtain fell closed and darkness surrounded them. His other senses heightened—the heat of her body, the soft sounds of her breath, the sweet scent of her hair. He gripped his thighs.

"You pick the props," he said, hoping she didn't notice the rasp in his voice.

Her gaze met his, something he couldn't identify in her eyes. Before he could say anything else, she leaned forward to the various props available. They took a few with glasses and top hats, and one with cutouts of champagne flutes. With each flash of the light bulb, the strain melted away, and soon they were laughing and posing, each snapshot more theatrical than the last.

Mia handed him a mustache and she grabbed a red pair of lips. She held them up in front of her own, batting her eyelashes.

"How do I look?"

"Like a cartoon."

"Really?" She held the lips in front of her face, eyeing them critically. "I always wished my lips were a little fuller. You know, like Angelina Jolie's? Hers are perfect. I can't imagine any man not wanting to kiss those."

She said the words conversationally, completely unaware of the bolt of desire that hit him like lightning. She laughed a little at herself and looked up, her eyes growing wide when she saw his face.

How clearly were his thoughts reflected there? He didn't have the fortitude to create a mask worth a damn. All he could do was stare at her pink lips and rasp, "Yours are pretty damn perfect."

That perfect mouth parted and a soft sound of surprise escaped. Just as he was about to lift his hand to slide his thumb across her lips, someone pounded on the side of the booth.

"You two done in there?" a man's voice slurred.

Mia blinked several times and gathered the props, shoving them back in the box as Noah pulled back the curtain, ignoring the crushing disappointment that filled him.

"All yours, buddy."

It was his dad's first week in retirement, and his presence was still very much at the architecture firm.

Well, in Noah's office at least.

Tuesday afternoon, Noah's phone rang, and he'd thought it was a joke when his dad's name flashed across the screen.

"Shouldn't you be lying by the pool or something?" Noah joked in greeting.

"Why haven't you submitted all your materials for the junior principal position?"

Noah's stomach dropped. "Uh…"

"I asked James about it at the party, and he kind of evaded the question. I just asked HR and they said your application isn't complete."

"I've been busy—"

"Bullshit. Nothing is more important than your career."

Noah's spine stiffened. "That's not true." His dad knew it, too. He'd always done a good job of balancing work and family.

"At this point in your life it is," his dad argued. "Now is the time to go hard and make yourself known, so you can slow down once you settle down and have a family."

"I have a family now, if you recall."

"I know you just got married, but that's not a good enough reason. Surely Mia wants this for you. What's going on?"

Noah leaned back in his chair. It was one thing to have this conversation with James…but with his dad? The man he wanted to make proud more than anyone else? He forced the words out. "I don't think I'm ready, Dad."

"Yes you are."

"There's too much competition. There's no point in applying when there are others with more experience." His dad might not buy that. In the past Noah had never had a problem at least trying things when it came to applying to colleges or jobs, even if he wasn't confident he'd get the spot. He'd learned from every process, regardless of outcome.

"This is unlike you, Noah." His dad sighed heavily into the speaker. "Is something wrong? Has something happened at the office I didn't know about?"

"No."

"Then I don't understand. You always said you wanted this. To be a part of the business I started and carry it forward. I thought you were proud to work there and be part of what we're accomplishing in this city."

Did he have to put it like that? "I do. I am." He stood and pushed his foot against the bottom of his chair, sending it wheeling across the room. "I just… I don't know. I guess I got distracted. I'll finish the application."

"You will?"

"Yeah."

"Good. I'm glad to hear it," his dad said. "I'll let you get to it, then. But Noah?"

"Yeah?"

"If I check on this again and find out you didn't at least try, I'll be very disappointed in you."

Noah's lungs burned and heart pounded with each smack of his shoes against the pavement. He paused at a crosswalk, jerking his head both ways to make sure he wasn't about to get creamed, and ran through the intersection without waiting for the signal to proceed.

He was too frustrated to care about jaywalking. Jayrunning? Whatever.

Climbing and camping were his preferred methods of stress relief. Getting out of the city and into the mountains was the best way to clear his head, and he'd always worked through problems best while hanging off the side of a rock, nothing else to focus on but his grip and the rope.

But it was Tuesday and an impromptu trip out of town wasn't possible. On the rare occasion something upset him on a day like this, he went for a run instead.

His father's words spoken that afternoon were on a scrolling marquee in his mind. Bright, flashing, and repetitive.

I thought you were proud to work there. I'll be very disappointed in you.

After work he'd immediately changed and hit the street, hoping to dispel the bitterness. By the time he made it home, he didn't feel much better.

Mia had gone to dinner with Claire and Reagan and wasn't there when he returned. He took a shower to rinse off, keeping the water cold to cool down his overheated body. As he stood under the spray, letting the frigid water rain down on his face, he suddenly had the sensation someone was watching him.

He lowered his head and opened his eyes, swiping a hand over his head to push his hair back.

Mia was standing in the hallway, eyes wide and mouth ajar. Apparently between thinking he was alone in the house and his mind being focused elsewhere, he hadn't thought to close the bathroom door. And no hot water meant the glass hadn't fogged up…

Her hand flew up to cover her eyes. "I'm sorry—"

He swiped a towel and turned off the water in one fluid movement. "No, it's—"

"I didn't—"

"Mia—"

But by the time he could get the word out, she was gone.

15

Mia shut herself in her room and had remained there for two hours. She knew from the slam of the front door Noah had left, but for some reason she still hadn't come out.

She currently lay faceup on her bed, staring at nothing, unable to see anything except Noah's naked body.

And it wasn't just a body. It was a sculpted, beautiful specimen of divine workmanship. Rivulets of water had streamed down the ridges and valleys of his chest and abs, and below... and all she'd been able to do was stand there, flushed and in awe, staring at him like a complete perv.

She could say two things with one hundred percent certainty.

One: she'd never been as attracted to another human being as she was to Noah Agnew.

Two: their friendship was officially ruined.

She covered her face with her hand and let out a groan. Why hadn't she just kept walking? She hadn't meant to glance into the bathroom as she passed, but she figured maybe he'd just turned the water on and hadn't gotten undressed yet. Neither of them had ever showered with the door open since moving in together. And for good reason—she could guarantee if he'd done that before, she'd have found some way to slide into his bed well before now.

She was climbing out of her skin with the desire to touch him. Run her hands over that smooth, taut skin. Trail her lips and tongue across his tattoos.

The look on his face, though. He'd been mortified. She wished she'd popped off with some funny comment to make them both laugh and lighten the moment, but no. After one look at his face, and realizing she'd just breached his privacy like a total creeper, she'd gotten the hell out of there.

How? How would they ever come back from this?

She had to apologize, explain she hadn't meant to see him. Or stare. Or ogle…however one wanted to describe it. Just as she decided to woman up and move to the living room to wait for him to return, her phone buzzed with an incoming text.

Graham: You're probably gonna need to come get your man. Don't think he's in any condition to drive.

Mia: Where is he?

Graham: We're at The Blue Lion.

Mia: I'm on my way.

She jumped out of bed, grabbed her purse, and headed to the pub. Guilt ate at her the entire drive, knowing he was so upset by what happened he'd gone somewhere to drink.

Noah rarely drank, and when he had more than one, it was usually because something was bothering him.

She wove through the dimly lit establishment, finally spotting him at a table near the back.

She'd know Noah's large form anywhere.

Instead of his usual confident stature, his shoulders slumped forward. His head was bent, forehead resting in his palm, his other hand wrapped around a glass tumbler.

Graham gave her a small smile when she walked up.

"Noah?"

He straightened and twisted around at the sound of her voice. His eyes were a little unfocused, but he looked nothing like Graham's message had led her to believe. She'd expected him to be half passed-out drunk.

"What are you doing here?" He didn't say it rudely. He seemed surprised to see her.

"Graham texted me."

Noah shot his friend a look and Graham shrugged unapologetically. "Seemed like y'all needed to talk something out." He stood and waved a hand across his empty chair. "All yours, milady." With a laugh and a wink, he disappeared into the crowd at the bar.

Mia looked at the chair, then back at Noah. "May I?"

"If you want."

Butterflies swarmed aggressively as she sat. She folded her hands in her lap, trying not to think about what he looked like under his jeans and T-shirt. "Noah, I'm so sorry. I didn't mea—"

"Don't worry about it," he interrupted. His cheeks were pink, and he wouldn't meet her eyes.

Shit. She'd really messed things up.

"Let me say this, please," she said, raising her voice when the track changed and a loud song blared through the overhead speakers.

He shook his head. "Not here."

"Let's go outside, then." She stood and held her hand out to him. He locked eyes with her, and she got the sense he wanted to decline. "Please."

He downed the rest of his drink and rose to his feet but didn't take her hand. He gestured for her to lead the way.

The cool evening air swept across her face as they exited the pub, and she kept walking, taking a few steps between two buildings where it was quiet and still.

"Please don't say anything. Just listen."

His jaw flexed, and he tucked his hands into his pockets. He gave her a curt nod.

"I'm so sorry for what happened earlier. I hadn't been like, standing there for a while or anything. I didn't mean to look—I mean, I didn't think you'd be—" She clamped her eyes shut, which only served to provide her a mental image of his full frontal, and pried them open again. "I completely invaded your privacy and I'm sorry."

He remained quiet for several beats, shifting on his feet.

"I was just surprised, I guess," she added.

Why, why had she said that?

His eyes snapped to hers. "What do you mean?"

Blood rushed through her veins, making her skin feel tight, and she couldn't seem to stop herself from telling the truth. Putting it all out there to see how he'd respond. "If I accidentally saw anyone else naked—Claire, Graham, anyone—I would have immediately turned the other way. But with you, I felt drawn in." She gripped her hands in front of her body. "This isn't coming out like I wanted. I just... I don't know about you, but I've been feeling things. Lately. I've thought about you in a different way than ever before. And when I saw you, my reaction wasn't to run away. I—I wanted to take off my clothes and get in there with you."

Something flared in his eyes before he twisted around and turned his back to her, running a hand through his hair. "Dammit."

"I'm sorry. I shouldn't have told you that." Shame spread through her. "Obviously you don't feel the same, or else you wouldn't have come here. I don't know what I was thinking. I guess I just hoped, maybe—"

Suddenly he was in front of her, and she took a step back. He followed her movement, only leaving a few inches between them. "Do you know why I never drink when I know I'll be around you?"

He was standing so close, it was hard to focus on what he said, much less string words together. It shouldn't have been a big deal—they'd been this close dozens of times. Maybe even hundreds. Hugs. Sitting next to each other, shoulders touching. They'd *kissed*, even if it was for show. But for some reason, the way he held his body so taut, heat coming off his skin in waves, made this feel different.

"Why?"

His usually bright eyes were hidden in the darkness. "Because I might say something I mean."

She tilted her head. What the hell did that mean? "Like what?"

He just looked at her for a few seconds, as if he stared hard enough, he'd be able to read her mind. Or see into her soul. She wasn't sure which.

He swayed toward her, his gaze dropping to her lips. "This."

His mouth came down on hers so hard and fast she gasped, sucking his breath into her lungs. He took a step into her body and her back hit the brick wall. His hand was behind her head—when had he done that?—to absorb the impact, fingers delving into her hair.

Her knees wobbled, and she scrambled to find purchase somewhere on his body. She was scrambling to do anything useful with her body, in fact, because her brain seemed to only be focused on her lips, and everything that was going on there.

And there was a lot going on. This was more than just a kiss.

This was a statement. A declaration. A punishment.

Of what and for what, she didn't quite know.

All she knew was this kiss was different. Wonderfully different. And she'd never accept anything less from him ever again.

This wasn't for show. No one was around. This was her and Noah, hidden from the world, but no longer hiding from each other.

There was no slow build. His tongue delved deep, claiming her mouth with passion and possession. Yet somehow the hand that cradled her face remained gentle, his thumb tracing her cheekbone with such care it was as if he worried she might break.

Her hands found their way to his neck and shoulders, one sliding down his back, her fingertips following the ridge of his spine, bracketed on either side by toned muscles. The other traveled up his neck and into his hair. As her thumb passed over the shell of his ear, a tremor ran through him.

"Fuck," he groaned. He stopped kissing her and put his forehead against hers, his heavy breath brushing across her face.

"Um," was all she could manage.

"Fuck," he said again. "I'm sorry." He stepped back and her arms dropped to her sides. "I don't—I didn't mean..."

She shook her head. "No." She waited for him to stop and focus on her before she continued. "You absolutely meant that. Don't you dare pretend otherwise."

His throat worked. "You're right."

Her hands trembled, and her heart thrashed at his admission. She'd been the one to say it first, but she hadn't expected him to agree so readily. "I am? You—you want me?"

He looked at her like she'd just asked if he liked to climb mountains. "Of course I do."

"For how long?"

"For forever."

She blinked as her mind raced to process what that meant. "Like, since that night in college?"

He released an incredulous laugh, though his expression remained serious. "Yes. And every night after."

"Why didn't you say anything?"

"You said you just wanted to be friends."

She stumbled over the words. "So did you."

"I lied," he said simply.

One breath. Then two. "So did I."

"Well, then." His eyes burned like fire. "Let's go home."

Noah's palm caressed her thigh the entire drive home, and it was a wonder she stayed on the road. Or didn't get pulled over for suspected drunk driving.

Which reminded her of the text Graham sent, and how much of a stretch it had been. Noah might have been buzzed enough to loosen his tongue, but he wasn't drunk.

She'd have to thank Graham.

Later, though. She had a husband to deal with tonight.

When they stepped inside and the front door clicked shut, they both paused. They stood on a precipice, about to leap into the unknown. It was terrifying and it was thrilling, and Mia searched his face, looking for any sign of uncertainty. But he just looked at her in that steady way he so often did.

Quiet, fierce, and determined.

He took two steps toward her, his stride purposeful and his eyes full of intent, at the same time she launched herself at him. He caught her in his arms and immediately hoisted her up, her legs wrapping around his waist. He didn't falter for a second and kept moving down the hallway, tilting his face up. Without a word she found his lips, eager and waiting. The second their mouths molded together, sparks popped beneath her skin. Noah knew how to kiss, and awe mixed with a feeling of *right* flowed through her veins, liquid sensations that had her mind and heart tripping over one another.

Her hands gripped the back of his head, angling his face just right. She sucked his full bottom lip into her mouth, instantly feeling crazed and out of control, and he groaned, the vibrations from his chest spurring her on even more.

In an instant they were in his bedroom, and her back hit the mattress.

His hands landed beside her head and he stretched above her, his lips insistent and everywhere. One of his palms worked down the side of her ribs, hips, and to her thigh, hitching her leg around his waist. He pressed his body into her and she sucked in a breath, fire exploding in her belly, flames licking through every nerve ending.

"Oh my gosh," she breathed. "I wanted this so bad. In the cabin."

"Me too." His lips moved to her ear, his breath hot on her

neck as he rasped, "You're my wife. My *wife*." He pressed an open-mouthed kiss to her skin. *"Mine."*

A thrill of satisfaction bloomed through her core at the possessiveness in his tone, so different than the way he usually spoke to her.

She wanted more.

His tongue traced the shell of her ear at the same time his large hand slid beneath her hips, bringing her even closer. She arched her neck with a moan, her hands sliding down his back to grasp at his shirt. His lips left her only long enough to reach behind his back and yank it over his head.

She kissed him again and his tongue dipped into her mouth, along with the faint taste of bourbon. Her hands roamed the hard muscles of his bare shoulders and slid along the smooth skin of his arms and back, cataloging in her mind each tattooed image her fingers passed over. Each one a beautiful reminder of who this man was.

They kissed feverishly for several moments, and she wiggled a little farther up the bed. She wove her arms between them to grasp the hem of her own shirt, sliding it off.

His lips came back to hers with a kiss that was so full of passion she released some sort of raw, muffled noise into his mouth. She meant to say his name, but couldn't quite find the brain cells to string the correct syllables together. Her hand slid to his waistband and inched lower.

Suddenly Noah was gone, and in her hazy state, it took her a minute to find him standing at the foot of the bed, his chest heaving and his eyes filled with fire.

"What's wrong?" she asked, her own breath coming fast. He was magnificent, standing there in just his jeans, abs rippling and tattooed arms tense by his sides. If he was having second thoughts and didn't want to do this...not only would her body burst into flame, but her heart would burn to ashes.

He gripped the back of his neck with one hand, his eyes wide like he was just realizing what was happening. His hair was sticking out in all directions. Because of *her* hands.

"I just, I just need..." He shook his head a little, his lips parted. "I want to slow this down."

Her heart still raced, and all she knew was she wanted the weight of him back on her. "Slow this down," she repeated on an exhale.

She went up on her elbows and his eyes tracked down her body, pausing at a few key areas, then slid back up to connect with hers.

He swallowed. "I've wanted this for so long. It's like I'm dreaming. But if this is real, and it's actually happening, I'm taking my fucking time."

She stared at him, noticing for the first time just how different he looked in this moment. He wasn't the same Noah she'd always known. His eyes were mostly the same, but they looked back at her now with a heat and raw power she didn't quite know what to do with. This wasn't Noah, her best friend. The one who spent hours bent over his computer, who ordered the same thing at restaurants because he didn't want to ruin a good thing, or who opened doors for her with a gentle hand on her back everywhere they went. This was a fierce, unrestrained Noah she'd never seen before.

They were at a tipping point. If they continued on, there was no going back. Noah and Mia would be forever changed, and for a split second, she wavered.

What if it's not as good?

And then when his brow furrowed the slightest bit, and

the corner of his full, bottom lip disappeared beneath white teeth, all hesitation fell away.

What if it's better?

She'd loved this man for years.

Decades.

A lifetime.

She sat up and scooted to the edge of the bed, letting her feet touch the floor. "You can take as long as you want. Take forever. Just don't *stop*."

He trembled a little, like a shiver ran through him, and he came close again, sliding his fingers through her hair, and her mind went blank.

He loomed over her, looking down at her like she was the most precious, beautiful thing he'd ever seen.

It was almost painful to look at him while he looked at her like that. She didn't deserve it. Didn't deserve him. Her heart swelled, her breath catching in her throat. She tentatively touched him again, tracing the pads of her fingers up his stomach and across his chest.

He sucked in a deep breath, his eyes falling closed as she traced his skin. His hips rocked forward a little, so slight it seemed unintentional. A primal, unconscious desire taking control. When he opened his eyes again, both his hands came to her temples, slowly smoothing her hair back before moving his hands to the sides of her face. He curved over her, still on his feet while she sat on the bed, dipping his head and whispering her name just before his lips touched hers.

She slipped her bra off and scooted back, pulling him with her. She inhaled sharply at the feel of his chest against hers, with nothing between them. They kissed deeply for several minutes, his hands moving over every inch of exposed skin with a patience she'd never possess. Compared to his measured movements, she felt like a fumbling, hurried teenager, but she couldn't seem to stop herself.

She just…wanted.

Tension wound tight within her, and she almost cried with relief when his hands went to the button on her jeans. He slid them down her legs, along with her underwear, and planted kisses along her thighs and ribs on the way back to her mouth.

This time when he rocked forward, her eyes almost rolled to the back of her head.

Somehow, she found her voice. "I'm completely naked and I'm gonna need you to meet me here."

He murmured something against her neck before he lifted his hips to give her access.

He kicked off his jeans and slowly, carefully resumed his prior position. Her knees bent on either side of his hips and she arched upward, feeling all of him. He made a choking noise and went still, closing his eyes as if trying to maintain control. He took a deep breath, then another, as she ran her hands through his hair, over and over.

When he opened his eyes, he carefully lowered his body, his forearms pressing into the mattress on either side of her head. He lay his forehead against hers, his blue eyes locked on hers. He spoke, his lips brushing hers with each word. "I adore you. I always have."

If she'd been standing, it would have brought her to her knees. As it was, she breathed the words in, pulling them deep inside her.

He kissed her softly and said it again, and the severity of emotion on his face was too much. Love and tenderness consumed her, filling her soul past the point of containment. Her eyes filled and a few tears escaped.

He didn't say anything right away. Just traced the wet trail with his tongue and caught one with his lips. "Don't do that."

"I can't help it," she whispered, unable to muster any embarrassment. The moment was too perfect.

"All the times I've imagined making love to you, you were never crying." A crooked grin tilted his lips. "Far from it."

Her return smile was automatic. "Get on with it then," she said, intending for it to be a challenge, but the slight whine in her tone belied the attempt.

"I'm taking my fucking time, remember?"

"Key word being f—"

His lips crashed against hers, swallowing any further conversation.

16

It no longer bothered Noah that he had a queen-size bed.

If Mia continued to be in it, maybe he'd even downsize. With the way they met in the middle and stayed wrapped up in each other all night, miles of mattress extended in both directions.

Light streamed through the windows, casting a soft glow on her skin. Propped on one elbow, he dragged a gentle finger down her temple, marveling at the softness of her hair. The crevices buried deep in his heart ached, and he couldn't tell whether the sensation stemmed from pleasure or pain.

The ramifications of what they'd done—the line they'd crossed—would come. But he'd become an expert at hiding emotions, and for now he'd pretend they could move forward and find a way to live happily ever after. Let himself live in the fairy tale for as long as he could, whether it lasted hours or weeks, and avoid reality as long as possible.

Reality never had served him well.

He continued stroking down her arm and to her hip. His ministrations would no doubt wake her soon, but he couldn't help himself. Being able to touch her like this, look at her like this…he'd dreamt about it his entire adult life. A fullness lodged in his throat and a smile pulled at the corners of his lips when her eyes fluttered open.

She slowly rolled onto her back, still mostly covered by the sheet, and his hand came to rest on her stomach. Her warm brown eyes met his, and her cheeks immediately flushed pink, her hands flying to her face.

"Hey," he said with a laugh. When was the last time he felt this happy? "Where'd you go?"

She split her fingers to peek at him. "I can't believe you and I…we…"

"Twice."

She squeaked.

"Left you speechless, huh?" He huffed on his fingers and rubbed them across his chest. "That's excellent."

The sound of her laugh filled the room and his soul. He rolled on top of her and pulled her hands away, stretching them above her head.

"Regrets?" he asked.

Her expression turned solemn and she shook her head. "You?"

"Never."

She lifted her head to meet his lips, and he followed her back down, his stomach dropping when she curved her legs around his. "Let's stay here all day," he said into her mouth.

"Mmm." She nipped at his bottom lip. "Don't you need to get ready for work?"

She twisted around to look at the clock on his bedside table, causing the sheet to slip lower. His body immediately tightened, and he released one of her hands to grasp her chin and bring her face back to his. "Nope."

Their eyes locked and her voice sounded breathless when she asked, "No?"

"I already called in sick."

He dropped his head to her neck, trailing kisses down to the curve of her shoulder.

"But," she sighed. "It's Wednesday…the weekly meeting…"

"Don't care." He was trying to encourage them to choose someone else for the promotion, anyway. "I have plans."

Her free hand wrapped around his neck and she scraped her nails along his scalp, sending a tremor through him. "You do?"

"Mmm-hmm." He traced his tongue along the shell of her ear. "Very pressing matters to attend to."

"Ohhhhkay," she murmured.

"What time do you have class?" he whispered.

"Class?" She sounded disoriented. "Um, one?"

Four hours before they needed to get out of bed. Not quite enough time for everything he had in mind, but he'd make it work.

"Good."

Two hours later, Noah lay on his back with his head propped on two pillows. Mia had draped herself across his chest, tracing one finger along his wing tattoo.

She kept her eyes on the design and asked, "Will you tell me about this now?"

He shifted his eyes from her face to the black ink, taking a few moments to study the intricate design. He'd considered the piece for a long time and had gone to a different tattoo artist—one who specialized in wings and feathers—than for his others.

He couldn't be happier with the artistry. The meaning behind it, however, wasn't so easy to explain.

"Wings usually represent being released or freed from something. From something that binds or holds you down. Sort of a liberation, I guess."

"Wings? Plural? You made it seem intentional that you only have one."

"I haven't quite gotten past my demons." He wanted to turn away from her so she couldn't see the sorrow and remorse on his face. They didn't belong in the perfect morning they'd shared. "I've tried to get away, but I never seem to get very far."

The sadness in her eyes was almost too much to bear. He ran his fingers through her hair, letting the silky strands fall to her back before starting again.

"Is it about Nathan?"

He nodded.

"I miss him too, you know," she said. "You were always my person, but being with you two together was something else. You complemented each other so well."

"He was larger than life."

"So are you."

"Not in the same way."

"No, that's true. You were similar, but at the same time so different."

He kept his eyes on his fingers disappearing into her hair, and delving back in after becoming visible again.

"I know there are things you've never told me about that night," she said.

He stilled. Oxygen stopped moving through his lungs.

"I wish you would."

He swallowed. "Why?"

"Because I want to know everything about you. I want inside your head. I want you to let me in. More than ever, now that I know how you feel about me, I want to know if it was something about that night that changed your mind about us."

Noah closed his eyes, feeling the warm weight of her body across his chest. Her breath brushing across his skin and the rhythmic beat of her heart. He focused on inhaling, exhaling, and repeating the action, considering his options.

Eventually, he resumed running his fingers through her hair.

"I'm the reason Nathan died."

She lifted her head. "What?" She shook her head. "How can you think that? A deer ran in front of the car. That's no one's fault."

"I know the *deer* wasn't my fault." His tone was harsher than he intended. "But I was the reason we were on the road that night. We were safe on the side of a mountain when Claire texted me that you were in the hospital. I'm not sure how much you were aware of then, because I didn't get to see you until several days after. But everyone was freaking out. That first night we thought it was cancer, or worse—whatever could even be worse than that—and when she said you were in the ICU, I sort of went crazy. I don't remember much, but I had to get to you and that was the only thing on my mind. We took my car up there, and if I hadn't been drinking, I'd have come down the mountain by myself. Sent my dad up there to get the guys the next morning, or something. But I couldn't drive, and Nathan had stopped drinking hours earlier. So he had to."

Slowly she sat up, and covered her mouth with her fingers. "So..." Her eyes filled with tears. "By proxy, I'm actually the one responsible."

Noah shot up to a sitting position. "What? No."

She wouldn't look him in the eye. "You wanted to come down the mountain in the middle of the night because of me."

"It's not your fault you got sick," he insisted. "I'm the one who made a *choice.* I'm the reason we were on that fucking road at three in the morning, and I'm the reason he was in the driver's seat. It should have been me, not him."

She shook her head and slid her palm to her collarbone. "Have you unconsciously blamed me all this time? Is that why, a few weeks later, you said we should just be friends?"

"No." He took her hand. "No. I never blamed you, not even for a second. I've *always* wanted to be with you, Mia. Those were the darkest days of my life and still, I never stopped wanting you. Which only made me hate myself more. Especially after seeing Rachel at the funeral."

She swiped at her eyes with her free hand. "Rachel? Nathan's fiancée?"

"We were camping that weekend for Nathan's bachelor party, remember? I approached her at the funeral. I wanted to tell her how sorry I was, and that I'd never forgive myself for what happened. The second she saw me she started crying and wouldn't talk to me. She left, and I've only seen her once since then. It was a few years later and I passed her on the Sixteenth Street Mall. I know she saw me. Again, I tried to talk to her, but she ducked into a store and I lost her.

"I don't blame her, really. I took the one person she loved in the entire world, and she hates me for it. My decision ruined her life. I guess I figured…who was I to find happiness when she was out there, heartbroken and alone?"

Mia pulled her hand back. "You were punishing yourself?"

"Not exactly," he began. He ran a hand across his jaw. "It's hard to explain. Yes, I feel immense guilt. I probably always will. I'm not sure I deserve happiness and love. But is that the only reason I hid my true feelings for you? No."

"Why then?"

"At first, I thought we just needed time. I was scared if we jumped into something new, like a relationship, right after everything that happened, we'd be destined to fail. I needed you too much to risk losing you. And you needed me."

Mia crossed her arms over her stomach. "I don't know what I would have done without you."

"That's why I initially suggested we stay friends, but I honestly thought it would be temporary. You agreed so quickly, and have stood by it ever since. You've always kept dating casual and you're so vocal about how you never want to get married. If I'd known it could have been like this, I would have done something a long time ago, self-hatred be damned. But you never gave me even a hint you wanted me. What was I supposed to do?"

"I don't know," she whispered.

"Not all of my decisions have been the right ones. But I know two that have: marrying you, and what happened last night."

A tear fell from her cheek, and he swiped the wet trail with his thumb.

"All the others are in the past," he said. "And I guess I'm just hoping we can stay here, together, even if it's just for a little while."

Say it's not temporary. Tell me you're ready to make this work for good.

She released a heavy sigh. "It's so complicated, Noah."

Not what he had in mind. But he'd waited nine years, and it wouldn't do any good to rush her now.

"Yeah. It is. But isn't every relationship?"

She leaned into his hand. "Not like ours."

"Even so, I don't want to be with anyone else."

Her eyes searched his, and he forced himself to remain still and silent while she thought. Would she ever accept that he wanted her, sick, healthy, and everything in between?

Finally, she leaned forward and pressed her soft lips to his. "Neither do I."

17

The next two weeks went by in a blissful haze. Mia went to class and studied as much as she possibly could while Noah was at work.

Because when he got home, all bets were off.

Sometimes they didn't even make it past the living room.

He would have respected her request if she asked for more time to focus on school in the evenings, but she thought about him constantly. By the time he walked through that door every day, it was all she could do not to throw herself at him.

She did once and had been very well received.

Her favorite discovery to date: Noah was more dominant in the bedroom than she would have expected. Forget coffee creamer or toothbrush arrangements, him taking her against the wall by the front door would be the thing she replayed in her mind when she was old and alone, thinking about the brief point in her life when she allowed herself to let go and be carefree with someone.

Sometimes he made love to her slow and sweet, as if he were trying to communicate from the very depths of his soul. Their bond felt unbreakable, and in those moments she didn't want the feeling to end.

But nothing compared to the times when his control slipped. The knowledge that she could turn her sweet, gentle, thoughtful husband into a crazed man hell-bent on making her scream his name turned her on beyond reason.

Which brought them to their current predicament: naked on the kitchen floor, which was neither comfortable nor particularly sanitary. The magic had happened on the kitchen table, but somehow they'd ended up here, sharing a plate of sugar-free cobbler Mia had pulled out of the oven minutes before he walked through the door.

Noah let out a satisfied hum. "If being a dietician doesn't work out, I second Claire's idea that you should open up a bakery."

She grinned. "I love the idea of baking as a complement to my job. Share my recipes to help kids and parents find ways to make foods healthier, but still taste good. And be creative when kids have allergies or food aversions."

"That works, too." He grinned. "I benefit either way."

After taking another bite, she leaned her head against the cabinet and studied him. She let her eyes roam his muscled body, and reached out to touch a small raised scar on his upper left thigh. "I'd never noticed this before."

"I don't think you had reason to see that area before recently."

She laughed. "True." She bit her lip and glanced at a nearby body part. "Speaking of, I don't know how you kept *that* hidden from me for so long."

The fork clattered to the plate. "Shit, Mia."

"I'm just saying. Damn."

"Weren't you trying to ask how I got my scar? Because you're quickly derailing my attention."

"I can see that."

"Alright." The plate hit the floor and he was on his feet, holding out his hand. As soon as she was standing he dipped down and hauled her over his shoulder.

She squealed and laughed as he carried her down the hall to the guest room. When her back hit the mattress, she looked around. "Why are we in here?"

"We haven't done it in here yet."

"Oh no. Don't tell me you're one of those men who wants to christen every room in the house."

He stood before her in all his naked glory. She'd never seen anything sexier. How had she not wanted to jump him every single day for the last nine years?

"Not just every room. Every surface."

"Impossible."

"Try me."

"The toilet."

He made a face. "Okay, every feasible surface."

She laughed and pulled him onto the bed, rolling on top of him. She sat up and ticked off her fingers. "We've taken care of your room, the living room, the entryway, and the kitchen."

He lifted his hips. "The guest room is as good as done."

She sucked in a breath. "Mmm-hmm…and um…" His large strong hands began massaging her thighs, and it was hard to think. "Sh-shower?"

"We can make that happen."

"Laundry room."

"Add it to the list." He slid one hand slowly up her back. "You done yet?"

"Hallway," she whispered as he put pressure on her neck to pull her down to his lips.

"Consider it done." He kissed her. "I'll never get enough of you, Mia Adrian."

She closed her eyes and pressed her mouth more firmly to his, hoping to distract him from her lack of response. It would be so easy to say it back. Tell him she never wanted this to end.

And it would be true.

But she couldn't only think of what she wanted. She had to consider the good and the bad, and the baggage that followed her wherever she went. Noah had his own to deal with—more than she'd even realized—and she couldn't pile more on his shoulders.

Couldn't and wouldn't.

Neither had said they loved each other out loud yet—at least not in the "I'm *in* love with you" way—even though she felt it, and she knew he did, too. It was as if they were both holding back just a tiny bit to keep their bubble intact for as long as possible.

If she said those words, it would be almost impossible to walk away. So she did the only thing she could for now and tried her best to show him.

The next evening Noah drove them to meet Claire, Graham, and Reagan at Top Golf.

She watched him drive for a few minutes, admiring his forearms on display and his strong hands gripping the wheel. "Hey. You never told me about the scar on your thigh."

"Technically, you never asked."

"You distracted me."

"Are you complaining?"

"Not even a little." Mia fidgeted in her seat. "But we can't do that now—"

"I don't know, we haven't done it in the car."

"Noah."

"Mia."

"We'll be late."

His lips thinned. "Fine."

"So how'd you get it?"

He sighed, a muscle in his cheek flexing. "It's a glass cut from the accident. I fell when I was climbing out through the window and a shard lodged in there pretty good."

Everything seemed to slow as Mia pictured the scene and how horrible it must have been. Losing Nathan had been awful, but the selfish part of her was deeply grateful that Noah made it out alive.

"I don't know what to say," she said softly. "I'm so sorry."

He reached across the console and took her hand. "Me too."

She held his hand tight for the rest of the drive, and only released it long enough for them to get out and meet at the hood of the car.

The others had already secured a bay on the third floor with couches that faced the open-air side of the building and the driving range beyond.

"You made it," Reagan greeted.

"Can't trust them to be anywhere on time these days," Claire remarked with a sly grin. Mia hadn't gone into much detail, but had let her best friend in on the recent development in her and Noah's relationship.

Her left ear was still ringing from Claire screaming through the phone.

"Lucky bastard," Graham muttered.

Noah clapped him on the back and sat on the couch, settling Mia close to his side. "Have you ordered anything yet?"

"Just drinks," Claire said.

"Have you ever been here?" Mia asked Reagan, who sat on the opposite end of the L-shaped couch.

"Nope. Never been golfing, either."

"That's okay, I suck, too," Claire said. "Mia's the best out of everyone."

"Excuse me," Graham interjected.

Noah rolled his eyes. "You know it's true."

Graham glared at him. "Fine. But I'm second best."

Claire studied her thumbnail. "Second best at hitting the ball or getting drunk while hitting the ball?"

"Both."

Mia pointed to Graham. "You're definitely better at getting drunk than me."

Graham did a fist pump and grabbed a club. "I'll get us started. Reagan! Watch and learn."

Mia settled against Noah's chest, watching Graham attempt to give Reagan a crash course in perfecting a golf swing. Noah's arm curved around her shoulder, his hand stroking up and down her arm while his pine-scented aftershave did something funny to her insides. The September weather was perfect, and she sighed with contentment.

She caught Claire watching them with a satisfied smile, and Mia made a mental note to thank her friend for helping them down this road. She'd always been Mia's cheerleader, encouraging her to do things she never would have considered on her own.

Drinks arrived, they ordered food, and began cycling through to take turns hitting the ball. Mia had grown up golfing with her dad, so she usually took the lead early on. She hadn't golfed much after her relationship with her parents became strained, so she always enjoyed coming here, even if it brought back memories. Half the places marked on her family's map of dream travel destinations had been linked to some golf course her dad wanted to play, and there was a time she'd thought maybe she'd get to go and play a few with him. A pang of sadness ripped through her earlier contentment, and she thought about the letter that remained in the duffel bag she'd brought from her old condo, still unopened.

A cheer from Reagan brought Mia out of her thoughts, and she forced herself to focus on the present.

Mia beat everyone the first two games, but second place was tied between Noah and Graham. As was typical when he'd had a few beers, Graham became Mr. Competitive.

"Best two out of three, my man," he said to Noah. "What do I get if I win?"

"Bragging rights?" Noah offered.

"Pfft. That's nothing."

"Okay...drinks are on me?"

Graham frowned. "That's better, but I don't know. I was thinking something bigger. Along the lines of you coming on the ice-climbing trip in November."

Mia looked up at that. "Ice-climbing trip?"

"Good Lord, he won't shut up about it," Claire said.

"It's true," Reagan agreed. "I know more about crampons and ice screws than I ever cared to."

Mia regarded Noah beside her, but his eyes were on Graham, expression hard. "What are they talking about?"

His gaze softened as he looked down at her. "Graham and some other guys are going ice climbing in Banff. He mentioned it a little while back, but I can't go."

Graham snorted. “Can’t? More like won’t.”

An edge entered Noah’s tone. “Either way, the outcome is the same. I’m not going.”

Mia looked between the two men, trying to decipher their standoff. Noah and Nathan had talked about ice climbing often, and it was something on both their bucket lists. They’d made her watch *K2*, their favorite climbing movie, three times before she put her foot down and said it was too depressing and had too little love story for her.

Would Noah really forgo something he’d always wanted to do because Nathan was gone?

Graham darted a loaded look in her direction before shaking his head and grabbing a driver.

Noah sat stiff beside her, his eyes locked somewhere beyond the open course. Reagan’s words from the day Mia moved out echoed in her brain.

He can’t be going out of town every weekend and leaving you alone.

Or did his reason have nothing to do with Nathan at all?

She thought about it the rest of the evening and considered asking Noah about it on the drive home. In the end she remained silent, unconvinced it was worth it to ask a question she didn’t really want to know the answer to.

18

There were several things Noah (probably) would never have experienced if it weren't for Mia.

The day after watching the pilot episode of *Modern Family*, Mia had declared it as her new favorite show and informed him they'd be watching it together every week from then on. It had quickly become one of his favorites, and he still watched reruns when he needed something light and familiar.

Without her, he'd never have known the rush of confidence he felt when he wore blue. He'd been seventeen the first time she told him how handsome he looked in that color, and he still remembered that moment as if it was yesterday.

He sure as hell wouldn't have joined a fraternity in college without her encouragement. If left to his own devices he'd have been a dorm hermit for sure. It was also possible he'd never have befriended Chris, the owner of a local outdoor supply store and Noah's primary climbing buddy other than Graham. Mia had been with him the first time he'd stopped into Chris's store in search of a new tent, and she'd chatted up Chris for a half hour after Noah had made his purchase. Not only had she charmed every employee in the whole damn place, she'd given Noah an in for getting first dibs on the best deals on outdoor gear from that day forward.

Each of those things had had an impact on his life in various ways, but they paled in comparison to what he'd shared with her over the past few weeks.

True intimacy.

He'd been close to his brother. His parents were easy to talk to and had kept open lines of communication when he was growing up. He had friends he could count on.

But no one had ever known him the way Mia did, and now that she'd seen every piece of him—even the darkest part—and still wanted to stick around? It was more than he could have ever hoped for.

Ever since that night at The Blue Lion they'd been inseparable. It was the first time he'd ever allowed himself to believe she felt as much and as deeply for him as he did her.

She was also borderline insatiable in the bedroom, which he wasn't complaining about. He just...damn. Wished they'd worked this out sooner. He could have pulled these all-nighters better when he was twenty-two.

His life at work, on the other hand, was miserable. He'd submitted a full application because he'd told his father he would. He had no clue if David knew about it or not.

Noah had been added to David's high school athletic arena project, and he suspected James had something to do with it. Noah was pulling most of the work—producing the documents, working out the details, and managing the schedules—but allowing David to be the face of the project, meeting with the client and presenting updates in their internal meetings. He kept his mouth shut, only jumping in when David misspoke because he hadn't been involved in the original discussions.

Just this morning he'd been working at his computer when he got a text about the multilevel athletic offices attached to the arena, the one piece of the project David was handling because of prior experience with similar structures.

David: When did the client want to see the plans of the office section?

Noah: Yesterday.

David: I'll get it finished by tomorrow. I'll send it to you and you can pass it on. Just tell them we got behind.

Noah refused to continue the conversation in writing and got up to talk to the asshole face-to-face. David looked up from his phone when Noah walked through the door and shut it behind him.

"Have a problem with my suggestion?" David said without preamble.

"You've already asked me to step aside for a promotion we both know I deserve. I won't take heat for your laziness, too."

David tsked. "This is a team effort, and I don't recall you reminding me they were due. Surely you've fumbled a deadline before. Or did your dad always help keep you on track?"

Noah ignored the comment about his dad. "You have the same schedule I do, and your tardiness makes us both look bad."

"Too late now." He tugged at his sleeve. "If it helps, it wasn't on purpose. I just need you to take care of it this time."

"No."

David cocked a brow. "No?" He moved a few papers around on his desk and held up a notepad with a phone number written on it. "This is the number for the insurance fraud hotline. Found it the other day. It's anonymous, too, which bodes well for me. It wouldn't look good for me to be going to these lengths for a promotion."

"Then why are you?" Noah bit out.

"Because you're the golden child who would step over everyone to climb the company ladder, and with Daddy at the top for so long, they would just smile and wave as you went. This is my only option."

It wasn't, but there was no point in arguing. Noah eyed the phone number and ground his teeth together. The bills and explanations of benefits for Mia's stay in the hospital a couple months ago had started rolling in, and even with insurance, it wasn't cheap. Without coverage, it would be astronomical.

"Fine. Send me the plans as soon as you're done."

David winked and dropped the notepad. "Glad we could work this out."

Noah walked back to his office on stiff legs, jerking his gaze to the clock. It was half an hour before he'd usually leave, but he was too wound up to be useful. He grabbed his bag and pulled out his phone.

Noah: What are you doing?

Mia: Just studying on the couch.

Noah: I'm heading out early. Hungry?

Mia: Always.

Noah: I'll bring something home. What sounds good?

Mia: Surprise me.

He smiled. Her adventurous nature was one of the many things he loved about her. Since he didn't share that attitude when it came to food, he ended up at Wings To Go for an order of plain wings and whatever new flavor Paula had going that week.

The smoky, salty aroma of chicken wings filled his car as he drove home and tried to push the interaction with David from his mind. He didn't want to start his evening with Mia in a bad mood. She could usually sense something was bothering him and would try to get him to talk about it.

What if he told her the truth? She was the only one he could talk to about it, and it might help. But as quickly as the thought came, he shut it down. She had enough to worry about, including an appointment with her nephrologist tomorrow. She saw her doctor regularly, but this was an extra visit he'd requested based on the results of the blood work she gave last week at her infusion appointment. She'd had to adjust her diet for a few days because apparently what she ate had a major impact on her kidney function. She said her doctor had mentioned dialysis for the first time, and while Noah didn't really know what that entailed, he sensed her trepidation.

He walked in the door ten minutes later, finding Mia exactly as she'd said: sitting cross-legged on the couch with a book in her lap.

She smiled and he went to her immediately, setting the bag of food on the coffee table. He took the book from her lap and pulled her to a standing position, wrapping his arms around her.

She let out a satisfied sound and hugged him back. "Well, hi."

"Hi." He rested his cheek on her head and closed his eyes, the tension leaving his body like it always did when she was in his personal space. They stood that way for long seconds, and he loved when she just let him hold her like this. She didn't pull away until he loosened his arms.

"Whatcha studying?"

"Dietary needs of teenagers."

He thought about his and Mia's standard diet from high school. "Pizza and frozen burritos?"

"Not quite," she said with a snort, and immediately dug into the bag. "How was your day?"

He headed to the kitchen for drinks.

"Fine," he called over his shoulder. "How was your test?"

"Good. There were only two I was unsure about."

He returned and sat down beside her. "That's awesome."

She flattened her lips. "I wish I'd known them all."

He laughed. "Don't be such a perfectionist."

"You're one to talk, Mr. Magna Cum Laude."

She opened the first container of wings and scrunched her nose. "Plain." She passed it over, then grabbed the next one. "What did you get me?"

"I left it up to Paula." He eyed her as she opened it.

Mia took one look at the wings and Noah's thighs went tense. The expression on her face…it was one she'd directed his way dozens of times over the past few weeks. And it usually meant something different.

He swallowed, telling his body to cool it. He smiled,

though, so wide his teeth were exposed. He even laughed a little.

"What?" she asked, confused.

He tried to shut it down and cleared his throat. "Nothing."

She snorted. "Nuh-uh. Tell me what you were thinking just now."

He leaned over and kissed her, smiling against her lips. "It's just… I realized sometimes you look at me the same way you look at chicken wings."

Mia's cheeks went pink. "I do?"

He nodded slowly, the grin widening on his face.

"And is that a good thing?"

"Hell yes."

"That's good, I guess," she murmured. Her eyes tracked down his body and back up, her tongue darting out to trace her lower lip. "But, Noah?"

His brain stopped working for a second. "Yeah?"

She leaned closer, her nearly black irises intense. "You're way better than chicken wings."

He cracked his beer and waved a hand at her food. "Better get going," he said, picking up a piece of chicken. He pointed it toward the hallway that led to the bedrooms. "Because as soon as we're done out here, we're going back there."

"I think I want a tattoo."

Noah traced the slope of her bare shoulder blade with his index finger. "You do?"

"Yeah. Maybe some flowers. I'm not sure if I want colors or just black. What do you think?"

"Either would look great. Where?"

"Here?" she traced her shoulder. "Or maybe along my side."

"The ribs hurt, but that would be sexy as hell." His eyes slid down her bare body curled against his. "Not that you need any help in that department."

She smiled, her dark eyes happy. "Wanna get one with me?"

He considered. "Maybe. I'd been thinking about another one. Something nature inspired." Then, like an idiot, he blurted out, "What if we got matching ones?"

She blinked, a sort of frown pinching her brows. "Like, each other's names?"

He laughed. "No."

"My parents did that. Tattooed each other's names on their bodies." She said it with a sad sort of laugh, like she'd always found it funny but wasn't sure how to handle it now that they weren't on good terms. "They got married pretty young."

He waited a few seconds to see if she might open up a little about how things were going with the three of them. When she didn't, he asked, "Want to talk about it?"

She shook her head.

"Okay." He switched back to his original suggestion. "We don't even have to get ones that have to be seen together to make sense. I thought it might be cool to get something just for us. To remember our time together."

"Oh."

He gathered her hair behind her head, tracing her cheek with his opposite thumb. He had no idea where his boldness came from, but he pressed on and said, "Or you could just stay married to me. Let our rings be the reminder, instead."

He felt her body tense. "Stay married?"

"Surely you've thought about it." How could his voice sound so steady with the way he was shaking inside? "Things have been perfect these last few weeks."

Slowly, she pulled away from his hands and sat up, wrapping the sheet around her body. "That wasn't our deal."

"Neither was this."

"Two years would have been a long time without this."

He took in a heavy breath. "Don't even think about saying this was just about sex. I know this means something to you."

"Of course it means something." Her voice went quiet. "It means everything."

He flexed his fingers before balling them into fists. "I can't go back to just being your friend, Mia. I can't."

She dropped her face into her hands. "Noah."

"Can you?" Would she really be able to walk away from him so easily? Move out of his house—*their* house—and slip that purple ring off her finger as if their relationship was as cheap as the band itself? Would she really be able to watch him go out with another woman and bring her back to this very bed?

The idea of Mia with another man made him want to crawl out of his skin.

Instead of answering his question, she said, "I need to ask you something."

He swallowed. "Okay."

"Why haven't you traveled since the accident?"

"What do you mean?"

"You know what I mean. For climbing. Camping."

"Graham and I go all the time."

"I don't mean to Eldo and Boulder. I mean outside Colorado. To Washington, to Canada. Places you and Nathan used to go."

He rubbed a hand across his forehead, and as she followed his movement her eyes narrowed. She knew him well enough to recognize it as a sign he was uncomfortable. He dropped his arm. "It didn't feel right after Nathan died, I guess."

"Is that the only reason?"

No. "What are you asking?"

She released an irritated breath. "Don't do that." Her brown eyes searched him beseechingly.

What was the point in lying? She already knew, or she wouldn't have brought it up. "I didn't want to be that far away from you."

Her expression told him that's what she'd expected. She didn't appear upset by the news. Resigned, rather.

He'd have preferred angry over resigned.

"Why not?" she asked.

He pushed himself farther up the bed to lean against the headboard. "Because once when I was several hours away, you almost died. I didn't know if I'd get back in time. I didn't know if I'd ever see you again. I've never known fear like that, Mia. It was paralyzing. When I say I don't remember anything after I got that text from Claire, I mean it. I don't know how we packed up, how I got to the car, or much about the accident. The one thing that's crystal clear is gut-wrenching fear. I'll never forget it."

He dragged a hand down his face, his stomach roiling at the memory. "I can't be in that position again, Mia. The only thing worse than the thought of losing you is the thought of losing you while I'm hundreds of miles away. What if I couldn't get to you? What if..."

She reached out as if she would take his hand, then changed her mind, returning hers to her lap. Her eyes were glassy. "I'm right here. I'm fine."

He just looked at her, his throat tight like a fist squeezed the breath from him, and said nothing.

"But don't you see? This is exactly why I stay single. I never want to make you feel that way. I don't want you to worry over me and stop living your life because of me."

"Nothing will stop me from wanting to be there for you."

She pressed a hand to her forehead, shaking her head. Her eyes drifted aimlessly before her, as if she wasn't really seeing him. "Noah, for nine years you've confined yourself to what, a hundred-mile radius around wherever I am? You've given up something you loved because of me. That's everything I *never* wanted. I have enough guilt for what happened with my parents, and I don't need to add you to it."

"Why does people loving you make you feel guilty?"

Her eyes widened slightly at him basically admitting he loved her. As he expected, she didn't comment on it directly. "Loving someone with a chronic illness is different. It's harder. Complicated. I'm the one living it, and yet the part that bothers me the most is seeing the people around me suffer. My parents. You. Claire. I'm lucky that I'm able to function normally most of the time. But when I was first diagnosed and every time I have a flare, the helplessness I see on your faces is ten times worse than the pain of my actual disease." She slipped out of bed and located her shirt, sliding it over her head. "I *hate* it, Noah."

"Not more than I hate watching you suffer."

"I very much doubt that," she said bitterly.

"Is this you saying you won't even consider staying with me? You won't even talk about it?"

Her brows came together and she squeezed her eyes shut. "If things were different…" She opened her eyes and met his gaze. "If things were different, nothing could keep me away from you."

Desperation clawed at his chest, as if he'd just slipped off a cliff, his hands and feet grasping for something to hold on to. Anything to give him a chance to climb back to safety. To *her*. "I don't want you different. I want you exactly as you are."

She swiped a hand across her cheeks. "You don't know what you're saying."

"I know exactly what I'm saying."

"You won't always feel that way."

"Don't tell me what I want," he said, anger seeping into his tone. "I want you. I always have and I always will."

She sniffed, and he watched helplessly as she pulled her yoga pants up her legs.

"Where are you going?"

She paused in the doorway. "I'm sleeping in the guest room."

"Why?"

Silence hung in the air. "I don't know," she admitted. "It just feels like the right thing to do tonight."

"For you or for me?"

"Both."

Another tear slid down her cheek when her eyes met his, and she left.

And he did nothing to stop her.

19

The following morning, Mia found Noah sitting shirtless at the kitchen table. The aroma of freshly brewed coffee filled the still-dark room and his hands were wrapped around a mug, his head bent low.

She watched him for a second, unsure if he sensed her presence. She'd slept terribly, thinking about him all night. Thinking about what they'd said, and how things had changed between them these last few weeks.

She wanted to stay with him so much it hurt.

He ran a hand through his hair, keeping his head bowed, and she walked up behind him, unable to stop herself from admiring the toned muscles in his back and shoulders. She touched him gently, sliding her palms across his shoulders and down his arms, curving her body around his. Her head came to rest next to his, her lips a breath away from the pulse in his corded neck. She inhaled deeply and took a moment to feel his hard, living body beneath hers.

He didn't move.

He didn't push her away, either.

"I'm sorry," she whispered. It changed nothing about their situation, but it was still the truth.

It took him several beats to respond. "I know."

There was nothing else to say, so she didn't even try. He wouldn't want useless words, anyway. She wasn't ready to walk away yet, though. From this moment or from their current relationship. Whatever they were doing and for however long it lasted, she intended to absorb every second.

He shifted and for a second, she thought he would get up and leave. Instead, he scooted his chair back and grabbed her waist to pull her into his lap. He buried his face in her hair, his thick arms holding her tight.

Her heart clenched, a lump forming in her throat. She blinked back tears and squeezed her eyes shut, focusing on his warm breath on her neck.

She loved this man more than she'd ever thought possible. Loved him beyond reason.

Beyond herself.

She was so desperate for him to be happy. He was a man who wanted to see the world and experience adventure. He loved to travel and push the limits of his body. He needed freedom. Being with her would only hold him back, even if he didn't see it now. In ten or twenty years, when he was too old to do those things anymore, he'd resent her for preventing him from going when he had the chance, even if he said it was self-imposed. He'd wish he'd done things differently, and they'd both know she was the reason.

She could bear his frustration with her now.

She'd never be able to live with his regret.

He spoke softly into her hair, his words muffled, and goose bumps flitted across her skin. Just as she was about to ask him to repeat himself, he spoke again.

"I'm in love with you."

Oxygen stalled in her lungs. The hollow in her chest expanded, filling with affection and agony, the most beautiful and painful sensation. Was this how women felt during childbirth—hating the pain but knowing with certainty it was worth it?

The tip of his nose brushed lightly across her skin and she shivered. His voice was deep and throaty as he said it again. "I love you, Mia. I love you so fucking much it hurts."

She turned, adjusting her legs to straddle him, taking his face in her palms. His hands anchored themselves on her lower back and his usually bright blue eyes were muted, the misery in their depths unfamiliar and hard to stomach.

She pressed her lips to his, savoring his soft, warm flesh. Pulling back, she waited until their gazes locked again. "I love you, too."

Nothing in his expression changed. She knew he heard her with the way his grip on her back tightened briefly, but he didn't respond. He simply stared at her, as if their love was a curse rather than a blessing.

Maybe he was right.

And then his hand slid up to curve around her neck and he pulled her mouth to his. This kiss was hot and rough, nothing like the featherlight brush from moments ago. He crushed her to his body and drove his tongue into her mouth as she gripped his shoulders, responding with equal urgency.

A groan rumbled in his chest, deep and raw, and she moaned. His hands slid low to hold her up as he stood and carried her to his room.

"Don't sleep in the guest room again," he growled into her ear as he approached the bed. "As long as you're here, this is where you belong."

"What did you bring us today?" Barbara asked, briskly rubbing her hands together.

An infusion pump beeped nearby. Mia grinned and reached for her purse, the stretched leather under her legs squeaking with the movement. "Energy balls."

Natasha, who had been setting up the IV access tray, paused and made a face. "Energy balls?"

"Don't look at me like that." Mia straightened and held out a small foil-wrapped package to each woman. "Try them. You'll see."

"I don't mean to complain about the free snacks…" Natasha started. "But I gotta ask, what's going on with you lately? Last week you brought mini scones from Whole Foods. They were delicious, but they were *store-bought*. And now energy balls? This is unlike you, Mia."

Mia held back a laugh. "They're no-bake. Took like, ten minutes to make."

"Why are you blushing?" Barbara asked curiously.

Her face got hotter and she pressed a fist against her thigh. "I, um… I used to bake in the evenings, you know? After work and stuff. But lately I've been…" She cleared her throat awkwardly. "Busy."

Natasha burst out laughing, and Barbara let out a low whistle. "Oh my. To be a newlywed again…"

"Anyway," Mia said pointedly. "You'll take these energy balls and keep quiet."

Barbara peeled back the wrapping and eyed one suspiciously.

"Seriously? It's not like I'm giving you Brussels sprouts."

"I love Brussels sprouts," Barbara defended.

"So do I," Mia said. "These are better."

"What's in them?"

"Peanut butter, chia seeds, sunflower butter, chocolate chips, oatmeal..."

"If you hadn't said chocolate I'd be out," Natasha said. "Let me know what you think, Barbara. Then I'll decide if I want to try it."

Mia frowned. "You're not gonna stick me twice are you?"

Natasha laughed. "Of course not."

As promised, she made quick work of starting Mia's IV (on the first try) and went back to her computer.

Mia's phone buzzed. It was a message from Noah that read Tattoo idea, followed by a drawing of Noah's ark.

She laughed and replied, Cute, but no. When she looked up her eye caught on the TV mounted on the wall, playing the Travel Channel as usual, and a sudden dullness settled in her chest.

"Everything okay?" Barbara asked from beside her.

Mia regarded the older woman who had become a friend. Barbara was kind, thoughtful, and easy to talk to, so rather than deflecting, she pointed at the screen. "That's Kingsbarns. It's this incredible golf course in Scotland. My dad and I used to talk about taking a trip to play there."

"It's beautiful," Barbara agreed. "So why on earth do you look like Natasha just told us she quit?"

She hesitated, unsure why she was about to talk to Barbara about her parents, but wanting to all the same. She'd been missing them more than usual lately. She'd found herself wanting to tell her mom about how wonderful it was being married to Noah and talk to her dad about her favorite professor at school. Getting an outside opinion sounded kind of nice, especially from someone who hadn't been there through the whole mess.

"Things with my parents are...difficult. We're not exactly estranged, but close to it."

"What happened?"

"Remember how I told you I'm adopted?"

Barbara nodded.

"I didn't know until two years ago. My parents never told me, and I don't think they planned to. It came out when I was first worked up to be put on the kidney transplant list. They asked everyone in my family to be tested because they'd be the most likely to be a match. My parents sort of had to come clean at that point." She looked down at her shoes. "I was completely blindsided. I've never been that angry. I felt so betrayed."

Barbara's lips dipped at the corners, her eyes sympathetic. "Oh, honey."

"I think what made it worse is I already felt so guilty because of my illness. Even though I take care of it now, because I was so young when I was diagnosed, they took on a lot of debt from all the early costs. That first hospital stay, plus months of specialists, scans, and procedures to figure out what was wrong, was ridiculously expensive. Watching them make sacrifices for me for years was tough already, and then during the stress of learning things were getting worse and I'd need a kidney transplant, they dropped that bomb on me. My parents got stuck with medical bills because of a genetic mutation I inherited from someone else. They had to sell the house I grew up in. They live in an apartment across town. My mother, who loved nothing more than to spend the entire weekend tending to her garden, doesn't even have a square foot of grass to take care of. They'll never have the money to travel all the places they wanted to go. And it's because of me."

Barbara waited a few seconds before she replied. "That sure is a lot to carry for something you had no control over."

Mia tucked her hands under her thighs. "There's a lot of bad luck in there," she agreed. "But there was also a secret they kept from me, and that was a choice. I was so overwhelmed when I found out, and I just… I didn't know what to think. Or do. We had a huge fight and I said I didn't want to see them anymore. I've only spoken to them on the phone a few times since."

Barbara's eyes darted to the television, still showing sweeping scenes of the lush greens overlooking the ocean, then came back to Mia. "You don't have to answer this, but did they ever give a reason? For not telling you?"

"They tried to explain, but I didn't want to hear it. I didn't, and still don't, see the point. Nothing would make that okay."

"Are you sure?" Barbara asked gently. "I'm not taking their side—I can only imagine how hurtful that was for you. And you have a right to know where you came from. But if they were loving parents up until that point, isn't it possible their side of the story is worth at least hearing?"

"No." The response was automatic, a justification for her actions for the past two years. But was it fair? "Maybe," she amended. "I don't know."

"I don't know, either." Barbara sighed with a little hum, like *this is a tough one.*

"Part of me wants to talk to them about it," Mia admitted. "But it's because I have this pipe dream things can go back to the way they used to be. Before I knew and before I got sick. And that will never happen, so I just…don't."

"I get that. I wish for some things in the past, too. But you don't seem content with how things are now. Are you?"

"No."

"So maybe just think about talking to them, you know? Hear them out. It might not help anything and you can go back to the way things are now. But on the other hand, maybe you'll get some answers you wish you'd had a long time ago and a relationship with them will be possible after all. If you want one, that is."

"I think I do. Someday." She just hadn't been ready, as evidenced by the unopened letter she'd carried to Noah's house. She was close, now, though. Closer than ever before.

Surely there was some explanation on those pages; she just had to gather the courage to open it.

20

"I can't believe I'm doing this."

Noah returned the book of tattoo designs to the table. "It's not too late to back out. Not until that needle touches your skin. Even then, you could say the word and just have a permanent freckle."

She laughed. "No, I want to do it. I'm still nervous, though."

She held a printed image of a floral design in her hand, for placement on the upper left side of her torso. His muscles twitched uncomfortably in anticipation of the pain she would experience. Most of his tattoos were on fleshy, muscular parts of his body. Bones supposedly hurt the most.

"Sticking with your choice?" he asked. "That's a pretty serious tattoo for your first."

"Go big or go home, that's what I always say."

"Not once have I heard you say that."

"Well, I do."

He gave her a look. "When?"

"I said it to myself right before I married you."

"No you didn't."

"I did." She arched a brow. "And back then I had no idea just how big I'd gone. Lucky me."

A laugh burst from his chest, along with a small measure of embarrassment. *"Mia."*

She laughed. "For a man who's so good in bed, you sure are a prude talking about it."

"I prefer action to talking."

"You can say that again." Her fingers slid across the sheet of paper. "Anyway, yes, this is the one. I know I'm supposed to have some serious reason I chose it, but I don't. Lilies are my favorite flowers, and I just want something beautiful on my body."

He leaned into her and whispered, "Everything about that body is beautiful."

She nudged him with her shoulder, and the smile on her face sent a rush of satisfaction through him. "Thanks for coming with me."

He hadn't had any important meetings today, so leaving the office after lunch had been an easy decision. "I wouldn't miss it."

"Mia?"

Ian, the large bald man who'd walked Mia through the paperwork, looked at them expectantly. They stood and followed him to a chair.

"So, how many tattoos do you have?" Mia asked as they went.

"Just one," Ian said. "I wanted more, but it hurts too bad."

Her mouth dropped open and she turned wide eyes on him.

Noah frowned. “Dude.”

“It’s true.” Ian shrugged, unapologetic. “Have a seat.”

Mia, looking uncertain, handed her purse to Noah and sat. He didn’t take his eyes off her while she lifted her shirt and Ian placed the stencil transfer. She stood to look at the placement in the nearby mirror, and Noah focused on taking slow, deep breaths. The intricate, feminine design curved just a few inches below the edge of her breast.

“What do you think?”

“It’s—” He cleared the rasp from his throat. “It’s perfect.”

“I agree,” Ian said appreciatively.

Noah tossed a glare his way before refocusing on Mia. She turned this way and that, studying the design, and finally gave a little lift of her chin. “That’s good.”

She returned to the chair and positioned herself per Ian’s instructions, then Ian prepared the machine.

“Sure?” Noah mouthed.

She smiled in reply.

“Here we go,” Ian said. “I’ll start for just a second then stop, so you know what to expect. Okay?”

Mia nodded, locking eyes with Noah. The buzzing started, and Noah wanted to grab her hand, but was afraid to jostle her.

“Good?” Ian asked.

“Yeah. It’s not so bad.”

Ian snorted.

“I’ve had worse.” Mia’s voice was steady and sharp, and Ian’s smirk faded. Noah couldn’t help the swell of pride beneath his own ribs as Ian continued, and Mia’s face barely registered the discomfort.

He leaned forward and gave her an encouraging smile. “You’re doing great.”

"Distract me?"

He reached into his pocket for his phone and carefully put an AirPod in her ear, taking the other for himself. He swiped through the songs on his playlist, found what he was looking for, and hit Play.

The moment the first notes of "Chasing Cars" flowed through, a familiar, soft smile tipped her lips. Her dark eyes met his as she listened, and his gaze swept her face, admiring the simple beauty of her. Her jaw relaxed and her eyes softened as the song played, and he just smiled at her, content to sit there and listen with her as long as she wanted.

The song paused for an incoming call and he quickly swiped to ignore it and set his phone to silent. It was just Julia—he'd call her back later.

She listened to a few more and during a break in the songs asked, "What's next?"

He'd come prepared. "Would you rather."

"Okay, hit me." She paused. "But not really, because this guy has a needle on my skin."

Noah chuckled. "Ready? Would you rather be forced to dance every time you heard music or be forced to sing along to any song you heard?"

"Sing." She grinned wryly. "I'm such a good dancer I don't think I'd be able to ward off all the men wanting to take me home."

Ian kept his head down, but his brow rose with interest, not having caught the dryness in her tone. Mia was a lot of things…a lot of wonderful things…but a good dancer wasn't one of them. Rhythm wasn't quite her forte.

"Would you rather travel the world for a year on a tight budget or live in luxury in one country for a year?"

"Travel."

Ian and Noah both nodded in agreement.

"Would you rather have free caramel lattes or free chicken wings for a year?"

Her eyes widened. "That's the hardest one you've ever asked me. I can't possibly choose."

"You have to."

She groaned. "Fine. Um… I'd have to give up the coffee. There's no way I could give up wings."

Ian paused. "A woman who can dance, wants to travel, and loves chicken wings? Are you single?"

The hell?

"Nope," Noah answered. "Check the rings, man."

"Sorry, didn't see one."

Noah leaned to the side, and sure enough, Mia's ring finger was bare.

She winced, and he didn't think it was from the tattoo. "I took it off when I was cooking earlier. I know exactly where it is—"

Ian stopped to wipe her skin with a cloth, and Noah took the opportunity to grab her hand. "It's fine."

She sighed and closed her eyes as he traced his thumb back and forth across her hand. He idly wondered how many men had hit on her over the past nine years. The possessiveness coursing through him was alarmingly potent. No man knew her like he did, but it didn't take much to want her.

One glimpse of that smile, one note of her laugh, and everyone wanted more of her. How many had succeeded? How deeply did they know her? How far into her life had she let them in?

That was the one part of her life she'd always kept hidden.

He couldn't fathom going back to that place. To wondering if she was with another man and where they were or what they were doing.

Noah wanted to be the only one to hear her intimate whispers, to know the gentle touch of her lips. To know the sweet, borderline annoying way she sometimes snored as she slept, and the way she always rubbed lotion on her legs before getting into bed every night.

He'd never considered himself a jealous man. Despite loving her all these years, he'd always kept his distance. Watched her live her life the way she wanted.

But that was before.

Before he stood in front of a judge and promised to provide for her and care for her. Before they lived together and shared a bed and their bodies. Before he knew the true meaning of the word intimacy and connection.

There was no part of him that wanted to go back to the way things were before this all started. Unfortunately, it might be his only option, because he couldn't let her out of his life completely.

Even if he was willing to try to go back to being just friends, he didn't have the first clue how to get there.

It was almost dinnertime when they walked out of the tattoo parlor. Just as he was about to ask if she wanted to grab something on the way home, Noah happened to glance at his phone.

"Shit."

Mia paused before opening the car door. "What's wrong?"

"I have a bunch of missed calls from work." Julia had called a second time, and James had called, too. Julia had texted as well, and he sat in the driver's seat and pulled up the messages.

Julia: Answer your damn phone.

Julia: David got fired.

Julia: James knows.

James knows. What did that mean? Did David tell him about Noah and Mia? Panic ripped through him as he tapped on the voicemail James had left. His tone was impossible to decipher.

"Noah, we need to talk. Call or come by my office before the end of the day. I'll be here until six. It's urgent."

His stomach plummeted. James knew. He had to.

"Is everything okay?"

His eyes darted to Mia, sitting beside him with concern in her brown eyes.

"Yeah, I think so. Sounds like there are some last-minute issues on a project I'm working on." The lie fell from his tongue too easily, but he wouldn't tell her anything until he knew how bad it was. "I'll drop you off at home and run up there, if that's okay. Shouldn't take long."

Her brow remained furrowed but she nodded. "Sure, that's fine."

He dropped her off and sent James a quick message to let him know he was on his way to talk. His mind raced with questions the entire drive, and by the time he pulled into the parking lot his stomach was in knots.

What the hell had happened? Had they made the promotion decision and David wasn't the one? It wouldn't be a surprise if they chose someone else, since David didn't deserve it and the principals weren't idiots. Still, surely the asshole realized Noah had no control over the situation. Even if David couldn't get over whatever issue he had with Noah, how could he do that to Mia?

The office was nearly empty. He straightened his shoulders as he moved down the hall, determined to face it head-on. His own door was open and as he passed, his gaze touched on the framed photo sitting next to the monitor.

When he'd gotten the images from the wedding—he'd asked Claire for them the next day—that one had immediately been his favorite. The way Mia looked at him…it had almost made him feel like that day was real. That it was about love and promises rather than necessity and deception. Her face was tilted up toward his, a secretive smile on her lips. Her dark eyes had locked on his as if she hadn't realized anyone else was even in the room.

With that image in his mind, and the reminder it brought about why he'd done this in the first place, he continued toward the door at the end of the hall. David's office was bare—lucky bastard got away before Noah could deal with him.

Noah knocked and leaned toward the door, waiting until he heard James's gravelly "Come in" before twisting the handle. He stuck his head in.

"Is now a good tim—"

"Yes. Come in and shut the door, please."

Resigned, Noah did as asked and sat in the chair opposite James. He looked the older man in the eye, refusing to cower or try to cover up what he'd done.

"I received an interesting piece of information this afternoon."

Noah fought the urge to fidget and said nothing. There was no question there.

A slight irritation flared in James's eyes at Noah's silence. "Any idea what it might have been?"

"I'm sure you're about to tell me, sir."

"You're too much like your father," James muttered. "Fine. If you won't say it, I will. We made the decision regarding the associate position. Julia accepted it this morning."

After an initial flood of surprise, Noah tilted his head and nodded. "Wow, that's great. Well deserved." He meant it, and felt ashamed he hadn't considered Julia might put in for it. She was an excellent architect, a hard worker, and great with clients. He'd been too wrapped up in everything with Mia and David, he hadn't even thought to ask if she was interested.

Which probably worked to her advantage, in all honesty.

"I agree." James steepled his fingers. "David didn't take the news so well."

"He wanted it pretty badly," Noah said carefully.

"It's a shame he didn't have the portfolio to back it up." James assessed Noah carefully. "It's what he said after I broke the news that I wanted to talk to you about."

"Okay."

"He claims you and Mia got married so she could quit and keep the company insurance for her medical condition. Is that true?"

"Yes."

James's brows shot up. "Yes?"

"Yes. That's why we got married."

The man who had been his mentor for years sat back in his gray leather chair. His expression was hard to read. "I've got to say, I didn't expect you to confirm it."

"I'm sorry."

"That you committed fraud, or that I found out?"

Noah inched forward in his seat. "Look, James. You've known me a long time. Since well before I was an architect. You've been a friend of my dad's, and a friend of our family, for decades. By proxy, you know Mia has been a part of my life for a long time. Our friendship was never a secret, even when we both worked here. In fact, I think most people knew that friendship was the reason my dad offered her this job without a day of administrative experience."

"She wasn't a bad employee."

"She was great. Doesn't mean she would have gotten the job if she'd walked in as a stranger off the street."

James tipped his head to concede that fact.

"My point is, our friendship was no secret. But how much I loved her was. I kept it from everyone. Even tried to talk myself out of it on occasion."

"I take it that didn't work out?"

Noah gave a humorless laugh. "I can't stop loving her any more than I can choose to stop breathing. When she had the opportunity to go back to school on a scholarship and pursue her dream job, I couldn't stand by and watch her give it up. I couldn't think of any other options, James. Our policy is antiquated and doesn't allow partner-based dependents without marriage. Even if it did, we couldn't wait until open enrollment in November. She deserved this chance, and God knows it was no hardship to marry her. It's real for me, if that makes it any easier to swallow. It always was."

"You should have come to me. Maybe we could have changed our policy, or made an exception."

Noah shook his head. "It wouldn't have been that easy. Besides, there wasn't time. She had to accept the scholarship to start this summer, and never would have done it if she wasn't confident she had coverage for the medicine she needed to live." He glanced at the photo of James's family on the bookcase. They vacationed at Seaside every summer, and they stood on the beach there, James's arm around his wife with their four children surrounding them. "What would you have done? If you were in my shoes and Sharon needed you, wouldn't you have done the same?"

James folded his arms across his chest. "It's the lie, Noah. I have a hard time criticizing you for taking care of Mia, you know that. Not only because I care about her too, but because it's plain as day how close you two were and how much she means to you. But this company was built on trust and integrity. I need to be able to believe in the people who work here. In their character. And everyone should expect the same from me."

"I understand."

"The fact that you lied, took advantage of the generous benefits we offer our employees—potentially putting our company at risk for audit and review, and then went along with some blackmail scheme with another employee to keep things quiet?" James frowned and his lips turned down at the corners. "I'm disappointed in you, Noah. So much so, I don't know how to move forward."

Noah swallowed, the reality and severity of the situation finally settling around him like dust after a storm.

"Do whatever you think is right, James. I take full responsibility for my actions, and I'll accept the consequences."

"I haven't made a final decision regarding your future with the company," James said slowly, as if the words were just as difficult for him to say as they were for Noah to hear. "I really hadn't expected it to be true. I wasn't prepared for this."

Neither was he. "I'm sorry."

"In all honesty, as long as there's a valid marriage license, I don't think there's anything any insurance company could do to try to prove it as fraudulent. It's the principle, though, and the prevarication. I can't just overlook what you did."

"I don't expect you to."

James dragged his hand down his temple and stood. "I'll have to discuss this with the other principals. I'll let you know as soon as we've come to a conclusion."

Noah stood. "Okay. Thank you, sir."

As he turned and walked to the door, James called out one last question.

"Noah?"

Noah looked back.

"If you'd known how this would turn out—that I'd eventually find out and your job would be in jeopardy, would you make the same decision again?"

Noah thought of Mia's beautiful, cheerful face and everything they'd shared these last few months. Of her excitement about what she was learning, and the new recipes she'd tried in preparation for future clients. He remembered countless nights on his couch, and the more recent ones in his bed. He thought of the things they'd talked about in the dark hours of the night—what they felt for each other and how complete his life felt.

The answer was clear. "Yes, sir. I would."

21

There was something he wasn't telling her, and it ate at Mia the entire time he was gone. She wrapped herself in his CU blanket and waited on the porch until his car turned down their street.

He parked in the driveway and despite giving her a small smile when he approached, his posture didn't carry his usual confidence. He stopped at her feet, leaned down, and tipped her chin up to kiss her.

"Get everything figured out?" she asked, trying to read his expression.

Instead of taking the seat beside her on the swing, he settled into the chair a few feet away. She frowned at the space between them.

"Not really."

"What? Why not?"

He slid his thumb and forefinger across his forehead, which sent a thread of unease through her. "Before I get into it, there are a few things I need to tell you."

Her skin prickled. "Okay."

"Do you remember that day in April when I put plastic wrap around your computer, and we talked about my marriage proposal in my office?"

"Yeah." She'd tried to keep working despite his handiwork, but had ended up needing to take a pair of scissors to it to get it off.

"Apparently David was in his office that morning. He heard our conversation, and knew our marriage was fake."

Noah kept careful eyes on her face as realization flooded her, and spoke again before she could respond.

"A few weeks later he came to my office and basically told me if I didn't help him get the promotion, he'd report us."

She stared at him, mouth open. "Wait." She shook her head then tilted it to the side, trying to stay calm. "Let me get this straight. David knew what we were doing, blackmailed you with it, tried to sabotage your promotion, and you've known this since *April*? And didn't tell me?"

A heavy exhale left him, and his shoulders seemed to sink even lower. "I'm sorry. I should have. But this was before we… before this was real. I wanted to protect you, and didn't want you to back out of it like I knew you would."

"I wouldn't have—"

"Mia."

Dammit. Why did he know her so well? "Okay, maybe I would have. I definitely would have." But this wasn't about that. "That's not the point. I can't believe you put your job at risk because of that asshole, and because I'm a selfish friend who put you in that position. You've worked hard and you deserve that promotion." First her parents, and now this? Would she ever stop ruining people's lives? "You didn't get it, did you? That's what this is about?"

Because of her.

"I didn't, but that doesn't matter. David got fired and he didn't take it well." He gripped the back of his neck. "Just like he threatened, he told James the truth about us."

A wave of dizziness crashed over her. "Oh no." *Don't pass out, don't pass out.* "Did you lose your job, too?"

"Not yet. James hasn't decided how to handle it."

She leaned forward and covered her face with her hands just in time to hide the tears filling her eyes. "I'm sorry. I'm so, so sorry, Noah. We never should have done this. This is your family business…and everything you've worked for—" Her voice caught and suddenly his warm body was beside hers, pulling her hands from her face.

"It's okay. I don't care about the job, Mia. And if I get let go, I'll find something else to make sure we still have insurance, I promise."

A rude, humorless laugh escaped. She yanked her arm away and glared at him. "Don't do that. Don't make this about me and downplay how hard it would be for you to leave Agnew."

Surprise flashed in his eyes for a beat. He didn't try to touch her again, and finally, he sighed. "Okay. You're right. I love that job and I love the company. Did I see myself there, someday taking on my dad's role? Sure. Did it feel good to see the look of pride on my dad's face every time I did something right? Yes. But everything will work out. None of that's more important than you. You matter more to me than all that, surely you know that by now."

Most people would love those words, but she wasn't most people.

She dropped her eyes, unable to look at him. "This wasn't how this was supposed to go," she whispered. "I wasn't supposed to drag you deeper into this."

"Into what? Your life?" She heard the frown in his tone. "That's exactly where I want to be."

A car blaring music drove by, and her eyes followed as it drove down the street.

"Has it been so bad having me there?" he asked, quieter.

Her eyes flickered to his, and she offered him the truth. "No. I've never been happier than these last few months. Being around you is my happy place. It didn't matter how awkward it was at first, it still felt right. And there's a part of me that wants to try this for real. To cancel the end date on this marriage and just be with you even when I have a job and don't need your insurance anymore. Because when I'm there it's like, this is where I belong, you know?"

"I don't know where you belong if it's not with me." The hope in his words was hard to hear, because she wasn't finished.

"But," she started, and he stiffened, gaze turning wary again. "There's always been this other part that says no. It won't work, it's not fair to you, it's not the right thing to do. I've tried to ignore that voice because I'm selfish and I've been so happy. But this, right here, is exactly why I know that's the one I have to listen to. I come with too much baggage and too many unknowns. You can't build a life around that. *We* can't."

"I knew you'd react this way." He raked his fingers through his hair. She didn't attempt to fix it. "Dammit, Mia, I love you. What can I do to convince you this is what I want? That my life without you is empty, and nothing about your health or your body changes that?"

She knew he meant what he was saying, but certain parts of his life were empty *because* of her, too. "I don't think you can. You're willing to give up too much for me. Maybe if I knew you wouldn't limit yourself because of me, we could have tried. But come on, Noah. You might have just lost your job. You don't travel with Graham like you used to. You won't even go ice climbing, something you've wanted to do your entire life, because of me. You and Nathan never shut up about ice climbing. You stopped doing things you love just because you're worried something will happen while you're gone. That's no way to live."

He didn't try to deny it. "Can't you see why? I've spent too much of my life wondering what-if. What if I had done something different, what if he'd lived, what if what if what if? So yeah, I do worry what will happen to you. But what if I let you go and I miss out on everything I feel when we're together? I don't care if that means I get to feel it for fifty years or five more hours. I don't care if I'm an architect at Agnew or working somewhere else while I do it. None of that matters." He gestured between them. "You and me together? We're perfect. Please, don't take that from me. From us."

She rubbed one hand down her thigh, frustrated. He'd been through so much, and she didn't want to hurt him. "There are parts that have been perfect," she agreed. "But you can't throw yourself on the fire for everyone. There will be nothing of you left. Nathan wouldn't want you to deny yourself because he's gone, and I don't want you to deny yourself because I'm here."

He leaned forward and propped his elbows on his knees, rubbing his hands down his face. "That's not what I'm doing."

Her eyelids burned, a ball of frustration swirling beneath her rib cage. "Do you remember what you said to me months ago, when we first talked about getting married?" she asked. "When I asked what was in it for you, you said it was helping me achieve my dream. You made this sacrifice for me—"

"It was hardly a sacrifice," he cut in.

She ignored the interruption. "You did that for me, and I want to do the same. I want to be with you, Noah. I love you. So much I'm tempted to be a selfish bitch and ask you to let me live in your house and sleep in your bed for as long as we both want to."

"So, forever then."

She looked down, a brief smile tipping the corners of her mouth before sorrow took over. "But I won't, because I want us to still pursue our dreams. *Both* of us. I'm going after mine, but you stopped going after yours."

"What if you're my dream?"

"I can't be your only one."

Noah regarded her, his blue eyes weary. "Have you already forgotten what I told you about Nathan and Rachel? For almost ten years, I've wished for you. Wished I hadn't done something so horrible, and ruined the life of my brother's fiancée. I wanted to deserve you, but I knew I didn't. If Nathan and Rachel couldn't live a happy, full life together, who was I to do that?"

Her heart ached with the pain in his words.

His voice shook, but he pressed on. "I still don't know if I deserve this. You. But I'm done punishing myself, and done living in denial. You're what I've always wanted, Mia. I wish you could feel how badly I want you, because if you did, you wouldn't be asking me to do something as stupid as go on trips to prove it."

"I'm not asking you to prove anything to me," she defended. "I want you to see for yourself that things will be okay if you go. You can't watch over me all the time, every second of every day. That's a life neither of us should have. You need to go on that trip with Graham. You need to see that I'll be fine, and so will you."

He stood and walked to the porch railing, his back to her. He didn't speak for several long moments. Then, finally, "I can't."

Her throat tightened. "Can't or won't?"

"Both." His voice was rough. "Please don't do this."

She pushed to her feet and approached him from behind, slowly sliding her arms around his waist and pressing her cheek to his back. He stilled, as if holding his breath. He didn't touch her.

"I love you, Noah. You've done so much for me, and I'll never be able to explain how much that means to me. But a strong relationship is a partnership that supports both members equally. I have to know you can take care of yourself as well as you take care of me, and right now, I don't think you can."

His head dropped forward. He dragged in a deep breath as if he'd fought it, but his lungs had taken over, demanding oxygen. "I don't know how," he whispered.

She tightened her hold around his body, selfish and stupid, memorizing the feel of him. Would this be the last time she'd hug him like this? The last time to mold her body along his? "I don't, either," she admitted. She'd never done well apart from him. "But I think we need to put some distance between us. I—I need space. So do you."

"Distance," he echoed. "Space."

She swallowed, hard. "Yes." How she didn't punctuate that with a question mark, she'd never know. Was this a mistake?

He pulled out of her embrace and stepped to the side. When he looked back at her she half expected him to argue again, but he just looked resigned. His voice was flat when he said, "Are you moving out, then?"

She opened her mouth, then closed it. Blinked. She hadn't even considered that, but it was a fair question. They needed to stay married because she still needed insurance, and he'd never ask her to end that, even if they broke up. Or stopped sleeping together. Or whatever the hell they were doing.

But now that James knew it was all a sham, did it matter if they kept up appearances?

"I, um. I don't have anywhere else to go." Graham had taken her old room at Claire's condo, and though after her conversation with Barbara she'd moved the letter from her parents from the duffel bag to her purse and carried it around for several days, she still hadn't read it. "I figured I'd just go back to the guest room. For now. I can look into other options."

A muscle flexed in his cheek and he stared straight ahead, seemingly at nothing. Finally, he nodded and went inside. The door hit the frame so hard she felt it in her bones, leaving her alone on the porch, darkness falling around her.

She sat back down in a daze, tucked his blanket around her body, inhaling his familiar scent, and let the tears fall.

22

Noah was a man who was pretty in tune with his emotions. He hid them well, but that didn't mean he didn't feel them, or give them the internal recognition they deserved.

So it was strange that defining how he felt in this moment was like groping around in the dark. Bumping into anger, stubbing his toe on frustration. Being forced to his knees by heartbreak.

He was at a loss.

He also had specific methods of dealing with said emotions. When he was angry, he went running. When he was frustrated, he went climbing. When he was heartbroken, he disappeared into the mountains.

He could do none of those things, mostly because he'd shut himself in his room and to leave he'd have to pass Mia again.

And for the first time in recent memory, he didn't want to see her.

I'm not enough.

She hadn't said those words exactly, but she might as well have.

For so long he'd lived his life content with being her best friend. It's what they'd always been, and it was beautiful. The piece of his heart that held something so much *more* for her had shrugged and gone into an indefinite hibernation, still there but not wreaking havoc or causing problems. Manageable.

But then they'd gotten married. They'd grown closer than ever before. And he'd kissed her and she'd kissed him back, and that dormant place woke with a vengeance, desperate and hungry to devour every piece of her he could get his hands on.

And a ridiculous, hopeful part of him had thought this would be it. Yes, they'd started this whole thing with the understanding it was temporary. She'd reminded him of that several times. And still, he hoped, because she was in love with him. She was meant to be his, a truth he felt deep in his bones.

But she was scared, and nothing he could say would fix that.

Everything he'd tried to be for her wasn't enough, which made him angry. At himself, mostly.

And the thought of losing her broke his fucking heart.

He paced around his room like a caged tiger until he heard the front door, followed by the sound of footsteps down the hallway. When the guest room door clicked shut, he grabbed his running shoes and got the hell out of there.

Noah's dad didn't take the news well.

After a terrible night's sleep, Noah had risen early and gone straight to his parents' house. Now that the promotion had been determined and James knew about the fraud, it was only a matter of time before his dad found out. Noah had figured it would be best coming from him.

His dad had been pissed. His mom was shocked, then she cried, but tried to keep things under control, especially after his dad started yelling about stupidity and using words like *irresponsible* and *ungrateful*. He'd stormed off and shut himself in his office two hours ago.

Noah had learned early that while his dad didn't handle being caught off guard well, he was usually pretty reasonable when he had time to cool off. When enough time had passed, Noah knocked on the heavy wood door of the home office.

"Come in."

His dad was behind the desk, leaning back in the leather chair with his hands behind his head.

Noah walked in and sat in the armchair in the corner. Though imposing, this room had always been his favorite in the house. Two walls were floor-to-ceiling bookcases filled with books ranging from nonfiction to fiction, architecture coffee-table books to crime mystery novels. When he was a kid he used to watch his dad sketch or roll out huge sheets of printed designs and ask him about every little notation, curious to know what everything meant and how on earth the buildings he passed in the back seat of his parents' car every day could possibly start from a drawing like this.

He had a lot of good memories in this room, but it wasn't so welcoming today.

"Your mother wants me to fix this for you," his dad announced. "Though I don't know why she thinks James listens to me. He hasn't for the last thirty years."

"This is my mess, not yours. I'll accept the consequences, whatever they are."

His dad seemed to accept this with something like respect. Noah would take all of that he could get right now.

"I'm sorry, Dad."

"Are you?"

This man was terrifying. But he appreciated honesty, and if Noah had to guess, he'd bet the deception was what bothered his dad the most. "I'm not sorry I married her. I love her and I had the chance to help her, and I'd do it again. But I am sorry I involved your company and that I may have jeopardized my position there. I'm sorry I didn't tell you the truth or ask you for advice."

"I'd have told you not to do it."

"I know."

"We could have figured something else out."

"Maybe." Maybe not. "What do you think James will do?" While he'd accepted the fact he could get fired, he didn't want to be.

His dad dropped his hands to his lap. "I don't know. You're an excellent architect, and I'm not saying that as your father. You're a model employee and he's always held you in high regard, before now. He's fair, but he doesn't like to cut slack."

It wasn't an answer, and it was pretty much everything Noah had considered, too.

"It would have been a joy to see you become the leader of that firm someday." Disappointment filled the room like smoke. For a son who respected his father, disappointment was about as bad as it got.

"I hope I still get the chance to."

His dad didn't seem convinced. "About Mia."

"What about her?"

"I'm surprised she went along with all of this."

"It took some convincing."

"Your mother is heartbroken the marriage won't last."

Leave it to his dad to bring up the sore spot. "I'm working on it."

His dad cocked a brow.

"It's real for me. It always has been. And even if it didn't start out that way, it's been real for both of us…for a while now. But we sort of got in a fight and I'm not sure what will happen now."

"What happened?"

"She got upset when I told her James found out about us and that my job was on the line. She carries a lot of guilt for what happened with her parents, and this just adds to it. She thinks it's all her fault, even though I told her the decision was mine and that I wanted to take the risk. She didn't like that at all."

His dad huffed out a breath. "I bet not."

Noah tipped his chin up. "What does that mean?"

His dad leaned forward to rest his forearms on the desk, which was no tidier now in retirement than before. "It means Mia's an intelligent woman. She knows what you'd give up for her. What you've already given up for her. It's not easy to watch someone you love suffer."

Noah's response lodged in his throat. *She* was watching *him* suffer? "What the hell are you talking about? She's the one dealing with a chronic illness." With strength and grace he'd never possess, on top of it all.

"You're terrified, son. You're so afraid of losing her because you lost someone else you love, and it's not easy to see someone you care about live in fear. Especially when it seems to drive everything they do. It can't be easy for her. I know this because I feel the same way, watching you."

Noah's pulse pushed against his veins, everything in him fighting to deny it.

"I lost Nathan, too, Noah. He was my *son.* Do I worry about something happening to you? To your mother? Am I sometimes paralyzed with fear when I know you've gone up into the mountains to go camping and will come down that same road where deer are as thick as trees? Yes. I do. But I haven't let it completely take over my life. I don't let it own me. I refuse to live that way, and I want the same for you. By the sound of it, so does Mia."

Everything in his body felt weighed down. "I'm working on it."

"Are you?"

Good God, did this man not give an inch? "I don't… I know I want to try."

His dad nodded, his blue eyes perceptive and understanding. "That's a start." He stood. "For what it's worth, I hope you figure it out and can make it work with her. Because a woman who cares about you that much is one you should never let go." He made his way to the door and turned back. "That and your mother will kill you if you don't."

Noah had been in his brother's old bedroom twice since he died.

Today was the second of the two.

Heart lodged in his throat, he opened the door, some stupid part of his brain half expecting Nathan to be lounging on the bed with his laptop, researching some new Flatiron route they'd try next week.

The room wasn't some creepy shrine kept for his brother—he'd been an adult not living at home when he died—but it seemed there were some things his mother hadn't had the heart to change.

The faded navy bedspread.

The bookcase filled with Nathan's things. Books, trophies, figurines.

The corkboard hanging above the desk filled with various notes, pages, and magazine clippings.

Noah stepped fully inside and closed the door behind him. He paused for a few seconds, hands in his pockets and head bowed.

Deep breath. In, out.

He continued on, drifting around the room, looking and thinking. Remembering.

Eventually he ended up in the desk chair, positioned near the window. Nathan's room overlooked the front of the house, whereas Noah's had been in the back corner. From here he could see Claire's parents' house across the street, and most of Mia's old front lawn, covered by an unseasonably early first snow that had arrived last night.

A young couple lived there now, and their kids had already been out to ravage nature's delivery, now marred with snow angel indentions, irregular patterns of footprints, and an honestly impressive family of snow people. A distinct contrast from the pristine white blanket of Noah's parents' yard.

He remained in Nathan's space for a long time. His attention shifted to the corkboard on the wall, and he smiled with recognition of several items on display. That smile faded at the article on "The Hidden Ice Caves of Banff," ripped from the spine of an old issue of *Outside* magazine.

Half rising from the chair, Noah reached up and pulled out the pushpin, sinking back into the chair with the pages in his hand. The photos were fantastic, meant to entice and inspire, but there was no way a picture could do that landscape justice. Those mountains—those climbs—were meant to be seen with your own eyes, experienced with your own hands and feet. At the top of the article, there was a handwritten note in Nathan's messy scrawl:

The thing we fear most has the greatest reward.

Noah stared at those words for a long time, a frown between his brows. His brother hadn't seemed afraid of anything. He'd gone after everything in life with confidence and fervor, everything from rock climbing to approaching women. He embodied the very definition of adventure.

When had he written that? What had he been thinking when he did?

Noah would never know.

He left the pages on the desk and left Nathan's room, but the words wouldn't leave his head. He came back to them again and again over the next few hours, unable to shake the feeling that there was something important there. Something he shouldn't ignore, like a shift in the wind that warned a storm was coming.

The thing we fear most has the greatest reward.

The answer was there, clear as day, though it took several more hours of warring within himself to admit it. To admit he knew what he had to do.

Finally, around midnight that evening, Noah slipped outside and climbed into the old tree house where he'd spent half his childhood. Settling in with his back against the tree, he slipped his phone from his pocket and called Graham.

His friend sounded groggy, but Noah got straight to the point.

"Is your trip to Banff still on?"

Graham yawned audibly. "Yeah. Leaving in three weeks. Why?"

Noah closed his eyes, heart pounding in his ears. "Got room for one more?"

23

Mia stood at the foot of the bed in the guest room, staring at the sealed envelope on the comforter. A standard-issue white envelope, it was nothing that should have caused her such deep turmoil.

To be fair, it wasn't the envelope so much as what was inside. And the familiar handwriting scrawled on the outside.

Her mother's handwriting.

It had arrived in her and Claire's mailbox shortly after the transplant discussion, when Mia had refused all contact with her parents. It had no address, which meant it had been hand delivered. Apparently, she'd made her point and her mom didn't bring it to the door. It was another year before Mia reopened the lines of communication with her parents, carefully maintaining a level of caution and distance.

Still, she'd never opened the letter, fearful of what she'd find inside.

Then, while getting her tattoo, she'd had a realization. When she was in the chair listening to Noah's playlist, there had been a song that reminded her of her mom, and for some reason in that moment she'd thought about the bouquet of flowers that had arrived every year on her birthday since she'd turned eighteen. They were different every year, each more beautiful than the last, and they all had one thing in common: lilies. The very thing she was permanently marking to her skin.

Tonight, I'll finally read it, she'd thought.

But then Noah had gotten that call from work, and when he came back they'd fought, and by the time she'd gone back inside that night—to the guest room—she'd figured she'd been through enough shit for one day.

That was two weeks ago and things had been…decent between her and Noah. Better than she'd thought they would be, especially after the way he'd reacted at the end of their argument. He'd gone to his parents that next morning and stayed there all weekend. She'd been worried he might move in with them temporarily, unwilling to even share the same space with her, but he came back Sunday night with an order of Wings To Go for both of them, and she'd taken it as a peace offering. She was still sleeping in the guest room and they hadn't done so much as kiss, but at least they were talking.

Even so, she was lonely. She missed the familiar routine she and Noah had fallen into. She'd told Claire about the argument with Noah, but her friend had been working a lot and hadn't been around much. The last few weeks had been lighter than usual at school, so she couldn't even rely on that to fill the time.

Which meant she'd been thinking about her parents, bringing her to this very moment.

Noah was out shopping for camping gear with Graham, and she was in the house alone. She didn't bother closing the door.

Taking a deep breath, she sat and picked up the envelope, sliding her finger across to open it.

Mia,

I have no idea how to start. Your dad says I shouldn't be writing this at all—that this isn't a conversation to be had via pen and paper no matter the circumstance—but it's been weeks and you haven't allowed me to explain in person. And I don't blame you. I wouldn't want to see me, either.

But I just want you to have all the facts. I also want to say I'm sorry for how you found out. I'm not sure I'm sorry about not telling you. Maybe I am. I don't know. Every time your dad and I talked about it as you were growing up he wavered, but the answer always seemed so clear to me. Time and time again I chose protecting you over hurting you. Maybe it was the wrong choice. It certainly feels that way now, with the way I've lost you. This is never what I intended. In fact, this is exactly what I was trying to avoid.

Anyway, right or wrong, this is where we are. I think about you every day. I love you and miss you. And I want you to know everything, and maybe have at least some explanation for why we handled things the way we did.

Your dad was a security guard once. I don't think you knew that, and it will probably come as a surprise. For a little while he was interested in going into law enforcement, but something happened that changed the course of his life—our lives—forever.

He worked the night shift at a community college, doing building checks and responding to alarm calls. One night he was walking the campus, and as he passed the auditorium he heard a sound. He thought it was a cat at first, or some other animal. But you know your dad, he can't stand the thought of anything being in pain, even a stray.

That's when he found you. Best we can guess, you were a few hours old. Wrapped in a blanket, still bloody, and crying your eyes out. It was March, and cold.

He found you abandoned in a dumpster—and that right there—that's the sentence I never wanted you to hear. I never wanted to say it or even write it, or have it be a reality that existed in your universe. Because no matter how we found you, you've been the joy of our lives, and our daughter. You're our true family and the reason for everything. Saying we wanted you feels like such an understatement. From the moment he first held you in his arms and wrapped his jacket around you, calling for help and then calling me in the middle of the night, we wanted to keep you.

We never could find your mother, or any information from anyone. I don't know what happened to her, and why she felt backed into a corner where she thought her only option was to leave you there. I can only imagine her fear and heartbreak. At least, that's what I try to focus on, otherwise I get insanely angry at her.

But if she hadn't made that choice, you wouldn't be mine. And it feels weird to say, but I'll always be thankful to her for that. I wish it would have happened differently, but I'd still want to end up with you as my child.

So there's the truth. The ugly part is we don't know where you came from, why someone left you there, or even when your actual birthday is. He found you a little after two in the morning, so it could have been the twelfth or the thirteenth. I never told you because I couldn't bear the thought of breaking your heart. Maybe that's selfish of me, but it's always you I've thought of.

The beautiful part is you felt like ours from the first moment. Your father said he felt an overwhelming need to protect you right away, and it tore his heart out when they took you to the hospital. We checked on you every single day, and immediately pursued adoption. Once we knew you'd be ours, your dad changed career paths and went into business administration. He didn't want to have a job where he'd be gone half of your life, working weird hours and at the risk of not coming home.

We would have handled things differently if it had been an open adoption, or even a closed one where the family surrendered you to an agency. In those situations you'd have the option to get in contact with your birth family, if both of you wanted to.

But that wasn't possible. There's no way to track down your family—believe me, we tried. Those first few months, that's all we did. I just couldn't justify shattering your world like that when there was nothing you could do about it. For better or worse, we're your only family, and you're ours.

The only thing left to say is I'm sorry I hurt you. We love you more than life itself. I'm not sure anyone can ever understand the love of a parent for their child until they have one of their own, but we'd do anything for you. Whatever responsibility you feel for your illness and the cost of your medical care, please know you mean more to us. We would do anything in our power to keep you healthy and happy. We'd sell every earthly possession we have, forgo every trip we ever planned. Everything we've done has been out of love, never out of obligation. We'd do it again and again, no matter whose genes make up the beautiful cells in your body.

We love you always, and I hope someday you'll find a way to forgive us.

Mom

The pages fluttered to the floor like snowflakes and Mia squeezed her eyes shut, tears sliding down her cheeks. She thought she might throw up, but focused on her breathing, and the sensation passed. Slowly, she crawled up the bed and pulled the covers over her body, curling into a ball and wiping her tears.

She lay there, staring at the wall. Absorbing, processing, considering.

He found you abandoned in a dumpster.

There's no way to track down your family.

You felt like ours from the first moment.

We love you always.

Mia thought back to her life before her diagnosis, and tried to come up with any instance when her parents had made her feel unwanted or like a burden.

She came up empty-handed, remembering only happiness and love. A sense of belonging.

The guilt she'd felt after getting sick had been her own doing.

But the betrayal…even thinking about the first time she heard the word *adopted* was like a swift punch to the gut, stealing her breath. No matter how they spun it, they'd lied to her. About where she came from. Information that was hers and hers alone and not theirs to keep.

Sometime later she registered the front door opening, and footsteps down the hall. After a few minutes, Noah's shadow darkened the doorway.

"Mia?" His voice was panicked and he started forward. "Are you okay?"

"I'm fine."

He stopped at the foot of the bed, seeing the pages on the floor. "What's this?"

She kept her eyes trained on the wall. "Read it."

The bed dipped under his weight, and she waited while he read the words her mother had written. He remained so silent, she could only hear her own breathing and the occasional crackle of paper when he flipped the pages over.

And then he moved. He came around to the side of the bed and knelt before her, grabbing her hand and forcing a fresh sob from her throat.

"Mia," he said hoarsely.

She gripped his forearm and squeezed her eyes shut. She wanted him to pull her into his arms and hold her, but they weren't doing things like that anymore. They'd kept careful physical distance because it would be too much, too hard.

Even so, no matter the state of their friendship, he was there for her, and right now she could do nothing but let him be. In typical Noah fashion, he said nothing. He knelt there beside her, a steady, strong presence, ready and willing to be whatever she needed.

He lifted his hand as if to brush her hair back, almost out

of habit, and seemed to catch himself. He dropped it back to his side.

She swallowed and dropped her eyes to his chest. "I think I want to go see them."

"Are you sure?"

"Yeah."

"Do you want me to come with you?"

She almost nodded. It would be so easy to say yes. So much easier to have Noah by her side, giving her strength. But she'd just lectured him on doing things on his own, hadn't she? Maybe he wasn't the only one who needed to take that advice. She'd relied on him a lot throughout her life, too—and this was something she needed to do on her own.

"No, but thank you."

If declining his offer hurt his feelings, he didn't let it show. He nodded and stood, and she swung her legs off the bed.

"Call if you need me, okay?"

She paused in her search for her shoes and glanced up at where he remained by her bed, hands in his pockets.

"I will."

Her stomach was in knots as she climbed the stairs to the third-floor apartment. She took a deep, shaky breath before she knocked.

Her dad opened the door and froze, his hand gripping the frame. He stared at her, his green eyes darting briefly outside and back to her.

A wayward thought crossed her mind, that she'd always been jealous of her dad's uniquely colored eyes, and as a teenager had frequently wondered why she hadn't inherited them.

"Mia," he said, his voice wobbly. They hadn't laid eyes on each other in two years.

"Hi," was all she said.

"Hi." He swallowed. Cleared his throat. "Do you want to come in?"

"Um, okay."

The apartment was average sized, with two bedrooms and a decent-sized living room with windows facing the mountains. They'd moved here several years ago, before the fight, and Mia had spent many evenings here sharing meals and celebrating holidays. Everything looked the same as it had then, but this time it felt…different.

"Scott, who was it—" Mia's mom entered from the kitchen and stopped short when her eyes alighted on Mia. She blinked several times as if convincing herself Mia was really there. "Oh."

They both looked so much older than the last time Mia saw them. Her dad's brown hair was peppered with gray, and her mom's previously shoulder-length dark hair was cropped short. Her dad had put on a little weight around the middle, while her mom appeared thinner.

The three of them stood awkwardly for several seconds before her dad sat in the recliner and said, "This is a nice surprise. Is everything alright?"

She wished Noah was here. She'd glance at him now, unsure how to begin, and he'd just stand there calm and silent. It would be enough to give her confidence to proceed.

"I read the letter."

Her mom's brows drew together and she gripped her hands in front of her. The misery emanating from her was tangible.

"I'm so sorry," her mom said, her voice breaking.

Mia swallowed, blinking back tears and making her choice. She took a deep breath, crossed the room, and walked into her mother's arms.

24

Noah stood in his bedroom staring into his closet.

He hadn't forgotten anything. He'd packed with careful attention and precision, as always.

He was stalling.

From the day he'd called Graham to see if it was possible to get in on the ice-climbing trip, part of him had hoped it weren't possible, or that something would fall through. But Graham had had no problem making arrangements, and the rest of October and first week of November passed by without a single bump in the road. Their friends Hugh and Chris were happy to have him along for a team of four.

Aside from feeling guilty for taking a vacation right after James had allowed him to return to work—on probation, of course—he'd almost called things off on his own twice. The first time was when Mia first made amends with her parents. It had hurt like hell when she'd declined his offer to go with her that day, like a direct hit to his already bruised heart. He'd been unsure how it would go, and wouldn't have left if she'd been in some kind of emotional turmoil over the whole thing. Was that reverting back to the very behavior that forced them apart a few weeks ago, and that Mia maintained was the whole reason they couldn't be together? Maybe.

Okay, yes.

But it wasn't a switch he could just turn off.

Turned out he didn't have to choose, though, because things seemed okay between them. She'd spent several hours with her parents that first day, and had had dinner with them twice more since. It was slow going, but things were going well. She even planned to spend Thanksgiving with them.

The change in Mia was noticeable, as if a burden had been lifted.

The second time he almost bailed was after an office visit with her nephrologist last week. The doctor had sent her straight from the office to the hospital for an overnight stay. Respecting her request that he not stay the night up there with her had been one of the hardest things he'd ever done. When he'd asked if everything was okay, she said she just needed help to filter things through her body because her kidneys weren't doing it well enough, like it wasn't a big deal.

Sure as hell sounded like it was.

"It's nothing to worry about," she'd said. "It just means I can get a transplant sooner, which is what we want."

He'd spent several nights since lying awake, thinking and worrying. The only reason he was still going away was because she'd seemed completely fine when she got home, and those words had been a scrolling marquee in his mind, his brother's voice a constant reminder:

The thing we fear most has the greatest reward.

"Let's go!" Graham called from the front of the house, pulling Noah out of his thoughts.

He let out a growl, even though no one could hear him.

A feminine voice sounded nearby. "What was that?"

He whirled around to find Mia a few feet behind him. She offered him a crooked smile and took several steps in his direction. Close enough he could smell her and see the few tiny freckles on the bridge of her nose.

"Are you hiding?" she asked.

He grunted, unsure how steady his voice would be.

She nodded thoughtfully, as if his response had been a normal one. "Graham's pacing out there. He's gonna wear a hole in your floor."

Your floor. For a while there, when things had been good, she'd begun referring to this house as theirs. *Ours.*

"He'll be fine," Noah finally said, wishing his voice didn't sound like he'd swallowed a handful of gravel.

A knowing look entered her eye. "So will I," she said quietly.

He dropped his chin to his chest and let out a shaky breath. *Don't make me do this*, he wanted to say.

But that wasn't fair. It wasn't just for her, as much as he wanted to pretend it was. This trip was important for him, too.

"It's the trip of a lifetime," she said. "If you don't go, you'll regret it."

His gut twisted with a swirl of emotions. "That's what Nathan always said. Ice climbing would be the experience of a lifetime." His brother had done so much research, convinced he'd go someday. If someone had told him he'd die before he got the chance, he'd have laughed in their face. One of the reasons why it hurt so damn much. "There are so many things I wish I could ask him. I wish I could tell him every detail."

Was it strange to talk to her like this with the way things were between them? They hadn't had any real conversations since their fight. But surely they'd always be friends, no matter what. She was the person who knew him better than anyone, and they'd been through a lot together.

They'd been through *everything* together.

Her soft gaze met his. "So ask him. Tell him. When you're on the mountain—because I guarantee if heaven is real, that's where he is—he'll be able to hear you."

He didn't have it in him to put up a front when she said things like that. And she was right, as usual. If he'd ever find closure, it would be while he was a thousand feet in the air, holding on with his fingers and toes with the wind at his back.

He failed to keep his voice steady. "And here I thought I wasn't going to cry today."

"I'll be thinking about you."

He ground his back teeth together as he looked at her. Her eyes were full of determination, but also something else, and he realized maybe she needed him to go, too. Maybe this was more than proving he'd taken her concerns to heart. What if she was nervous too, and needed to prove to herself she'd be fine without him after months of being together?

He hated the space between them right now. He hadn't touched her in weeks, his empty hands, bed, and heart taunting him for his mistakes. For taking this back to the very place it started. Back to the what ifs.

But it had to be this way, because if he touched her now as he teetered on this precipice, he couldn't be responsible for his actions. Chances were he'd drop to his knees and beg her to kiss him, and forgo the trip altogether.

So when she took a step forward, he sucked in a breath and moved back an inch, his back hitting the wall. She stopped short, closer but not touching. Her lips parted and her eyes searched his.

No telling what she saw reflected there, but for some reason it made her sway toward him.

"Fuck's sake," Graham mumbled from the doorway. "You had all night to say goodbye."

Mia spun around and stepped away. Noah remained where he was, chest tight and muscles tense.

If only they'd spent last night the way Graham assumed, maybe he wouldn't be such a mess right now.

Or maybe he'd be worse.

"Yeah. I'm coming." He pushed off the wall and passed her as he followed Graham to the door.

Claire was in the kitchen with a cookie in her hand, scrolling through her phone.

Graham opened the door and put his hand on the wood. "Hey, Claire, you gonna give me some sugar before I go?"

"Nope."

"Then why are you even here?"

"Mia said Noah would be more likely to leave if I pretended like I'd be staying here with her while he's gone."

Noah shot up from where he'd bent down to get his backpack. "Wait, you're not—"

"Claire!" Mia whisper-yelled, giving Noah a push from behind. That contact alone sent a shock through him, and he barely processed her muttered, "Stop worrying and just go," before finding himself with Graham on the porch, the door slammed shut behind them.

Graham blinked. "Damn."

Noah frowned, glancing back and resettling his bag on his shoulder. "I know."

Graham shrugged, already over it. He clapped his hands and rubbed them together with excitement. "Ready for this?"

Noah's legs felt like concrete as he followed his friend down the steps. "As I'll ever be."

Noah and Graham met their friends at the airport, and two hours later were on a plane to the Great White North. Graham sat next to Noah, calm as could be, while Noah signaled to the flight attendant for another rum and Coke.

"Dude," Graham said with a laugh. "Chill."

Noah ignored him and leaned his head against the seat.

Hugh and Chris had claimed seats in the row in front of them. Hugh appeared in Noah's line of vision, his face pressed in the space between the seats. "Noah, you okay, man?"

Chris's hand appeared at the top of the seat in front of Graham, and he went up on one knee to twist around and regard Graham and Noah behind him. He never was one to miss out on a conversation. "Yeah, what's going on?"

"I'm fine, guys."

Graham shook his head solemnly. "Is this what love does to you? If so, I want no part of it."

Chris laid his chin on the headrest, still facing them. He fluttered his eyelashes and grinned at Noah. "Aw, are you in love, Noah?"

Noah glared at him, but Chris only laughed. He cracked his knuckles, wishing he could relax and laugh with them. But he felt like a caged animal, pacing in a tiny space, desperate to get out. He'd never been claustrophobic or afraid of flying, and certainly not afraid of heights, or else rock climbing would have been a terrible recreational choice. What was his deal all of a sudden? Unease prickled the back of his neck, and his heart raced.

He focused on breathing and told himself Mia would be fine.

He hadn't wanted to leave her, but it wasn't just that. This felt like more than concern for his wife.

Graham's smile faded as he eyed Noah. He shoved his hand forward through the split in the seats, pushing Hugh back.

"What the—" Hugh protested.

Graham waved his hand at Chris hanging off the back of his seat. "Give us a minute, will you?"

Chris's eyebrows rose, but he did as asked.

Graham spoke loud enough for Noah to hear, but low enough that the low roar of the engine ensured no one around them could.

"You're thinking about Nathan, aren't you?"

Noah darted his gaze to the restrooms at either end of the plane, and found both lights on, indicating they were occupied.

Dammit.

"Come on. Let's get everything out in the open now," Graham continued. "This is gonna be a long damn trip if this is what I'll be dealing with."

Noah snapped his gaze to his friend's. "Doesn't this feel wrong to you?"

"Wrong?" Graham appeared taken aback. "Of course it feels wrong. It feels that way every time we climb without our third man. I think about it every damn time we're hanging off the side of a mountain and I remember his stupid laugh, or his steady 'place hand, move feet' chant, and how he'd cry every time we made it to the top like some pansy-ass. Climbing made him so fucking happy, and it's never been the same since he's been gone."

Stunned, Noah could only stare at him. They rarely spoke of Nathan, and even though Noah assumed Graham missed him, he hadn't realized just how much.

Graham turned away to face to the window for a few long beats, and Noah stared at the navy leather of the seat in the row ahead of him.

"But," Graham finally said, voice thick. "Remembering how much it meant to him is exactly why I won't stop. It's my way of honoring him and his legacy. I love it, don't get me wrong. Nothing compares to standing at the top of a mountain I just climbed with my bare hands. I've never found anything else that makes me feel so powerful, while at the same time so insignificant. But when I think about skipping a trip, or taking a break for a while, I always think, 'Nathan would have wanted to go. And since he can't, I should do it for him.'"

Noah gripped his thighs, wishing the flight attendant would arrive with his drink already. It was too early in the morning for a conversation of this magnitude.

But Graham was right—it was best to get past everything now. For the safety of every person on the trip, he needed to be able to focus once they were on the ice.

"I know what you mean," Noah said. "You know part of the reason I've limited myself is because I didn't want to leave Mia. But that aside, when it comes to Nathan, it's different for me than it is for you."

Graham nodded. "I know. He was your brother."

"I don't mean just that. I mean the fact that I'm the reason he died. I struggle with the idea of doing these things he can't, because if it weren't for me, he'd still be here."

Graham's subdued expression transformed to shock. "What in the hell are you talking about?"

Noah crushed the empty plastic cup in his hand. "I made Nathan drive that night. It was the middle of the night and I'd been drinking, and I should have waited until morning, but I didn't care. I'm the reason we were on the road in the dark, and if it wasn't for me he'd still be here."

Scratching at his cheek, Graham appeared confused. "We've never talked about that night, but it sounds like this conversation is long overdue."

"What do you mean?"

"I mean I always remembered you were out of it that night."

It was the understatement of the century, and nothing Noah didn't already know. It was the next thing Graham said that caught him off guard.

"But I never realized how much. Because what you just said isn't how I remember things going at all."

25

The one thing Mia hadn't counted on when Noah left was how much she'd worry about him. It was usually the other way around, and she quickly concluded she didn't like the feeling.

He'd been gone two days and she'd barely stopped thinking about him. Even from her current spot in the infusion center for her regular visit, she couldn't turn it off.

She'd been so scatterbrained she hadn't even brought Natasha a treat.

There were so many things that could go wrong—a faulty rope, a loose piece of ice, bad weather. Were they safe from avalanches, bears, frostbite? Were those even valid concerns, or was she being completely ridiculous?

Why hadn't she asked for more information?

Right—she'd avoided bringing it up to make sure neither

of them talked him out of going. Based on the places her mind was going, she was just as likely to have done so.

This trip felt important. Could it be what he needed to finally come to terms with what happened? Find closure and make peace with his brother's death? Maybe even absolve himself from the guilt he carried around like a backpack? She wished for that, for him, so badly.

She hoped they were having fun, too. With Graham there, it was almost a guarantee, and Noah deserved a break and time to enjoy himself. But, not too much...surely there weren't women with them, right?

She frowned. That was a stupid assumption—there were tons of women climbers in Colorado. What if their guide was a woman? A sexy, healthy, ice-climbing Aphrodite?

She hadn't so much as thought about other men since they got married, much less looked at one with interest. Especially not since they'd admitted their feelings and slept together.

But they'd put a stop to that. *She'd* put a stop to that, and didn't know if they'd ever come back together. She had no claim on him (no *real* claim, anyway).

Still, she couldn't help the burn of jealousy at the thought of him with another woman. An idea she'd completely just made up, but isn't that what love did to people? Made them irrational?

She picked up her phone with a sudden urge to send him a message. Other than a single text he'd sent letting her know they arrived in Canada safely, they hadn't spoken since he left. She'd figured they both needed this time apart, but now she was second-guessing herself.

Mia: At my infusion appointment, and you know what that means: chicken wings. Thinking about you. Hope you're staying safe and having a great time.

Her thumb hovered over Send. Was the *thinking about you* too much? It was true, but saying things like that to each other only made this whole situation more difficult, didn't it? This trip was a step in the right direction, but it didn't mean they could go back to the way things were.

She decided to go with it, pressed Send, and settled into the leather chair, a relieved smile spreading across her face when she spotted Barbara walking toward her.

She adored Barbara, and she'd take any distraction she could get.

They exchanged pleasantries and Barbara asked how school was going, then told Mia about a new carrot cake recipe she'd tried over the weekend. Mia thought she was doing a good job hiding the fact that her mind kept going back to Noah every few seconds until during a break in conversation, Barbara called her out.

"You seem distracted today."

"Oh. I'm sorry. Um, I'm not. I'm fine."

Barbara offered a bemused smile. "Honey, you're a terrible liar."

It was so true. She gripped her hands in her lap. "Can I ask you something?"

"Sure."

"It's personal."

Barbara cocked a brow. "That's okay. I think."

"A while back, you told me your husband died of cancer several years ago." She hadn't seemed to mind talking about it, or else Mia wouldn't have mentioned it.

"Yes. Gastric cancer. He battled it for two years before he finally let go."

Sadness weighed on Mia's shoulders, and she swallowed,

asking the question slowly, carefully. "What's it like, to take care of someone you love when they're sick like that?"

Barbara looked at her thoughtfully for a few seconds. "I'm not going to lie. It's hard. But I'm not sure I even had the full experience."

"What do you mean?"

"When I say George battled cancer for two years, that's what I mean. *He* battled it. Not we. Almost immediately after his diagnosis, he started to withdraw from me. It was subtle at first, and I didn't realize what he was doing. He started shutting himself in the den more and more, and I thought he was tired and depressed about the diagnosis. Which was probably true, but it wasn't just that. He'd always been one of those 'do it yourself' men, but we shared our lives with each other. We used to read at opposite ends of the couch on Saturday evenings, but he started taking his books to the other room. I used to iron his dress shirts on Sundays, and he said he wanted to start doing it himself. Finally, I realized he was distancing himself."

Oh, George. I know exactly how you felt. "He didn't want to be a burden," Mia offered.

"Maybe. He never would talk about it." Barbara adjusted the tubing around her arm. "When I think about those last few months—the last year, even—it breaks my heart. Not even because he was sick. I hated that too, but it was more that he shut me out. We'd been married twenty-seven years. Been through a lot together, and had a beautiful story. I thought so, at least. I wanted to be with him when he was sick and be the one taking care of him. It was like I lost him before I really lost him, you know? Our time together was cut short well before he actually passed away. That's what hurts the most, and that's the part I've had the hardest time forgiving him for. For leaving me in such a painful way."

Mia forced a swallow down her dry throat. "I'm so sorry, Barbara. I shouldn't have brought it up."

"It's alright. I don't mind talking about it." Her shrewd green eyes connected with Mia's. "Why do you ask? What are you worried about, honey? Is this about your parents?"

Mia shook her head. "I'm…having a hard time with Noah. Like George did. You know how I felt about what my illness did to my parents, and I never planned to get married. Never planned to bleed into someone else's life like that."

"And then you did."

"And then I did," Mia agreed. "Noah and I have been friends since we were kids. I've loved him basically my entire life."

"So, he knew what he was getting into."

"Does anyone really know, though? There are so many unknowns. I married him, yes—because I couldn't seem to stop myself. But now that we're here, I can't stop worrying about what it's doing to him. What he's missing out on, and what he might miss out on in the future. Last week we found out my kidneys are getting worse. I've known for a while because I've been in more pain, but have tried my best to hide it from him. But he knows, and his anxiety is palpable. Is his life, his experience on this earth, going to be stressful and limited because he's with me? It feels so damn selfish to let that happen."

"If I may, speaking from experience, it's selfish to push him away, too."

Mia balked at that, and Barbara hurried to continue.

"It hurts when someone you love pushes you away. It feels like a punishment. If he's anything like me, and he loves you half as much as I loved George—and I expect he does—he wants to be there with you. Take care of you. He *wants* to, Mia. And by refusing him, you're stealing his blessing. You're stealing something that's his to give before he can even offer it."

"I—I don't think I'm doing that," Mia said weakly. She'd never thought about it like that. A memory from a few months ago surfaced, when he'd asked if she'd rather be a ninja or a pirate. She'd reasoned she didn't want to be a pirate because she didn't want to be a thief.

"There's something else I think you should consider. I tried to put myself in George's shoes so I could be more understanding about what he was going through, and I wish he'd done the same for me. So think about if the situation were reversed: What would you do if Noah got sick and wouldn't let you help? How would you feel if he was in the hospital and wouldn't let you in his room?"

Mia stared at a speck on the floor in front of her chair, discomfort washing over her in punishing waves, each one more forceful than the last. She glanced up at the bag of fluid hanging from the pole beside her.

Suddenly all she wanted to do was disconnect and get out of there.

"That question bothers you," Barbara said.

Mia nodded.

"Why?"

She felt tears gathering, but refused to let one fall. "If that's what he wanted, I would respect that."

Lies.

She'd scale the wall and climb through the damn window if she had to.

Mia clenched her jaw and stared straight ahead for several long moments before finally meeting Barbara's shrewd gaze.

She sighed heavily, admitting defeat. "Damn you, Barb."

★★★

Mia stretched her arms over her head, trying to focus on the open book in her lap. She had an exam tomorrow in Medical Nutrition Therapy, the most difficult course of the semester. She'd worked her ass off to hold an A so far and couldn't let her wandering thoughts ruin that.

She wanted to do well and be at the top of the program. She owed it to the scholarship donors and Noah, to prove she took it seriously and wouldn't waste the opportunity they'd so selflessly given her.

Had it really only been seven months since she received that acceptance email? Since she and Noah first broached the subject of marriage?

Her heart lurched at the memory of the first time he suggested they get married.

Focus. Stop thinking about him.

Easier said than done, and the conversation with Barbara a couple of days ago hadn't helped, either. She oscillated between thinking about Noah, that conversation, and back to Noah again.

She closed the book, giving up for the night and tossing it on the table. The coasters she'd given him as a gift sat neatly stacked near the edge, a few inches from the two food-inspired coffee-table books he'd bought the last time he tagged along to her bookstore café date with Anita and Bridget. Fading daylight streamed through the sheer curtains she'd hung when she first moved in, casting soft shadows across the couch and the plush CU blanket draped across her lap. She pressed her face to the black fleece and inhaled deeply, Noah's familiar scent flooding her senses.

It suddenly hit her she hadn't gone this long without seeing him in...actually, she couldn't remember a time she'd gone this long without seeing him. At least not since she was diagnosed. Even before they got married, he never went out of town for more than a long three-day weekend, and she always saw him at work before or after.

The shrill ringtone assigned to her doctor's office pierced the silence, startling her. She frowned, checking the time—seven fifteen—and wondered why on earth Dr. Cowley would be calling her right now. She swiped across the screen to answer.

"Hello?"

"Mia? It's Dr. Cowley. I have great news."

She was afraid to ask and pressed a hand to her mouth.

"We found you a kidney."

Claire showed up fifteen minutes later. Eventually she had to push Mia into a kitchen chair and declare she'd do the packing. Mia's hands were shaking and her thoughts were all over the place as she tried to process everything Dr. Cowley had said.

Deceased donor.

A possible match.

She needed to go to the hospital within the hour for workup and transplant prep if everything lined up.

Was this really happening? Finally? After years of waiting and wondering?

"I think I got enough clothes," Claire said, tossing a gym bag on the floor. "Toiletries are next. Anything I forget I can just come back for. I'll call the school tomorrow and make sure your professors know. Did you call your parents?"

"Yeah, right after I called you."

"Noah?"

Mia closed her mouth.

Claire paused on her trajectory to the hallway and turned. "Mia? Did you call Noah?"

She shook her head, dropping her gaze.

Out of the corner of her eye, Mia saw Claire's hands go to her hips.

"You have to tell him."

Mia closed her eyes. "You of all people should understand why I don't want to call him right now. It's nine years ago all over again."

Claire came closer and put her hand on Mia's shoulder. "This is different. You're not in the ICU with some unknown illness. This is what you've been waiting for."

"It doesn't matter. It's still a big deal. Something could go wrong. They're supposed to be there three more days but he'll freak out and try to come back."

"How he reacts is up to him. That's not in your control, as much as I know you wish it was." Her face was more serious than Mia had ever seen it. "You *have* to tell him."

In that exact moment, almost as if a higher power was at work, Noah texted her.

Noah: Hey. I'm glad you texted. I've been thinking about you, too.

She almost broke down right there, wishing he was here to stand beside her and hold her hand. Her heart and her brain were on two completely different wavelengths, trying to discern what she wanted versus what was best for him. For them.

Claire was right, though. She had to tell him, and time was running out. She smoothed her hair behind her ears, and hit the FaceTime button.

Within seconds Noah's ruggedly handsome, familiar face

was on the screen, a sweetly surprised, if uncertain, smile shaping his lips. "Hi."

"Hey," she said, tears coming out of nowhere and flowing down her cheeks. The stress of everything that had happened in the last half hour, combined with seeing him, suddenly overwhelmed her.

His expression fell. "Hey. What's wrong?"

She shook her head, swiping the wetness away with her hand. "I'm sorry. It's just…good to see you."

His brow stayed furrowed and the image on her screen got larger, as if he held the phone a little closer. "It's good to see you, too."

Getting a hold of herself, she took in his unkempt red hair, bright blue eyes, and rosy cheeks. "How cold is it there?"

"Fucking freezing," he said with a slight laugh. "But we were prepared."

"Are you glad you went?"

He tilted his head to the side. "Yeah. I am."

"Good." She swallowed, catching another warm tear that escaped.

"Are you okay?" he asked gently. She could see the worry in his eyes.

"Um…" She switched hands and gripped the phone tighter. "They, um, might have found a kidney for me."

His expression didn't change for a few seconds, like it took him some time to process what she'd said. Then a beautiful smile lit up his face. "What? Mia, that's incredible. What's the plan? When will they schedule the procedure?"

"Well, that's the thing. I know we'd expected a live donor, and there'd be more time to prepare, but it's a cadaver. I'm about to leave for the hospital."

Noah's face paled. "Right now?"

She nodded.

The screen jostled and Noah was on his feet, moving around the tent. His head was out of the shot for a few seconds and she heard a muffled, "Graham!" He sounded panicked.

"Noah," she urged. "Stop. You don't have to leave."

He paused his movements, his eyes back on hers. "The hell I won't."

A fresh wave of tears came and her hand started to tremble. "You can't. It's too much like the last time."

"Mia, listen to me. I can and I am." His voice was fierce and determined. "I'll always come back for you. Always."

A sob broke from her chest, and she dropped her forehead into her palm.

Rustling noises continued through the speaker, as if he was packing. She heard a few low murmurs and recognized Graham's voice.

"Hey."

She looked back at the screen to find Noah focused on his phone. On her.

"Please," he begged. "Don't ask me not to come back. I can't stay here knowing you're about to go into surgery. Tell me you understand, and you want me there with you."

She sniffed, taking measured breaths through the thickness in her throat. "Did you at least get what you needed from the trip?"

A sad but contented smile settled on his face. "I'll tell you when I get there."

She hated hospital gowns. Every time she'd been admitted over the years, the first thing Mia asked of Claire was to bring her a change of clothes.

It wasn't an option, now, what with her about to go into

surgery. She had no idea what time it was, only that it was in the early hours of the morning. She'd seen the tiniest hint of the sunrise from the window of the pre-op area, and exhaustion from not having slept all night caught up with her.

Guess it was a good thing she was about to go to sleep for a while.

She gave blood immediately upon arrival, and shortly after, they'd confirmed the match. She didn't allow herself to focus on the fact that someone else had died to give her this opportunity. She figured she'd have weeks of recovery for reflection, and couldn't let her mind go anywhere other than hoping nothing went wrong during the surgery.

The surgeon said the procedure would only take about three hours as long as there were no complications. She signed a ton of paperwork and was formally admitted to the solid organ transplant service.

Her parents had met them at the hospital and set up shop with Claire in the waiting room. She hadn't even tried to tell them they didn't need to stay.

Progress, she supposed.

Claire had spoken to Noah once more while Mia was being prepped, and confirmed he was on his way. Claire had handed Mia the phone, and he'd quickly told her he'd be there as soon as he could before he had to hang up to go through airport security. She'd never admit it, but she was relieved at the news. Now that she knew this was happening—that she was about to be cut open and have a foreign organ placed inside her body, the fear was real. He wouldn't make it back before she woke up, but she still took comfort in knowing he'd be there soon to hold her hand and be the calming presence she'd come to depend on.

A hand pulled the curtain aside and the surgeon's face popped through. "Ready?"

"As I'll ever be."

A nurse slid in beside him and wheeled Mia into a white-walled room filled with monitors and shiny metal equipment. A man who introduced himself as the anesthesiologist placed a nasal cannula around her head and slid the device into her nostrils.

The last thing she remembered was his smile.

"See you in a bit."

26

It took Noah three times as long to get from Calgary to Denver as it had going up there. The only available route on such short notice took him through Vancouver, and he wasn't scheduled to arrive at the hospital until two o'clock the next afternoon.

It was a last-minute trip and a completely unlikely event that he'd be at the Vancouver airport on that exact day, at that exact time, which made what happened to him during the forty minutes he was in that building seem impossible.

Almost like fate.

He'd been rushing through Terminal B to get to his next flight, and as he errantly surveyed the gate numbers above the crowd around him, his gaze landed on someone familiar.

He froze in his tracks, half wondering if he was hallucinating because of exhaustion.

"Rachel?"

He would have stopped for no one else. She was the one person he'd pause for, though a tiny part of his brain continued to urge him to locate Gate 37. He didn't turn toward her completely, in an effort to signal his need to continue on, but…she was the woman whose life he'd ruined, and who had never stuck around long enough for him to apologize. And there she stood, looking as shocked as he did, her hands gripping the handle of a stroller.

He stared at her for a second, then looked down at the baby and back to her face. Thoughts whirled through his brain, there and gone in an instant, too quick for him to grab one and hang on. He blinked, trying to make sense of what he was seeing. What it meant.

"Hey, Noah." She smiled at him.

Smiled. Looked him straight in the eye and seemed…happy.

A man appeared at her side. "Flight's delayed by an hour. Want to get some coffee?"

When Rachel didn't immediately reply to the man, he seemed to notice Noah standing there.

"Um, Noah, this is my husband, Brian." Something passed over her features. "Brian, this is Noah. He's—was—Nathan's little brother."

Rachel was married? With a baby?

And she'd told her husband about Nathan?

Understanding dawned on Brian's face, and he held out his hand. "Oh. Wow, it's nice to meet you, man."

Noah woodenly shook the other man's hand, still in shock. "You too."

"I can't believe you're here," Rachel said. "What are you—"

In that moment a voice came over the loudspeaker for a boarding call for United Flight 3623 to Denver.

"Shit, that's me," Noah said, coming out of his stupor. "I'm sorry, I have to go."

"Oh, of course," Rachel said. "It was good to see you." It sounded like she meant it.

"Yeah," Noah said. "You too."

She gave a little wave and Brian offered a head nod before Noah took off at a jog. He'd think about what just happened later. Right now, he'd focus on Mia.

By the time the plane landed his stomach was in knots. He'd grabbed an Uber, not even stopping at home first. He was tired, dirty, and had a massive hiking backpack on his shoulders as he walked through the hospital doors. He followed Claire's directions to the family waiting room on the fifth floor. Claire was there with Mia's dad, and they filled him in with as much as they knew. The procedure had gone well, she'd been out of surgery for several hours, and after briefly waking from anesthesia had been asleep ever since.

Hospital policy allowed only one family member in her room at a time, and Noah was relieved her mother allowed him to take her place at the bedside. He'd like to think he was above arguing with a woman twenty-five years his senior, but probably best not to test it.

Mia looked peaceful, lying there surrounded by white, her dark hair spread across the pillow. Her skin was pale, but her lips had color. He wished he could hug her tight and wondered how long it would be until he'd be allowed to.

He carefully pulled the chair as close to the single bed as possible and settled in, his eyes leaving her face only when the machines to his right occasionally beeped. Each sound caused his pulse to spike, but he rationalized if a nurse wasn't running into the room with fear in her eyes, everything was probably okay.

Exhaustion pressed down on him, and he wondered how long he'd last. He held her left hand between both of his, feeling the warmth of her skin, and watched the rhythmic rise and fall of her chest.

Thoughts scrolled through his head, of his life spent with Mia and the last seven months as her husband. When she moved into his house, she'd brought a light he hadn't known was missing. Or maybe he had known, he just hadn't wanted to admit it. Hadn't wanted to admit he'd been living his life as half a man, wallowing in the past and too afraid to step forward and move on. He thought of Nathan and the accident, and the discussion with Graham about that night. That plane ride had been fraught with revelations and discoveries that became clearer to Noah with each passing day.

And what the hell had he just witnessed in the Vancouver airport? Rachel had apparently moved on, too. She hadn't run away crying, too full of misery to even look at Noah and his likeness to her dead fiancé. She'd smiled and introduced him to another man she'd come to love.

He tried to process everything, but wasn't sure how. Could the human brain deal with so much information in the span of five days?

Mia shifted in her sleep, bringing his focus back to her.

"I have so much to tell you, beautiful," he whispered. "I love you so much."

He pressed his lips to the back of her hand and gently laid his head on the mattress beside her arm, keeping one hand wrapped around hers as he drifted off to sleep.

★★★

Noah woke to the soothing sensation of someone running their fingers through his hair. His eyes blinked open and when the machine behind him beeped, he remembered where he was.

He sat up to find Mia watching him, her lips spread in a soft smile. She dropped the hand that had been stroking his head, her other one still clasped in his.

Leaning forward, he lifted her arm and pressed the back of her hand to his lips.

Her eyes followed his movement, and thank God she didn't chastise him or pull away. "Hi."

"Hey. I'm sorry I fell asleep."

"Don't be."

"How do you feel?"

She took a deep breath and winced.

He straightened. "Does it hurt?" He kept her hand in one of his and searched for the call button on her bed with the other. "I'll call the nurse."

"It's not so bad," she said, but didn't decline the offer.

He reached up to brush hair back from her temple.

She leaned into his touch. "I'm so glad you're here."

"Me too."

He arched his back in a stretch, stiff from being bent over her bed, and looked at the clock. He'd been there a little over two hours. Her attention was on him, her cheeks pink and her eyes alert.

"What a whirlwind, huh?" he asked.

"I'm still stunned, I think. I vaguely remember talking to the surgeon after the procedure, but I was pretty out of it. I'm guessing everything went okay?"

"Far as I know," Noah said. "Your mom said the doctor would be by this evening."

"Are they still here? My parents, I mean?"

"Yep. Claire, too."

She nodded.

Maybe she'd finally accepted that everyone wanted to be there for her.

The door opened and a young blonde woman in scrubs walked in. "You're awake," she said with a smile. "I'm Abby, your nurse."

"Hi," Mia said.

That was enough pleasantries. "She's hurting," Noah cut in.

"Noah," Mia chided.

He ignored her and addressed the nurse. "Is there something you can give her?"

Abby cast him an amused glance. "Absolutely. Can you tell me where it hurts?"

Mia answered the nurse's questions, including where the pain was, that it was dull and aching, and ranked at a six out of ten.

When Abby left, Noah bounced his knee up and down, starting an internal countdown until he'd call the nurse again if she didn't return quickly with the meds.

Six out of ten? He'd accept nothing less than a one. *Maybe* a two.

"How was—"

"Shh," he interrupted. "Let's wait until you feel better. We'll have plenty of time to talk about it."

"The pain meds will probably knock me out again."

"That's okay. You need to rest."

Her dark eyes caressed his face, and she smiled wryly. "Who do you think you are, charging in here and being all bossy?"

"Your doting husband."

"Overbearing, more like."

His mouth twitched. "Protective?"

She pursed her lips. "Fine. But if you won't tell me about your trip yet, figure something else out to distract me until she brings the drugs."

He thought for a second, then pulled his phone from his pocket. He opened the music app and set it on the blanket just as the first few notes of "Chasing Cars" drifted through the speakers.

She closed her eyes and mouthed the words, entwining her fingers with his.

Noah let his heart fill to the brim with the knowledge she was here and awake and content to let him stay here beside her.

As his favorite lyrics from the song played, he realized he'd never agreed with them more.

Those three words *weren't* enough. They didn't even come close to describing what he felt for this woman, but maybe that was okay.

Because if it wasn't enough to say it, he'd just have to show her.

27

After three days in the ICU, Mia was finally moved to a room on the regular floor. There was no telling how long she'd be in the hospital, as it all depended on the new kidney and when it started working.

If it did at all.

She'd always thought of herself as a patient person. But the waiting was unbearable. Every day she gave blood and kept one eye on the door until the doctor came in with the results.

Every day she wondered: How were the numbers? Were they improving? Was the kidney functioning?

Did her body seem to be accepting it, or were there signs of rejection?

So far there were no signs of that, which was good. But no sign of resumed function either, which wasn't.

The pain was quite a bit better, but without the need for medications that kept her in a state of drowsy comfort, her anxiety steadily increased.

She was rarely alone. Aside from nurses that cycled in and out every few hours to take her vitals or give her one of the fifteen medications she now had to take, the chair in the corner was always occupied. Sometimes it was Claire or one of her parents, and for about half an hour yesterday Graham had stopped by.

But mostly, it was Noah. He got grumpy when anyone suggested it was their turn and asked him to step out, and it seemed they'd all decided it wasn't worth the fight. Only when he needed food or a shower did he leave willingly.

One day she'd gently reminded him he had a job, but the death glare he'd directed at her had her cowering in the bed.

Today was the first day she felt back to normal, or close to it. She had energy and an appetite, and after walking the halls for a while was feisty enough to complain about the special menu offerings for "immunocompromised patients." She vaguely remembered learning about dietary restrictions during the patient education seminar she'd had to attend to get on the transplant list, but that had been years ago.

"I can't believe I forgot I can't have fresh fruit," she whined.

"I can't, either. You're the one who wants to be a dietician. Even I remembered that," Noah quipped.

"How?"

"You talked about it for like a week after." His cheeks went pink when he added, "And I did a little reading recently about life post-transplant. After you said they moved you higher on the list."

"Oh."

She didn't deserve this man.

It slowly sank in how intense things would be for a while. She'd come into the hospital on three medications for her kidney disease, but would leave with four times that many.

Drugs to suppress her immune system so her body didn't reject the new kidney.

With a weakened immune system, she also needed drugs to protect her from infection.

She had to be careful where she went, and what she exposed herself to. Travel and being around crowds wouldn't be possible for a while.

There would be frequent blood draws and doctor visits, especially at the beginning.

It would be a never-ending cycle for months. Maybe even years.

Thinking about it with Noah beside her, looking at her as if he was ready to handle anything and demonstrating his willingness to do just that over the last few days, was enough to send a wave of panic coursing through her. It was insistent and familiar, the same thing she'd feared ever since she said *I do.*

And yet it was different because this time, she *hated* it. She thought about everything they'd been through, the fact that he'd faced his fears and gone to Banff and still come back for her. She thought about what Barb had said about letting people love her, and allowed gratitude to wash over her. This time, she rejected that fear out of hand.

She was so tired of pushing him away. If he hadn't been scared off yet, it didn't seem like anything would change that.

Thank God for that.

He watched her, brows together and lips flattened into a straight line, probably wondering why she was being so quiet.

She smiled. "Will you tell me about the trip now?"

He ran a hand through his hair and gave a little nod before scooting his chair closer to the bed.

"Ice climbing is..." A slight smile tipped his lips and he exhaled. "It's like nothing else I've ever experienced. It's a whole different side of nature. The terrain was completely different. Rocks are sturdy and constant, while the ice is like this ever-changing wall of uncertainty. The risks were more evident, and it was definitely more physical. I don't really climb for the thrill, but I see why people do. It really felt like man versus nature, and like we were defying what the human body was meant to do."

"If anyone can challenge a mountain, it's you."

He dropped his eyes to his knees. "Nathan was the one who liked to challenge nature. I just want to be in it and enjoy it."

Mia leaned forward to gently brush his hair back, any excuse to touch him in that moment.

His blue eyes met hers. "I realized some things while I was gone."

She sat up a little more and waited for him to continue.

"Did you know Graham and I never talked about the accident after it happened?"

She frowned. "Never?"

"Not really. We're both good at avoiding things when we want to."

She hummed. "That I believe."

"But this trip was all Nathan, through and through. He was bound to come up. We finally talked about it, and Graham filled in some gaps my memory hadn't held on to."

"What kind of gaps?"

He flattened his palms on the white blanket, flexing his fingers. "I thought I was the one who forced Nathan and Graham to pack up and leave the campsite that night. But that was just an assumption, because I was drunk, knew I couldn't drive, and it seems like something I'd do if I was worried about you."

"Did Graham remember it another way?"

Noah's throat worked and he curled his hands into fists. "When I got the call, I was completely out of my head. All I wanted was to get back to town, but you know us. When we go to a good camping spot, it's in the middle of nowhere. No Ubers, taxis, nothing. Graham said I started calling fraternity brothers to see if anyone was familiar enough with the area to come get me. But Nathan took my phone away and insisted he wanted to go. You were like family to him, too. He wanted to come and wouldn't hear otherwise, and he's the one who packed up and pushed me in the car. He kept saying, 'She'll be okay, man. She'll be okay.' I hadn't remembered it until Graham said that. And then, when you called me and told me about the transplant and I was in a car heading down the mountain, I could hear his voice clear as day, saying 'she'll be okay.' He knew back then I had to be with you." His voice broke. "He still does."

His face crumpled, and he dropped his forehead to his hands. Mia reached forward to tug at him, pulling him up so he was half draped across her chest, wishing she could climb out of bed and wrap herself around him.

"Noah," she murmured, warm tears spilling over. "I want that, too. I love you. I missed you so much."

He anchored one hand at her side and cupped her cheek with the other, kissing her fiercely. She covered his hand with hers, squeezing her eyes shut as she pressed closer.

When he pulled back his lashes were wet.

Her heart thrashed against her ribs. "What have I ever done to deserve you?" she asked hoarsely. "All I've done is push you away."

"No," he said. "You didn't."

"I did."

"You tried to pretend you did, but I knew better. I knew you didn't really want me to move on, even if you didn't." He traced her cheek with his thumb. "Besides, I had my own shit to work through. We just needed time."

Her throat tightened with uncertainty. "This is too one-sided," she said. "You've always been there for me. Watching out for me and taking care of me. You've loved me despite my illness and stubborn attitude. Other than loving you, what could I possibly offer you that can compare?"

"Your love is all I need. But you take care of me too, you know. You always have."

She forced a swallow. "How?"

"I always felt like I was in Nathan's shadow, but you saw me. You were the first person to choose me as I was, and never made me feel like I had to be different, or more than." His lips tipped up in the most adorable grin. "When Brittany broke up with me in eighth grade because I was too shy and wouldn't kiss her in the cafeteria, you pushed her lunch tray on the floor."

A laugh slipped past her lips. "I hated her for that."

"When I didn't make the football team sophomore year, you suggested I join the rock climbing club instead. You turned me on to one of the biggest passions of my life."

Tears were falling freely now. She didn't even try to stop them.

"When I had the flu a few years ago I couldn't get rid of you. You bring me my favorite chicken wings every week. But..." He leaned in conspiratorially. "I need to let you in on a little secret. It's not the wings I want so much as an excuse to see you for dinner every week."

"Same," she managed to get out.

"And you've always encouraged me to date other women because you thought it was best for me. I can't believe that's what you really wanted."

"Never," she admitted, blinking through her tears. "I had myself convinced there for a while, but deep down, the idea of you with anyone else ripped my heart out."

"See? Even then, you were trying to protect me. The funny part is, it was from the only thing I've ever wanted."

She pulled him closer and kissed him again. "I'm sorry," she whispered.

"Me too." He kissed her once more.

"I love you."

"Yeah?" He smiled. "Well. I loved you first."

28

Mia made him go into work the next day, which was probably a good idea for a guy on probation.

He left early, though.

When he stepped into her room that afternoon, she was sitting cross-legged on the hospital bed in black leggings and a white tank top, her thick black hair piled on top of her head. As soon as he laid eyes on her, want hit him like the lash of a whip. His inhale lodged in his throat and he paused in the doorway, clenching his jaw.

It had been too damn long since he'd seen her naked. She'd been through a lot and her body was healing, and he'd wait as long as he needed to.

But fuck, she was the most beautiful thing he'd ever seen. He couldn't wait to caress her body and hear her whispers in the dark. After the freeing realizations from his trip and the fear of knowing she was undergoing surgery while he was on a plane—every day with her seemed more precious than the last.

He'd never been so happy he married this woman.

She looked up and smiled, which did nothing to cool his ardor. "Hey, you."

"Hey, beautiful."

She wrinkled her nose and ran an absent hand over her messy hair. "Oh, please."

He approached the bed slowly, devouring her with his gaze as he went. She dropped her hand to her lap, her lips parting when he was at her side. He put one hand and a knee on the mattress and leaned in, cupping the back of her head with his other hand. With effort, he kissed her gently, ignoring the way his body screamed at him to be rough, take and give back to her, and put him out of his misery. Both of them, if she felt even a fraction of the desire he did.

"You make it hard to breathe," he whispered against her lips.

"Oh," she murmured, and captured his lips again, her fist grasping his shirt to pull him closer.

He smiled and tore his lips away before he did something stupid like climb up there with her. This hospital bed wasn't made for what he had in mind.

"Why'd you stop?" she whined, her cheeks flushed in a delicate pink.

He swallowed. "Just trying not to get kicked out of here," he half joked.

She smoothed her hands across her stomach and took several cleansing breaths. "Okay, yeah. You're right."

"How was your day?" he asked.

"Boring. But my creatinine is almost where it needs to be,

which means the kidney is working. There's a chance I can go home tomorrow."

"Really? That's great."

"Since it's flu season they said it's best for me to get out of the hospital as soon as possible. Be at home with less exposure."

He pouted. "Does that mean we can't have that huge welcome home rave I'd planned?"

She snorted. "Like we have enough friends for a rave."

"You do," he retorted. "You've made friends with half the city of Denver while waiting in lines."

She giggled, an adorable, girlish sound, and he tucked it away in his heart. They'd had too many moments without laughter and he lived for those moments of joy.

"Speaking of going home," she started, her smile fading. "There was something I wanted to talk to you about."

He pulled the chair close and sat, the way she said it putting him on edge. "Okay."

She looked down at her hands, scratching at one thumb nail with the other. He took one in his, hoping to calm her. "I don't know if you remember this, but now that I've had a transplant, I qualify for Medicare."

No, he hadn't remembered that.

What was her point?

"I could have my own insurance now. I don't need yours." She locked eyes with him. "I don't need you to be my husband anymore."

What in the actual… *What?* He slid his hand from hers and dropped it to the bed, staring at her.

She pursed her lips and leaned forward to grab his hand again. "Don't go all quiet on me. I'm not saying I don't want to stay married. I'm just saying our options are different now, and we need to talk about it. Make sure this is still what we both want when we have no obligation to stay together. I'd much rather you be with me because you want to rather than because you're fulfilling a duty as my protector and friend."

He laughed once. At least, he thought it was a laugh...it was hard to tell. The sound was rough and emotional, involuntary and forced from his chest from somewhere deep inside. "You don't think I want to be with you?"

"I do think you want to. But we made this decision really fast, and you didn't have time to think it through. I'm not saying we shouldn't be together. All I'm saying is we don't have to stay married. We can get a divorce and date and go through the process from the beginning again, like a normal couple. Do I want to be your wife? Yes. Do I also want the choice to be my husband to be a free one for you, one to make based on love alone and not out of a sense of duty? Also yes."

He tucked his lower lip between his teeth, nodding slowly. "I'm going to tell you a few things, and I want you to listen carefully."

She blinked at him, eyes wide.

He stood and placed a hand on either side of her legs, leaning over to kiss her. "I don't need to think this through because you've been on my mind since I was eighteen years old. People date and take their time because they need to get to know each other. You and me? We know each other inside out." He inched forward and brushed his nose against hers. "The inside part more recently."

A tiny whimper left her throat.

"I've waited my entire life to get to where we are. I'm not interested in going back or starting over. Are you?"

"No," she whispered. "I don't want to start over."

"I love where we are."

"Me too."

He brushed his lips across hers again, soft and sweet. "Good."

He slowly lowered himself back into the chair and regarded her seriously. "If we're done with that nonsense…"

She laughed.

"Maybe I should get us new rings. Real ones."

She immediately shook her head. "I love the one you gave me."

"Really?"

"Yes," she said on an exhale. "If you only knew how I felt the night you gave it to me…"

Seriously? "Tell me."

Her long, dark lashes brushed her cheek as she looked down at her left hand. "Terrified. Amazed. Breathless." She met his gaze. "Take your pick."

"Pretty good description of how I feel every moment I'm with you."

"Well." She smiled, so damn beautiful. "I guess it's a good thing you like adventure, then."

"I thought I told you to wait in the car."

Mia shrugged from where she sat in the corner of the tree house, unapologetic. "You were taking too long, and I love it up here."

He pulled himself up the rest of the way. His mom had made them several freezer meals to take home after Mia was discharged, and in the five minutes it took him to go inside and pack them up, she'd snuck out back. "I'm pretty sure climbing trees is on the list of things you're not supposed to do after surgery."

"I feel great."

He grunted and settled in beside her, blowing into his

cupped hands. She angled the space heater in his direction, smiling.

"You must be dead on your feet. Let's get you home and in bed."

"I'm fine."

"Mia." His tone held a note of warning.

"Noah. I mean it. I want to sit here with you for a few minutes. Maybe make out a little like the last time we were up here."

"Absolutely not."

She lurched to a sitting position. "Excuse me?"

"You just got out of the hospital. You need to take it easy."

She glared at him and climbed over him, settling in to recreate the position of their last kiss in this tree. She slid her hips across his, bracing on his shoulders for balance, and he groaned.

"Don't," he whispered.

"I just want a kiss," she said. "Give me that and I'll stop."

"Really?" A hint of teasing colored his tone. "That's all you want?"

"No. But I'll take what I can get."

His palm spread across her back and he pulled her close, their mouths crashing together with a sigh of relief that seemed to originate from both of them at once. He worshipped her mouth, alternating between soft and needy, but never taking it further. When she placed her hand on his chest and he flinched, she jerked back.

"Did I hurt you?"

"A little," he said. "I, um, have a new tattoo there."

She leaned back farther. "You do?"

He nodded and slowly unzipped his fleece. "I've gone several times over the last few days because I didn't want to be away for too long," he said as he shrugged out of it. "He finished it up this morning, so it's still tender."

He lifted his T-shirt to reveal a second wing, identical to the first, on the opposite side of his chest. The skin around the upper corner was red and splotchy. Right where she'd touched him.

She traced a light finger along the bottom, just below the ink, careful not to hurt him. "You finished it."

"Yeah," he rasped. "I finally feel free."

Their gazes collided and a multitude of experiences and emotions passed between them. Years of friendship, struggles, pain, and devotion.

"I love it," she murmured. "And I love you."

"Same," he said. He dropped his shirt and leaned forward to kiss her softly. "I have a question for you, then I'm taking you home."

"Okay."

He caressed her cheek with his thumb. "Would you rather do this life separate or together?"

She smiled, covering his hand with hers.

"Together."

EPILOGUE

"Are you two hiding?"

At the sound of Claire's voice Mia startled and jumped back, swiping a hand across her lips.

"Hey," Noah said. "Don't wipe my kiss off your mouth."

Mia gave him a look that said, *shhhh*, trying to ignore how sexy he looked with those hooded eyes and flushed cheeks, and regarded Claire standing in the doorway.

Even from their location in the guest bedroom, the hum of voices and music filtered from the living room of Noah's parents' house and likely into the patio and yard beyond.

Claire arched a knowing brow. "It's your graduation party, Mia." Her voice was stern but she looked as if she was holding back a smile. "These people are here to celebrate you. Meanwhile you're back here doing God knows what with Noah."

Mia scrunched her nose, smoothing her hair.

"She is my wife, you know," Noah put in. He still leaned against the wall where Mia had pinned him with her body just a few seconds ago.

Mia bit her lip. "It's just… James has kept him superbusy since his promotion last month and he just got back from a trip to Index. We, um, haven't had much time alone—"

Claire held up a hand. "I don't need to know. Just finish up, okay? I'll try to get this party wrapped up—no pun intended—in the next hour and you can do whatever you need to do. At *home*."

With that, she disappeared.

Noah's arm snaked around Mia's waist and dragged her close again. He kissed her hard, then pulled back. "There."

She smiled, reaching up to fix his hair. "Ready?"

"I guess." He pushed off the wall and took her hand. "Claire's probably right, we should be out there. But it's a good thing we have two days off after this. I don't plan on doing anything but you."

Mia's neck flushed with heat. *"Noah."*

"What?" He didn't sound the least bit apologetic.

She just shook her head and grinned as they made their way to the living room. Noah's dad intercepted him, pulling him away almost immediately, probably to discuss some new hobby he'd picked up. So far in retirement he'd gone through several, from things like organic gardening to tracing his entire family ancestry. A couple of months ago he'd almost bought a boat before Noah talked him out of it.

Mia's mom waved to her from the food table, and Mia's stomach growled. She made her way over and gave her mom a side hug as she perused the options.

"This is a great turnout," her mom said.

Mia's heart swelled as she looked at the family and friends

filling the room. "It feels surreal. I can't believe I'm finally done."

Her mom squeezed her arm, careful not to jostle the plate Mia was piling high with food. "We're so proud of you."

"Thanks, Mom."

After she'd finished eating she made her way around the room, chatting and accepting congratulations and well wishes from everyone. Some asked what her plans were, and she was happy to report she already had a job lined up with a local pediatrics group.

An hour had passed and she kept looking for Noah, but had only seen a glimpse of him once.

Suddenly a warm, large hand gripped hers and his familiar scent filled her senses. He pressed a kiss to her cheek before he winked and walked away again, leaving her with a frown on her face and a folded piece of paper in her hand.

She unfolded the small note, and laughed.

Meet me at the tree house in 5?

She cast her gaze around the room, searching for her husband. He was by the kitchen island, leaning one arm against the granite, perfectly at ease. He'd already joined a conversation with someone, but must have felt her looking at him and lifted his eyes. He grinned, a secret, sexy smile just for her, and cocked one brow.

With a saucy look of her own, Mia gave him a little nod and glanced at the clock.

Let the countdown begin.

*****

ACKNOWLEDGMENTS

I loved the idea of this book so much that I waited months to start writing it, terrified I couldn't do Mia and Noah justice. In the end, I'm so unbelievably happy with how it turned out, and it never would have gotten here without the following people.

My agent, Kim Lionetti, for seeing the potential in the story and believing it deserved to be in the hands of romance readers, and my editor, Margot Mallinson, for choosing to work with me, loving Mia and Noah, and bringing this book to its full potential.

Special thanks to my cousin Angela Conrad for answering all my questions about architects and for reading a messy early draft of this book to check those pieces for accuracy.

Thank you to the early readers—critique partners and betas. I'm the worst at keeping a list early on like everyone says I should, so by this point I'm not even sure who all read it, but I'll do my best: Denise Williams (ride or die), Heather Gearhart (CPFL), Falon Ballard, Haley Kral, Lindsey Jesionowski, Anne Furasek, Staci Klugh, Abby Barnett, Misty Miller, Anna Grissom, Fransen McGinley, and Ashtin Taylor. And a special shout-out to Katie Rose, who not only reads my early drafts but texts me reader reactions in real time, which is my favorite thing in the whole world. To Brittany Kelley for being my daily scream-into-the-void partner as we went through the querying and sub process once again. You're my favorite. To Lianna, my favorite bookstagrammer, who just happened to stumble across my debut and became one of my favorite Canadians—I hope this one lived up to your expectations.

Thanks to my parents and my sister, who encourage me and are always there for me. To my husband for supporting me and giving me time to write even though he's the furthest from a romance reader I could possibly find.

And a huge thank-you to all the romance readers out there who continue to buy books like this one and never stop believing in the power of love. You're the reason I'm able to keep writing, and as long as you want to read them, I can't imagine I'll ever stop.